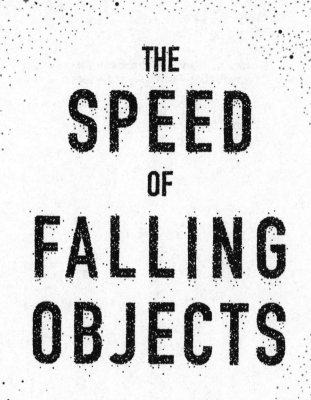

THE
SPEED
OF
FALLING
OBJECTS

**Books by Nancy Richardson Fischer
available from Inkyard Press**

When Elephants Fly
The Speed of Falling Objects

THE
SPEED
OF
FALLING
OBJECTS

NANCY RICHARDSON FISCHER

ink
yard
press

ISBN-13: 978-1-335-92824-5

The Speed of Falling Objects

This book is dedicated to my husband and best friend, Henry.

To say that I'm not a fan of creepy crawlies
or creatures that slither is, as you know, an understatement.
But I would live in the Amazon to be with you.

1

I don't remember impact.

There's silence, followed by individual sounds, like someone conducting a nature symphony—first birds with different songs, then the deep vibration of frogs, the buzz of myriad insects and an undercurrent of slithering that might be my imagination. I don't know. I've never been in the rain forest before.

The world is dark, just a pinhole, that slowly expands. Splashes of iridescent paint turn into birds taking wing. Below, flowers explode like fireworks—crimson, hot pink, cobalt. Twisted roots tunnel into coffee-colored earth. The rich smell of organic matter mingles with the musty funk of decomposition. Above my feet, I see every possible shade of green made from clusters of leaves. Massive palm fronds reveal temporary slivers of a stormy sky. Lightning licks its dark gray fabric.

A wave of vertigo hits and I'm spinning again. Screams echo. Are they Cass's, Jupiter's or mine? All I know for sure is that they're not Cougar's.

My world is upside down.

No. I'm upside down, still strapped in, feet above my head tangled in a thorny vine that is suffocating a tree's thick limb. The airplane seat beside me remains connected to mine but it's empty, the metal caught in the bough of a massive tree that suspends me two stories above the ground. My stomach, despite the painful compression of the seat belt, lurches.

Where's Sean? He was sitting next to me when… We were talking about surfing and then…

Raindrops patter down on my face. They're hot. Rivulets leak into my mouth, tasting like copper, salt. I touch my tongue. My finger comes away stained red. I look up, a little bit to the left, and then close my eyes, brain scrambling for a different explanation.

I hear my mom's no-nonsense voice like a siren in my brain: *List everything that scares you. When you give your fears a name, it takes away their power.*

The nightmares began when I was eight and lasted an entire year. After each one, my mom would make me list the things that scared me, then everything I liked, then what I wanted to be when I grew up. It became my mantra—a way to cut the dark dream threads. The list changed over the years, but now I revert to my eight-year-old self.

I am afraid of…

Heights. Snakes. The dark. Dancing in public. Headaches… Spiders. Wrong choices. Surprises. Playing sports. Losing friends. Guns… Blindness. Disappointing people. New places. Hospitals.

Did I say snakes already? Bees. Migraines. Speed… Being an anchor, a problem or an embarrassment… Bad dreams.

More droplets patter down on my forehead, dribble into my hair. I refuse to look up again.

I like…

Flannel sheets. Some Thursdays. My mom's smile. Milk Duds. Writing letters. Carrot cake… Making people laugh. Creating dioramas. Dancing if no one is watching. My dad's phone calls. The Phantom Tollbooth. *Dogs. I like dogs that I know. Dad's show.*

My head is pounding so hard that my skull may explode. If I pass out upside down, will I die? The ground is far, probably twenty feet. Unlike my father, I'm not a coordinated cat with nine lives. My neck will snap if I land on my head. Death if I'm lucky. Paralysis if I'm not. Both ankles will break if I come down on my feet, possibly fracturing tibiae and fibulae, too. Maybe only my ribs will splinter if I land on my side, but that could puncture a lung. If my back and pelvis break like twigs, there's no way I'll be able to drag myself out of this place.

A hysterical giggle burbles to the surface. I don't even know where I am. My vision blurs.

When I grow up I want to be…

Adventurous. Strong. Athletic. Popular. Brave. A propeller. The solution. Cougar.

I unbuckle my seat belt and drop.

2

Four Days Earlier

"Let's call her Lady Bacon."

The fetal pig lying in a dissection pan on our lab table appears to shudder. Its once-pink skin is now a mottled tan. A rough tongue hangs sideways from a body that feels like plastic but has the weight of something once alive. *She deserves respect.* "We'll call her Poppy."

Trix scowls. "Why do you get to name her?"

"Because I'm the one doing all the cutting." I tie a string around one of our pig's forelegs, pass it under the pan, stretch it tight, then tie it to the other foreleg. I do the same thing with the back legs. The hard sternum is easy to find. I follow it down to the bottom of the rib cage, pick up a scalpel and begin an upside-down V incision. If our teacher had some nylon thread for sutures, a needle holder and forceps, it'd be fun to try to close up the incision with the stitches my mom taught me one rainy afternoon using a banana instead of a piglet.

When the smell of formaldehyde rises from the long slices, Trix gags. "Don't barf on our pig." I don't mind the smell. It's part of the environment of a lab where everything is controlled, clean and in its proper place.

Using the dissecting scissors, I cut through the muscle of the pig's belly. The next two incisions are down and around the umbilical cord, then above the hind legs. When I peel back all the flaps of skin there's still membrane attached to the muscle. I consider asking Trix to cut it but she looks kind of green.

"Please tell me you're done mutilating Poppy," Trix says.

"Almost."

"Did someone actually raise this pig just to kill it for our biology class?" Sarah asks from her seat at the lab table in front of us. The overhead fluorescents highlight skin that's such a pale white that it has a greenish hue, and lank, greasy hair. In fourth grade a group of kids created a giant calendar to document when she changed her clothes or showered. Turned out it wasn't often. They posted the calendar in the cafeteria.

Mr. Petri's fingers twist the tiny island of gray hair in the center of his otherwise bald, black dome. "These pigs are a by-product of the pork industry. We don't use 'em, they become fertilizer. You have an hour to dissect, identify and flag what we've studied, so less talking, more slicing."

Trix's eyes water when I make an incision up through the chest, then cut away the rib cage and sternum. The final two cuts expose the pig's neck. I resist the urge to twist my head to see each exposed organ more clearly.

"Look at Pigeon dig in," Nate says from the table to our left, and I look up. A grin splits open the lower half of a pasty face dotted with acne.

The scrutiny of the entire class crawls along my skin like ants. Kids rarely use my old nickname. They call me Danny now, and the snickers don't happen that often anymore. I've changed. But so has my dad. He became Cougar Warren when I was twelve, star of his own NetCom TV show, *COUGAR*. He travels around the world, sometimes alone, other times with celebrities, surviving the desert, the jungle, the mountains or even the ocean in a makeshift raft. The show's tagline: Wits. Strength. Ingenuity. Having a dad who's famous, especially one who kicks ass every week and hangs with rappers, actors and pop stars, definitely cuts down on harassment. There are a lot of kids in my class who want to meet him. Thing is, Cougar left my mom when I was seven. He rarely visits. But they don't know that.

"Pigeon, did you skip breakfast?" Lander asks me. He's Nate's lab partner and fellow baseball player, sports identical brush-cut hair, though his brown skin is acne-free, and he follows his buddy around like a puppy. No surprise that Lander needs to make a joke about me, too.

Trix peers over at their pig. "Wow, the big, tough jocks haven't even picked up their scalpel. Maybe their little piggy isn't the only one missing its balls?"

Lander sneers and gives her the finger.

Trix tenses. I say, "Let it go," then pin flags to their corresponding organs before moving to Poppy's right side. "It's kind of amazing," I say, tracing the fetal pig's heart.

Trix pinches her nose with gloved fingers. "How much it stinks?"

She's the toughest girl I know, but bad smells are her downfall. "No, how—"

"How you're afraid of spiders," Trix interrupts, "scary movies, the dark, thunderstorms, swing sets, worms, ticks, riding a bike, lumpy food and flies."

I stick in another flag. "Horseflies bite. Ticks carry Lyme disease. The rusty chains on swings are an accident waiting to happen."

"But you can cut open Poppy without a problem?"

"What's amazing," I say, "is that every living organism starts with a single cell that divides, communicates with other cells, keeps dividing until it eventually makes us, and Poppy here, with all our parts in the right places."

Trix isn't listening. She's playing with the gold hoop in her right nostril. It's the latest of her nine piercings. They're all new. Last year she was preppy—plaids, pinks combined with parrot green, high socks and shiny loafers. The year before she was into black lipstick and nail polish, dark trench coats, and eyes ringed so thickly with liner and mascara it was a miracle she could see. The only sure things with Trix are that she's bound to change her look and she'll always be my best friend.

Right now Trix has locked eyes with the new kid, Tim Hunt. For today, he's her type—shaggy black hair, a nose ring, skin so washed-out that he looks like a vampire. They'll probably go out this weekend. By *go out*, I mean get at least partially naked.

What would it be like to be Trix? I'm basically invisible to guys. The only boy I've fooled around with is George McCay. He goes to Jesuit. We met at a party Trix dragged me to, and both of us were buzzed on cheap beer. We made out. He had braces and a mouth that tasted like Doritos. I counted to sixty, then said I needed to head back to the party. I don't think George was disappointed to see me go.

Mr. Petri is watching us. "Do something," I say with a nudge.

Trix unlocks her green eyes from Tim's. "Fine."

She identifies the rest of the items on our list and when our teacher looks away, I correct her mistakes. Then I take a moment to appreciate the neat dissection. While I'm leaning over the fetal pig, I inhale to breathe in its essence.

Trix laughs. "I thought we broke that tired routine."

I blush. "Old habit." After the accident when I lost my eye, I had this stupid idea that if I found a dead butterfly, bird or squirrel and breathed them in it'd somehow make me whole again. In my defense, I was young and, while I thought my actions were subtle, some people did notice.

She peels off her gloves. "Done. Gotta love teamwork."

"I'm the *work* part of that equation. Truth." *Truth* is what we say when there's zero bullshit.

Trix nods. "We all have our skills." Again, she eyes Tim. "Yours just happens to be the science part of our equation. Admit it, you love this stuff."

"I do it because you suck at it. Do tell, what do you bring to the mix?"

"Fun."

I snort. We met in detention in the fourth grade. Trix had

cursed out her teacher, Mrs. Glass, who made the mistake of telling my friend that being aggressive in gym class wasn't ladylike. I'd done nothing to deserve detention. I'd just ducked into the room as an alternative to an afternoon home alone. It's been the two of us since that day.

Trix leans in and takes a selfie of us. "Stop," I say, putting up my hand too late. She checks out the photo. *What does she see?* A pretty girl with creamy white skin, perfect curves and pink hair, though she's a natural blonde, beside a homely one in glasses who has two different-colored eyes—gray and blue—a bad decision I made at age eight. I'm a skinny five-eight with dirty-blond hair that washes out my sallow, white skin. My hair is always in a braid so that it doesn't obscure my view. I've been told I have a great smile and an easygoing personality. Other than that, I'm nothing special. So I'm beyond lucky to have a friend like Trix who doesn't care about surface stuff like looks, or that I'm unpopular, and even defends me when I act weird.

She says, "I'll pick you up Saturday night at seven."

I consider arguing, then shrug my acceptance. Trix will show up at my door the night of whatever stupid dance the school is having and won't leave until I go with her. "You do get that my going to a dance is a waste, right?" I don't dance in public. Not since seventh grade. That was when a group of kids, including Nate and Lander, came up with their own dance. It was called "The Pigeon." They stood in a circle flapping their arms like wings and poked their heads left and right, imitating me.

I'd never realized that was how I looked. I was just trying to see better because having only one working eye makes judging depth and the speed of moving objects, like people dancing with abandon, a bitch. Until then, though, I'd thought I was doing a pretty good job. Funny how a single moment changed my self-perception forever.

Later that night Trix looked up facts about pigeons to make me feel better about my new nickname. Like they can fly up to fifty miles per hour, make great pets because they always find their way home, and can morph their wings into different shapes to fly in storms. It didn't help, but I appreciated her effort.

The good news is that I'm more coordinated now. When you lose your eye as a little kid, as opposed to as an adult, your brain has an easier time adjusting to the new normal, and eventually adaptation becomes mostly automatic. I'll always have a blind spot on my left side, and I'll never be a great tennis player, but the trick to fitting in is never putting myself in situations where my monocular vision is exposed.

Trix helped me get through whatever torture our gym teacher planned in junior high. We had verbal cues for when I should swing a bat, kick a ball or leap over a hurdle. Sometimes it worked. Now I take bowling for gym. It's a benefit of going to a broken-down old high school that has a few lanes in the basement. My friend also helped me break the habit of turning my head by pinching me hard enough to leave a bruise every time I did it around her. And I never dance, because even though I no longer move like a pigeon, deep down that bird still flutters around inside me.

Trix asks, "Come over tonight?"

I shake my head. "I need to study."

"I'm getting the results from my private investigator."

Trix nibbles her lower lip, a nervous tick. I could tell her she has a great family already and that she'll always have me, but she's been obsessed with finding her biological parents and it's my job to have her back, so I say, "I'll be there."

3

There's a note on the fridge: *Pull flank steak out.* I take off my glasses, make a quick kale salad, a ginger marinade for the meat, do my homework, then grab one of the medical journals my mother leaves on every surface of our place in northwest Portland. It's her version of decorating. Mine is creating dioramas, three-dimensional boxes depicting different scenes. They're scattered throughout our apartment.

I like working in miniature so I use jewelry boxes for my creations. My favorite is in a rectangular bracelet box that rests on the kitchen windowsill. It's a scene from the arctic, complete with an igloo, mini-glaciers, several people, a pack of dogs and a polar bear I made out of toothbrush bristles. With each diorama, I use the scalpel my mom gave me, once she was sure I wouldn't slice an artery, to cut elements from balsa wood. Then I hand paint or cover them with textured material. The last step is a visit to our local antique and junk shop, for a surprise to place inside each scene. My favorite discovery so far is a miniature pocket watch. It's hung around the polar bear's neck, like he knows, with the glaciers melting, that his time may be running out.

Other than my dioramas, nothing has changed since we moved into our two-bedroom, one-bath apartment when I was eight. Early on, mom hung framed posters of the skeletal and circulatory systems and detailed renderings of the body's organs on the living room walls. I'm not sure if I memorized them or if they seeped into my brain through osmosis. She also taped a handprint turkey I drew in kindergarten, now faded to pastels, to the dented stainless steel fridge. An interior designer wouldn't be impressed, but the apartment is like a comfortable old shoe and it's home.

I sit down at the kitchen table and let the medical journal fall open.

Case XXI: Nineteen-year-old male. Working with handheld drill while on a ladder. Ladder tipped, resulting in a ten-foot fall. Landed on 18″ drill bit, face-first. Bit went through right ocular cavity. Exited back of skull. Right eye destroyed...

My mouth has gone dry. A key scrapes in the door lock. It swings open, letting in a rush of icy December air and my mom, also a force of nature.

"Hey, Danny. Glasses?"

I put them back on as she dumps an overloaded messenger bag on the kitchen table. She shrugs off her down jacket, red scarf and hat. Her cheeks are pink circles on a smooth white canvas, jaw-length blond hair alive with static. Even though she's my mother, I recognize that Samantha McCord is beautiful. Nice for her but embarrassing for me as I fall far from that tree.

"Which case are you reading about?"

"Drill bit."

"Worst part was that he was uninsured. Over $100,000 in medical bills."

My mom is obsessed with insurance, mostly medical, but also car, fire, life and wrongful death. It makes sense in a morbid way. Her own mother died in a car wreck when she was eighteen. There was a small life insurance policy. Four months later her father was diagnosed with stage IV colon cancer. He was dead in six weeks. The combined policies got my mom through college. My dad didn't have the same safety net. He was eleven when his parents died and there were no insurance policies.

I turn on the broiler and put the steak in the oven while my mom massages her feet. If the ER is busy, she rarely sits down at work.

She says, "Brain injuries."

This is the game we play every night before dinner. She baits a hook, tosses it into the water. I usually bite. My mom enjoys it. "Yes?"

"They don't require a huge blow. A small fall on a ski slope can put a kid in a coma, even kill them, while an old woman can get trampled by a horse and wind up with a headache."

I ask, "So how do you figure out what a patient needs when they come to the ER?"

"If they're responsive, ask questions. If not, get information from the family to see if the patient has a history of illness or drug use. Take scans. Sometimes a patient will seem fine, lucid, but later have migraines, ask repetitive questions or have seizures." She opens the oven, flips the steak over and puts it back under the broiler.

"Why?"

"There's bleeding or swelling in the brain that, over time, creates so much pressure inside the skull that it damages the brain tissue, sometimes irreparably."

"Sounds painful."

"Unbearable."

I remember how I felt after the accident. Like a bomb kept exploding inside my skull. Samantha pulls out the flank steak and expertly slices it. I ask, "How long does it take until the patient dies?"

"Minutes to days. But they don't always. What would you do to save them?"

She sets the steak and salad on the table, then sits across from me. We both dig in. "The skull is like a football helmet, right?"

"Meaning?"

"There's no give. So I guess I'd find a way to get rid of the pressure. Maybe drill holes through the patient's head? Or is that too brutal?" I stab a piece of meat and pop it into my mouth.

"Not brutal at all," she says between bites. "A neurosurgeon can either drill a hole in the skull and put in a shunt to drain the fluid or remove a piece of the patient's skull to give their swollen brain room."

My mom's eyes gleam. She was planning to be a surgeon, but my parents met halfway through her undergrad at Berkeley and she got pregnant. They married. Cougar started working on the first iteration of his show, traveling a ton, and Sam was left struggling to get through college while taking care of me. Money was tight. Everything Cougar made went right back into his show. When she finally graduated, my mom had to figure out a way to make a living, fast. She chose nursing. When she couldn't afford a sitter, she'd bring me to the hospitals where she worked. I'd do my homework in the emergency department's waiting room.

"Earth to Danny?"

"Do you ever wish we had more family?"

Samantha eats another piece of steak. "Why?"

"It would've been easier on you." My parents don't even have siblings.

She wipes her mouth with a napkin. "Wishing for something you don't have is a waste of time."

Cougar's nickname for my mother is Commander Sam. She hates it, but in a way it's a compliment. She's pragmatic, determined and, like a tank barreling toward enemy lines, nothing stands in her way. Both her parents were in the army. She doesn't talk about them much, but does say that they taught her there are problems and solutions, right and wrong. My dad falls in the *wrong* category—tried, found guilty, with no execution but also no reprieve.

"I took Friday and Monday off."

For my seventeenth birthday, which is next Friday, we're going on a road trip to check out a few Oregon colleges. Early December isn't the best time for college tours. It'll be cold, rainy and gray. "You do realize that you're way ahead of schedule?" I'm only a junior.

One brow arches. That single brow lift means she's quietly lining up her arsenal, ready to pick off any protest like a sniper. "Scholarships go fast."

"What about a state school in California?"

She frowns. "We can't afford out-of-state tuition."

Both of us were crazy hungry so we polished off our meal in record time. Mom jumps into cleaning up. If I went to the University of Southern California or the University of California, Los Angeles, I'd be close to where my dad lives when he's not filming, maybe get to know him better. I take a deep breath before entering enemy territory. "We could let Cougar help with tuition?"

She lets my question dangle, which isn't a surprise. I was seven when my parents divorced. It was only a few months after my accident. Sam refused child support, which wouldn't have been much in the early days but could've helped a little. Even now that Cougar is successful and wealthy, she won't take a dime or let me take anything other than birthday and Christmas gifts. She says her decisions are based on keeping me safe, but I'm not seven anymore.

I've poked the bear and wait to see if she's going to attack. Samantha rinses the steak pan, then dries off her hands and says, "Danny, have you thought more about what you want to study in college? Nurses can always find a job."

She's watching me, her jaw tilted like she's ready for a fight. My suggestion doesn't merit a response. I guess college in dreary Oregon isn't the worst thing in the world.

"Danny?"

"I'm still not sure what I want to study." Trix's plans change every five minutes and her parents just smile about it. One day she's going to be a fireman, like her dad, the next a shoe designer or join Cirque du Soleil. Me? I'm interested in science, but I want to be everything I'm not and different from my mom, who is equal parts drive, anger and regret.

The phone rings—a momentary reprieve.

"Hello…? Fine, Cougar," my mom says.

My stomach clenches a tiny bit, like always. Sam hands me the phone. "Hi, Dad."

4

"Hey, guess where your dad is right now?"

I say, "Africa, Thailand, Mongolia?" He really could be anywhere in the world.

"Nope. LA, sitting poolside at Chateau Marmont."

"Cool."

"Cool? Yeah, pretty much *the* coolest hangout in Los Angeles. I just had a meeting with Gus Price's people. Drumroll. He's in for an episode of *COUGAR*. He has a few days open, and there's a tie-in with his next project, so we're filming in a week. Three days, the Peruvian rain forest. It'll be epic. Given Gus's visibility, a great episode might even get me a movie deal. We have a script, just need to hook a major studio for backing. Be pretty cool if your dad made the leap to the silver screen, huh?"

"Really cool. But you're already famous."

"True. But this would launch me into the stratosphere. Goodbye, Venice Beach. Hello, Malibu. Cougar Warren, action-adventure hero. Move over, the Rock, right?"

I smile so he can hear it in my voice. "Right." I'd reconciled myself to him forgetting my birthday was coming up. He's a busy guy.

"You don't know who Gus is, do you?"

My mom is staring at me, a deep groove forming between her eyebrows. "He's an actor." I know only because Trix dragged me to his last movie, a remake of an old film called *American Gigolo* that starred Richard Gere. The original was about a high-price male escort who gets framed for murder. Gus's version is about a homeless kid who's *rescued* from the street by a glamorous female pimp. She sets him up in an expensive apartment, then sends him out to sleep with older women. "In Gus's last movie, he was framed for murder but ended up being given an alibi by one of his famous clients," I say to show my dad I'm tracking. What I don't add is that Gus's eyes are pretty amazing and he's so good at acting that I actually believed he was that homeless kid.

"Exactly! Gus is *the* hottest teen actor in the world right now and he's going to do my show. Gus Price, in the rain forest? Add flash floods, venomous snakes, spiders that paralyze, stingrays and electric eels—it doesn't get hotter than that. You still terrified of bugs?"

"Pretty much." He laughs so I do, too. When I was eight, my dad showed up for a rare visit. We went to an entomology exhibit at the local science museum. It featured live bugs from around the world. Kids could touch and even hold the ones that didn't bite or sting. I remember there were hickory horned devils—giant yellow caterpillars with orange horns sprouting from their heads—long-legged katydids that looked like green leaves with sticklike legs and ant lions, bristly, brown spiderlike bugs with curved jaws.

Before the accident, I would've loved the exhibit. I was the kid who wasn't scared of anything, just like my dad. But having one eye changed things. When Cougar put a giant black-and-white-striped goliath beetle on my left shoulder, my blind spot, and I felt it crawling up my neck, I FREAKED out. Cougar took me outside and asked, *What is wrong with you?* I couldn't articulate my terror, but it was the idea that on one side I was now defenseless. That was the day Cougar started calling me by my nickname, Danny, instead of my first name.

"I'm not planning a career in entomology," I admit.

Cougar chuckles. "Yeah. You're not cut out for that."

He's right, but inside I wince.

My dad visited only a few more times since that day. When I was nine he was in town to do local press. He took me swimming at the coast. The news had just run a story about a shark attack—a great white bit off a surfer's leg below the knee. Cougar and I were playing in the shallow water, splashing and having fun, when the sand suddenly dropped away and I was in over my head. Petrified, I forgot how to swim. He dragged me out, choking and spluttering. When he said I needed to go back in the ocean and conquer my fears, I grew so hysterical that a couple on the beach intervened. Cougar hissed in my ear, *Stop it!* On the drive home my dad told me he was sorry and not to worry about it. But he could barely look at me. I sensed that I hadn't just humiliated myself. I'd embarrassed him.

Cougar asks, "Ready for the big surprise?"

"Um."

"I've cleared it for *you* to come along!"

I hold the phone a few inches away until the reverberations die down. "Excuse me?"

"You, me, Gus and a few remaining crew members who couldn't make the trip with the production team are going to Peru on Sunday. I'll have my assistant FedEx your ticket. You have a passport, right?"

"Yes." Last year there was a school trip to Mexico. I got a passport, just in case we could pull together enough money for me to go. It didn't work out, so I drove to Vancouver with my mom and sat through a weekend seminar on streamlining hospital emergency rooms. My leg starts jiggling. I can't help it—hope launches like a rocket.

"We'll meet in LA, fly to Lima together, then on to Iquitos."

His enthusiasm is infectious. "Where's that, exactly?"

"Eastern Peru. It's the gateway into national parks with hundreds of millions of hectares of unexplored tropical Amazonian rain forests. There's not even a name for where we're going. It's one of the most remote, rugged, deadly parts of Peru. If we're going to see jaguars, it's there. Are you stoked, Danielle?"

Danielle. My insides contract, and this time I'm ten years old again. Cougar was in town for a single afternoon. We rented bikes to ride along the Willamette River. Before the accident I was a whiz on a two-wheeler. I was only four when

I learned to ride without training wheels. My dad always crowed that I was a superior athlete, like him. That day, on the flat, paved path, I crashed five times. In my defense, it was the first time I'd tried to ride with one eye and my depth perception was way off, plus I was nervous. Cougar kept looking back, shaking his head. He didn't have to say the word *inferior*. I understood, even then, it was the opposite of being superior. When he dropped me off at the apartment, he said, "Goodbye, Danielle." It was the first time in my entire life that he'd ever called me by the given middle name on my birth certificate. As soon as I got inside and shut the door, I vomited. Cougar called me Danielle from that day on.

"Danielle?"

Despite the name, excitement makes my body hum. *This is my chance to spend more than a few hours with my dad.* "Yes! I'm down!"

The expression on my mom's face reads, *Why are you still on the phone with that ass?* Hope falters midair. There's no way she'll let me go to Peru with my dad. When I was little, she barely let him take me out of the house during visits. Excitement is replaced by heaviness in my bones, like gravity is working hand in hand with reality to pin me to my boring life. I remind myself that it's still interesting to hear about my dad's adventures. "Being so cut off... Won't that make it hard to film?"

"Hell yes. It'll take hours in a power canoe to get upstream to our start location. You might get to see pink dolphins, alligators called caimans, freshwater sharks, monkeys, plus some of the most poisonous frogs, snakes and spiders in the world."

The idea that my dad thinks what he's describing is a plus makes me laugh. "Wow!"

"I know! You'll need about a week off school."

I glance at my mom. Hurricane Samantha is about to unleash. "I don't think—"

"Just hand Commander Sam the phone. I'll take care of it," Cougar says. "Is this the best sixteenth birthday present any kid in the world will ever get? Damn straight!"

He remembered. He's just a year off. For a second disappointment makes my insides slump. I hand the phone to my mom and leave the room. "I'm headed to Trix's to study," I call over my shoulder. Trix won't mind if I show up a bit early. If I stay, I'll be able to hear their fight from anywhere in the apartment.

5

Trix lies in the center of her parents' bed wearing a cropped white T-shirt that shows off the sapphire stud piercing in her belly button, and tight black leggings. Her parents let us study in their bedroom since Trix shares hers with a little sister and it's impossible to get anything done when Mai is around. Trix is holding the letter from the private detective she hired with her babysitting money. I drop my backpack, shrug off the waterproof down jacket I scored at Goodwill and take a seat on the orange '70s-style swivel chair that fits perfectly in the faux-wood-paneled bedroom.

"Flame out," Trix says.

In a nutshell, the private detective couldn't find Trix's biological mother, Meredith. He did find out a few things. Trix's mom was a foster kid, but if there were any known family those records were lost in the system. Meredith spent most of her childhood in trouble and was sent to prison for a drug conviction when Trix was two, released three years later, then disappeared. That means Meredith violated her probation. There's a standing warrant for her arrest so she has a good reason to hide out. The detective said she could be anywhere—living off the grid or even passed away. Trix's bio dad was never listed on the birth certificate so that's a dead end, too.

"Waste of all my money," Trix mutters. "Now I'll never know why I'm named after a cereal."

"I'm sorry. But you have an amazing family. They *chose* you."

"And I love them, like, a ton, but how can I know where I'm going if I don't know where I came from?"

Mrs. Robinson pokes her head into the room, a baby on one shoulder. "Hey, Danny."

Trix's adoptive mom is an imposing six foot two with brown skin and dimples that never quit. Mai, four years old, her shiny black hair in pigtails, hugs Mrs. R's leg. Three-year-old Joe darts into the room wearing a fireman's hat and nothing else. You can hardly see the scar from his recent cleft palate surgery. Mr. and Mrs. R adopted all seven of their kids. Trix was born addicted to crack. After her mom ditched, the Robinsons took her on as a foster baby and adopted her a few years later. Their home is too small, always chaotic, but overflowing with love.

"Don't stay up too late, girls," Mrs. R says, then leads the little kids away like the Pied Piper.

Trix sighs. "I probably have, like, a ton of hidden talents, but I'll never know about them because I'll never know my biological parents."

"Knowing who your bio parents are doesn't necessarily help. I know my mom. She's obsessed with insurance policies and science, being bossy and sucking the joy out of my life." Trix laughs. "And I know Cougar's talents, but that only makes me feel like I'm totally inferior."

"You can't follow in Cougar's footsteps so it's almost like you don't have a bio dad, either. Truth."

If there's a hole in my heart, it just widened.

"Change of subject," Trix says, possibly reading my expression. "I'm going out with Tim Friday night."

I exhale to release the tension in my body. "Try not to devour him in one bite."

Trix licks her lips. "I think it's going to be the other way around."

"Why's that?"

"Guys always tell you who they are up front. Tim said he's into sex, not commitment."

My head spins. Last year Trix wanted to date one guy until graduation. This year a guy who only wants sex is a plus. "Maybe Tim isn't the best—"

"We could find you a date if you'd put in a little effort."

My face gets warm. I shift in the chair, glance down—old Levis, a flannel shirt and double-knotted high-top sneakers. *Safety first.* "My Saturday night is already booked." There's a *COUGAR* marathon on NetCom. I unzip my backpack and pull out our biology textbook. "Ready to do some studying?"

"Nope."

Sighing, I climb onto the bed and lie down beside Trix. We

stare up at the yellow smiley-face mobile Mai made for her parents. "Cougar called. He invited me to watch the filming of an episode of his show. He said it's my birthday present. It's going to be in the Peruvian rain forest…with Gus Price."

Trix gasps, hands and feet pounding the mattress. She turns to stare at me. "No way!"

"Truth. Unexpected, right?"

"More like bizarre. Cougar rarely remembers your birthday."

She's right but her words prick further. "Maybe now that I'm older he wants to spend more time together?"

Trix snorts. "What'd Samantha say?"

"She didn't have to say anything. The answer is always no." The annoyed look on my mom's face when she was talking to my dad flashes through my mind. "I hate the way she says his name. *Cougar*, like he's a joke."

"Well, isn't his real name John?"

"That's not the point. She's awful to him. No wonder he bailed."

Trix toys with the gold hoop in her eyebrow. "Do you want to go?"

I've seen every one of my dad's shows, watched when my mom isn't home. Cougar eats snakes, bugs, raw eggs and maggots to survive. He suffers in extreme heat, cold and torrential rainstorms that make his skin blister, pucker, crack, bleed. In one episode my dad almost died from a killer bee attack. In another, he was charged by a grizzly bear.

"It's so not you." Trix giggles, then notices I'm not laughing. "Come on, it's funny."

I scowl. "This is the first time my dad has invited me on a trip. The first time he's included me in his job, his life. It's a chance to spend more than a few hours with him. So what if I have to sleep in a mud hut or eat cockroaches?"

"Seriously?"

I can't help a little smile. "Okay, I'd rather starve than eat a roach. But a few days without food and sleep won't kill me. Maybe I'll discover I have high cheekbones and a future as a supermodel. Plus it might be fun to try some of the stuff my dad does."

"Danny, no offense, but you're not going to be a super-model regardless of cheekbones, and you're the most unco-ordinated person I know."

"Ouch. Thanks a lot, best friend."

"Sorry. But come on. Your dad rappels down mountains and jumps off cliffs and shit. Heights freak you out. You're not a good swimmer. D, your favorite sport is bowling."

"And vacuuming." There's something about the symmetry of vacuuming a room that I find soothing.

"Don't leopards, crocodiles and those nasty fish with teeth... What're they called?"

"Piranha."

"Yeah, piranha. Don't all those things live in the rain forest? You'd be freaking terrified!"

I sigh. She's right. I've been known to run from an ant. "WWCD?"

"What Would Cougar Do does not apply. Cougar would tell your mom to kiss off, make the trip, catch piranha with bare hands and fry that fishy up for dinner. But you're not him and you won't be able to fake it in Peru."

Trix is right. The old game we played to deal with prob-lems, like bullies in my case, and Trix's boyfriend dilemmas, *WWCD*, doesn't work in this instance. "I still kind of want to go." After I say it, it hits just how much I mean it. I want to go on a trip with my dad, sit next to him on a plane, scramble through the rain forest, build stuff, catch things and shiver in a downpour beside him. I want to know him and to show him that I can be a daughter who doesn't embarrass him, who's more like him than like my mom. If Cougar knew that, things could be different.

"Look, I'd kill to spend a night in the Amazon with Gus Price. He's *the* hottest eighteen-year-old guy on the planet. When I slept with Ben, I imagined it was Gus. Richie, too, even though he has great hands. There was this thing he did, twining his fingers together, then—"

"Stop!"

Trix cackles. "Anyway, I agree with your mom."

"Why?"

She rolls onto her side and braids a loose strand of my long hair. "You'll just end up disappointed."

What she means is that I'd disappoint my dad. *COUGAR*'s tagline—Wits. Strength. Ingenuity—is a million miles from mine: Defective. Inferior. Embarrassment. "Maybe things will be different this time," I venture.

Trix shakes her head. "Look, if you and Cougar were going to have a close father-daughter relationship, you would have one. Truth."

It hurts enough to make my eyes sting. This is Trix's version of tough love, but today it's too harsh. I turn my head away.

"Danny?"

"Give me a sec." I can count on two hands the hours spent with my father in the nine years since he left. Phone calls are sporadic, rarely for Christmas, off and on for my birthday, usually from an airport, after a celebrity-filled party, or from halfway around the world. I roll off the bed, grab my back-pack and jacket, head to the door. I tug on a still-damp hat and steel myself for the cold walk home.

Trix calls out, "I'm just trying to protect you."

I hesitate, then turn around. "I used to be a tomboy."

Her eyebrows shoot up. "Excuse me?"

"Truth."

She scrunches up her face, like she's trying to imagine the impossible. "O-kay."

"When my dad was around we climbed trees, swam in rivers, even went rock climbing. I had zero fears of heights, the dark, water, speed or the snakes we saw at our campsite." Trix is giving me a super skeptical look so I don't add that we once saw a bear. We crouched behind a bush until it fin-ished eating berries and wandered off. Cougar called me his *best buddy* as we walked back to camp.

Trix points out, "You're scared of everything *now*."

I nod. "What happened changed me. Which is weird, since losing my eye wasn't the result of some death-defying act or bear attack, just a run-of-the-mill accident."

Trix slithers on her belly to the end of her parents' bed and rests her chin on folded hands. "You never talk about that night."

"Talking doesn't change it."

Trix holds up the detective's letter. "Neither does hiring a private investigator. We're in the same boat."

But she's wrong. I had a chance to be Cougar's buddy for-ever. I'd do anything to take back that moment in the woods. The split second when it all went wrong. Trix doesn't un-derstand. Cougar doesn't want to be my father and it's my fault. *Truth.*

6

My mom sits at the kitchen table with a small tape recorder beside her laptop, earbuds in. She's transcribing one of the ER doctors' notes to make extra money. She doesn't look up, mention her fight with my dad, the trip, or ask if I want to go to Peru. I don't mention it, either. Every relationship is a balancing act. As long as we don't mention my dad, ours remains steady.

I give her shoulder a squeeze as I pass. "Night." My mom squeezes my hand back. That's as close as we ever come to a hug. Sometimes I think it's because I used up all her physical affection after the accident. I was terrified to be alone and always wanted her on my right side, where I could see her, refusing to sleep unless her hand rested in mine.

★ ★ ★

At the top of the stairs, I pause. Instead of going into my bedroom, I walk to the end of the hall. Above the linen closet is the outline of a door leading to the attic. Using the pole kept in the closet, I hook the handle, pull down a folding ladder and then hesitate. The attic is dark, dusty, and there are spiderwebs in every corner and crevice. The worst part is that I have to walk five steps in total darkness before my outstretched fingers find the string hanging from the bulb.

I climb up and manage not to trip over the dark threshold. Even now, at almost seventeen, my heart knocks like bony knees until I find the string. Weak light illuminates the unopened boxes my mom packed after her parents died. Old prints lean against the walls beside stacks of textbooks from premed classes. A steamer trunk rests in the corner. It contains climbing ropes, harnesses and shoes my mom put away after she got pregnant. A pang shoots through my chest. This attic is the place dreams go to die.

The first time I climbed up here alone, I was nine. I'd had a nightmare that my dad's sky blue eyes were filled with black ink that leaked down his cheeks. His mouth was gone, replaced with a patch of white skin, and his light brown hair had turned white. When I woke, I'd desperately needed to see a picture of my dad, but I knew my mom had put them all in a box when we'd moved. So I crept past my mom's bedroom and up the ladder, petrified of the dark, but more terrified that Cougar's face had been mutilated. In a cardboard box hidden behind biology and chemistry books, I found photos of my dad and tried to memorize his face.

I'm in the attic now to find my passport. It'll be here

somewhere, because my mom believes in the adage *out of sight, out of mind*. I get that I'm not going to Peru, that it's best to let the idea of the trip drift away like a cloud. But I guess I just want to hold my passport...to know that someday I can go somewhere with my dad.

Sitting cross-legged, I open a cardboard box. On top are framed pictures. There's a blurry shot of my parents setting up a tent. It's probably the summer they met. My dad was teaching a rock-climbing course in Yosemite. My mom was his student. In the shot, her hair is in a messy ponytail, huge grin lopsided. My dad is laughing. They look young, happy and free.

The next photo is of my mom in the hospital with me in her arms. She's looking down like she can't believe what she's holding; like maybe there was a mistake and someone will take this baby back so she can return to her real life. Cougar stands to the side of the bed. One hand grips the metal rail. He's looking out the window. When I was six and they were fighting more than talking, my mom told me that my dad never wanted children. People think little kids won't remember the things they say, but they do if it's bad enough.

The final framed picture in the box is an eight-by-ten of a campsite in Yosemite. I know I'm seven because it's the last photo I willingly let anyone take of me. The late-afternoon light makes the pine trees in the background look like tombstones. I'm standing by a tent wearing a bright blue hat, my blond braids running halfway down my jacket, and jeans ripped over one knee. Cougar works on the fire, his red plaid shirt lit by the flames. My mom is peeling potatoes, head down, long hair twisted into a tight bun. We're separate, foreshadowing the end of our family. A friend of Cougar's took the shot. My mom was furious he was there. It was supposed to be a family weekend, but Cougar wanted to climb with his buddy. So she had to hang at camp with me. That was the night everything changed. A ghost pain sears through my left eye.

If you and Cougar were going to have a close father-daughter relationship, you would have one. Truth, Trix reminds me.

Deeper in the box is a Velcro strap attached to a small sticky leather patch. I wore the patch for several months to hide my mangled eyeball and again after the enucleation. That's the surgery that removed my damaged eye and replaced it with an orbital implant. Later, my prosthetic eye was fitted over the implant so that it would move like a normal eye and no one would know I was a freak. *Out of sight, out of mind.* I toss the patch aside, but something stuck to the back plunks to the wooden floor. It's a red disk. Turning it over in my fingers, I recall the feel of the rough clay before the memory of what it is rises to the surface.

Cougar couldn't be there for my surgery, so he'd sent his favorite book, *The Phantom Tollbooth.* My mom read it to me each night until the painkillers kicked in. It was about a little boy named Milo who gets a package in the mail. It's a make-believe tollbooth. He uses a coin to drive through the booth in his electric car and suddenly finds himself in the Lands Beyond, where he has incredible adventures that are designed to give him the insights and knowledge he needs to fight demons, save princesses and find his way home.

After I went back to school, I made a coin in ceramics class to match the red plastic one that came with my book and sent it to my dad in one of the countless letters I wrote him. He'd picked the story. I was sure that if he had the coin, we could meet in the Lands Beyond. My little kid brain figured it was a place he'd love to go. A place where we could return to being buddies and he could show me how to be brave again. But he never wrote back.

Blood whooshes in my ears as it pushes through arteries, returning to my heart, then surging again. *Why is the coin I sent Cougar in this box?* I should leave the past alone. I *should.*

Mining beneath a mound of hospital bills, I find a stack of letters bound with a string. My childish handwriting in red crayon is on the front of each envelope. Beneath it is my mother's neat cursive. I remember watching her address every letter. I licked the back of the envelopes, put on the stamps. She took them to work to mail them. *Right?* There must be at least fifty letters in this pile. I didn't give up writing for over a year and wrote more after the nightmares started. Tearing open the top envelope, I withdraw a lined sheet of paper with messy letters that slant to the right.

Dear Dad,
I'm sorry. I was bad. I miss u.
xo Danny

I rifle through more…

Dear Dad,
My eye hurtz. I have headakes that make me barf. Mom says I look like a pirite with my patch. I hate it. I'm sory.
xo Danny

Dear Dad,

I have a plastik eye. It does not moov. It's not the 4-ever one. I get that laytr. I have nightmares. I'm scared of the dark. I'm afraid of every thing I cant see. I need you to make me brave again. Where are you?

xo Danny

Dear Dad,

I'm sending you a coyne for the tolboth. I will meet u in the Lands Beyond. I am sorry. I miss you. I'm sorry.

xo Danny

Dear Dad,

Today I picked the color of my new eye. I choze the same blue as your eyes. It will move like my other eye. That will make me look betr. Almost like b-4. I know what happened was my fault. Mom says it's yours. Don't believe her. U R THE BEST!!! Mom is angry all the time. I think she hates me. Please come home so I can be your best buddy again…

xo Danny

The letters slide from my hands, a stack of apologies, pleas, missed opportunities, lost love. My heart hurts like someone stomped on it. My dad never read what I was going through. He didn't know how much I missed him or how sorry I was for what happened.

I don't understand.

All the things my mom ever said about Cougar rattle around my brain. *Selfish. Childish. Careless. Cruel. Impulsive.*

43

Egomaniac. Narcissist. She hates him. *That much?* "Yes. That much."

I dig through three more boxes until I find my passport. With shaking fingers I put it in the pocket of my jeans, leave the light on and climb down the ladder.

7

Heart hammering, I dump the unsent letters on the kitchen table. My mom takes a long time to look up. That's when I drop the ceramic coin on her notes. It spins, then settles, making a soft whisper like the sound of a page being turned.

Commander Sam pulls out her earbuds. "I can explain."

There's a part of me that hopes she can. I want to believe that my mom wouldn't do this to me, couldn't. "Try."

She squares her shoulders, like a fighter about to throw the first punch. "He left, Danielle."

Disappointment tastes like acid. I swallow and it's gravel going down my throat. "Don't call me that. I wrote at least fifty letters. I thought Dad didn't want me after what happened. He probably thought I blamed him, too—"

"You should have."

The dam holding back my fury bursts open. "It was my fault! He told me to stay in the tent. I followed you guys into the woods, hid. You called him a selfish bastard. He called you a jealous bitch, an anchor, not a propeller. I remember every word! Especially the part where you said he'd ruined your life, but what you really meant was that having *me* ruined it."

My mom's eyes get that shine that comes before tears. I've never seen her cry. Ever. "You don't need to pretend. Not anymore."

Her face flushes. "Danielle... Danny, I was struggling to take care of you, do my job, pay the bills. At times it was suffocating. Your dad married me when I got pregnant, but in reality? I was always a single mom. Cougar was only home a few months total a year. He barely contributed to our household. Every dollar went back into his damn TV show. It was all about building the brand, getting picked up by a network, then a bigger network. He was never satisfied."

"He had a dream."

My mom slams her fists on the table. "So did I! You can't possibly understand."

"I can't understand?" I want to hit something, too, but my arms remain stiff with outrage. "Maybe my big dream was to have a dad."

"You do. Just not one who cared enough to stick around."

Her words twist the knife embedded in my back. "Why'd you even keep the letters?"

She throws her hands in the air. "I forgot they were there."

"You *forgot*?"

"Danny, I was beyond exhausted. After the accident you

barely slept. When you did, you had horrific nightmares. It stayed that way for over a year. I had to emotionally support you plus work overtime to pay for the surgeries and prosthetic—"

"You could've asked Cougar for help."

My mom snaps, "He was too self-involved to visit. I wasn't going to take his money so he could clear his conscience."

The knife plunges deeper. "So to punish him you never sent my letters? And you resented me even though you wouldn't take his money."

"I was there before, during and after the surgery. I'm the one who got up every night you screamed in your sleep—the parent who held you, read to you, taught you how to adapt to a new normal and get over panic attacks. Cougar didn't deserve those letters!"

The truth is like being submerged in ice water. I've never known my mom. I'm seeing who she really is for the very first time—an angry, controlling ex-wife who'd use her kid to hurt her ex. "What about me? Didn't I deserve the chance to have a relationship with him?"

"Do you know the definition of a narcissist?" She doesn't wait for my answer. "It's a person with excessive interest or admiration of themselves and the psychological need for power. You were better off without Cougar in your life."

I back away from her. "I'm going to Peru with my father."

My mom's hands grip the edge of the table. "You're a minor and I have primary physical custody."

WWCD? "If you want to have any type of relationship with me after I turn eighteen, you won't try to stop me."

We stare at each other until there's a shift in my mom's

body, like she was a snake ready to strike but now uncoils. "I was protecting you."

"Thanks for that."

"He's reckless. Dangerous. At best, he'll only disappoint you."

"At least I'll give him that chance."

48

8

"Danielle!" my dad shouts as I come down the escalator at LAX. He's standing at the bottom, dressed in jeans, a loose denim shirt and worn cowboy boots. His sunglasses reflect the clicking cameras of a handful of paparazzi. When he waves to me, they swing around. The flashes momentarily blind me. I pause until the spots clear from my vision before descending the moving steps. Tripping would be a catastrophic way to start what I hope is the beginning of a new father-daughter relationship. Especially when I've spent the past few days and the entire flight reading about the Amazon rain forest to impress my dad.

People stare as the escalator descends. They're trying to connect the dots, taking quick shots of Cougar with their phones and a few of me, just in case I'm someone important they don't recognize. The idea of me being anyone special almost makes me laugh.

My dad wraps me in a bear hug. "I've missed you so much, buddy."

Buddy. The sweet nickname he used to call me makes my heart swell. He smells the way I remembered. Like fresh soap, the outdoors, wind. I haven't seen him in person for over two years, but when I pull back from the hug he looks the same— tall, muscular, tanned skin. He rests sunglasses in wavy, light brown hair. The new lines around his blue eyes make him even more handsome.

"If it's okay, I go by Danny now."

Cougar nods, like he understands I'm trying to build a bridge closer to the old us. "This is my daughter," he tells the photographers. "Danny, this is Cass, my personal assistant." He nods at the dark-haired woman to his right, who's balancing a handheld video camera that obscures her face. "I couldn't survive without her."

Cass says, "Hey, Danny," without taking her eye from the viewfinder. "How's it feel to be here?"

"Um. Great."

"Don't mind the camera. I'm making a behind-the-scenes video diary for this episode that the director may use."

"Sure. Okay."

Cass asks, "Excited about the trip?"

"My kid is coming to Peru to shoot my little show," Cougar tells the paparazzi. "It's an episode with Gus Price. She's got a huge crush on the guy. Who doesn't? So this trip is her sixteenth birthday present."

A huge crush? My face goes up in flames. Cougar tugs at

my braid, which I redid four times before I got off the plane. I probably should tell him that it'll be my seventeenth birthday, but it doesn't really matter.

The paparazzi shout their questions…

"When did Gus commit to the show?"

"He's been trying to get on for some time," Cougar says with a shrug. "But I couldn't say no to Vonyay. He's the hottest singer on the planet, or Ella, right? How many guys get to jump off a cliff with a scared supermodel?"

"Where will the episode be filmed?"

My dad rubs his hands together like an excited kid. "Peru. Deep in the Amazon rain forest. Place doesn't even have a name it's so remote. Lots of things can kill you there—poisonous vipers, big cats, gnarly spiders, boa constrictors. If we're lucky we'll see them all."

Every hair on my body stands up, like they're trying to get my attention, wave me toward the nearest exit. I smile, my lips sticking to my front teeth so that I look more beaver than girl.

The last reporter, a paunch hanging over his ripped jeans, asks, "Are you dating Carmen Fox? Rumor is you're having twins."

Cougar chuckles. "Sadly, neither the lady nor twins are in my immediate future. But I'd sure like to try." The paparazzi all laugh. "That's all for now, boys and girls. I want to spend some quality time with my daughter."

My dad squeezes my shoulder. I hide a wince. My arm still hurts from the yellow fever, tetanus, hepatitis A and B, and typhoid fever shots. I'm sure Commander Sam made them hurt more than necessary to punish me for going to Peru. My stomach gurgles. It definitely doesn't like the malaria pills I swore to take every day. Cass grabs my bag from the carousel. We rush into the perpetual sunshine of LA and the waiting black Escalade.

"Are we going to your house in Venice Beach?" I ask Cougar as the Escalade pulls away from the curb. I've never seen it except for photos in *Architectural Digest*.

"Nope, we're going to a hotel in Beverly Hills called K's. Our flight takes off late tonight so K's will be our base until then."

I hide my disappointment. Hopefully, after this trip, there will be plenty of time to hang at my dad's house. Maybe he'll even let me stay with him, finish high school in California. I have no reason to return to Portland.

When we reach the hotel there are more paparazzi waiting. How these guys know my dad's every move is beyond me. The camera flashes are blinding, but thankfully the reporters don't follow us into the lobby. The hotel is gorgeous, marble floors, leather chairs and floor-to-ceiling bookcases. There's even a piano. It looks like a super wealthy family's library, but with chandeliers. Several people in the lobby are trying to watch my dad without looking like they care. Even the staff is drawn to him, like moths to a bright light. Maybe they feel like I do, like if they look away, he'll vanish.

"Thanks again," I say. "This means a lot."

Cougar says, "To me, too."

I hear a flash go off but it's on my blind side so it doesn't affect me.

"New glasses?"

I push the heavy rectangular frames up the bridge of my nose. "Mom picked them out."

"They hide your gorgeous eyes."

My heart seems to smile. I joke, "Safety first." But the truth is that I have only one eye left. It has twenty-twenty vision, but it's still beyond important to protect it. Just the idea that something could happen, that I could end up blind, makes me nauseated.

We had a blind substitute social studies teacher in seventh grade. Mrs. Ballard. A few of the guys silently moved their desks so that when she walked through the rows, she hit dead ends. My face burned as she struggled to figure out what had happened, but I didn't speak up. Self-loathing won over doing the right thing. The idea that I could become that helpless, ridiculed for a condition I wouldn't be able to change, and that people could make the world even more terrifying than spending every day in the dark, still fills me with dread.

"I doubt there's much danger in the lobby of K's," Cougar says.

My dad is right. I'm in the lobby of a five-star hotel. I tamp down my fears, slide my glasses off and stuff them into a pocket. *What does he see?* Hair two shades darker than my mom's, skin pale from Oregon's rainy winter, no muscles. But I hope he also notices that the blue of my left eye is identical to his own.

Cass picks up a key card at the front desk, hands it to me. Without the camera hiding her face, I can now see she's gorgeous. Asian heritage, with flawless skin, long black hair and a perfect smile.

"Why don't you freshen up, then meet us in Cougar's room for your preinterview?" Cass says. "Room 837. It's supposed to have a balcony and great view. Feel free to raid the mini-bar. When you're ready we're in 861."

"Preinterview?"

Cougar winks. "All part of the birthday fun."

I ride the elevator alone, then follow an arrow to my room. It's beautiful—wood floors, cream-colored carpets and white furniture with silver pulls. The queen-size bed is covered in linens so crisp that they must've been ironed. I open the French doors but don't step onto the small balcony. Clear blue sky above, the city stretched out below. I make myself a promise: I will get to know my father on this trip and become the person I was meant to be.

I shrug on a white T-shirt, the slightly ripped jeans with embroidered flowers down one side that Trix made me buy at a vintage shop last September and sneakers. After brushing my hair until all the snarls are out, I put it in two loose braids.

Quickly, I text my mom: In LA. Dad met my flight. Leaving early morning. It's short, to the point and more than she deserves.

My pulse trips over itself as I walk down the hall to my dad's room. I shouldn't be nervous to spend time with him, but I've seen him only a dozen or so times in the past eight years. We're strangers who share DNA and a sprinkling of phone calls. But we used to have everything in common. We can again.

Cass answers the door on the third knock and waves me in. This suite makes mine look like a shoebox. The living room has a giant built-in TV, modern leather chairs and an L-shaped couch. There are massive black-and-white prints of beach scenes, the models in retro-style bathing suits. The entire far wall of the suite is made of sliding windows that open onto a long deck.

"Danny! I'll be with you in a few minutes," Cougar says from his seat at an antique desk. There are notes in front of him, a Bluetooth mic in one ear. He laughs at something the person on the other line says. "No, you're the sexy tiger. Yes, you are…"

I wander into the next room. A massive wooden headboard frames a king-size bed that's across from a window with an expansive view of LA. The leather furniture in here is a deep brown, and a plush red-and-blue Persian-style runner leads to an enormous bathroom with gray marble double sinks and a shower that looks like a car wash. This is the bathroom of Trix's dreams. She's always complaining about cold showers because of all her siblings. I'd text her photos, but the phone call we had when I told her what Commander Sam had done rings in my ears.

That totally sucks, Danny. But imagine what your life would've been like if you'd ended up spending half your time with Cougar. You have zero in common.

You're missing the point. My mom pretended to send my letters. She lied about it for almost ten years! She let me think, let my dad think, that neither one of us cared.

Stop yelling, okay? Regardless of what your mom did, and it was definitely shitty, your dad should've been there for you. You weren't a priority. It's the same thing with my birth dad.

I'm going to Peru.

What? Bad idea! You don't belong in the rain forest. Come on, you'd look like a fool.

Thanks for your support. Do you want to tell me how uncoordinated I am next? That I'll never be a model? Maybe call me Pigeon?

I'm trying to protect you. Look, I understand why you want to go. Really, I do. But the ugly fact is that none of our bio parents ever really wanted us. Look at the bright side. At least we're in this together.

I stare into the hotel mirror, and my reflection grimaces back. Our fight grew worse...

We're not the same. My birth mom kept me and my biological dad wants a relationship with me.

Danny, you're freaking delusional. Let it go and move on. It's okay to be you.

Really? Then why search for your birth parents when you have an amazing family? Why change how you act and dress every year? Why pierce holes in your face, dye your hair and have sex with people you don't give a shit about who just want to use you?

Now who's being a crappy friend?

So why be my friend at all? Oh yeah, because you're miserable about your bio parents and I am, too. Except now I have a chance to have a relationship with my dad, to have everything I've ever wanted, which you already have with your adoptive father, and you want to steal it from me.

Take it back.

Which part?

All of it.

No.

"We're not the same," I tell my reflection in the mirror. "Cougar would've been there if he'd known that I didn't blame him, that I loved and needed him."

"Danny," Cass says, appearing in the mirror behind me, the video camera at her side. "You ready?"

My face goes blotchy red. *Did she hear me?* "For what, ex-actly?"

Cass gives me a funny look. "Kiddo, your dad wants you in this episode, too."

"Like helping you?"

"No. In front of the camera."

I shiver, suddenly ice-cold. "What?"

Cass smiles. "You heard me. Incredible, right?"

"That's not... I'm not... I don't think that's a good idea." What I don't say is that this is my chance to prove to my dad that I can be the kid he used to love. That won't happen if I'm forced to do things that accentuate my flaws.

Cass says, "I'm going to let you in on a secret. What Cougar wants, Cougar gets. Come on, we'll do the interview on the balcony while your dad finishes his calls." She walks out of the bathroom. Over her shoulder, she asks, "You coming?"

WWCD? "Yes."

9

Two chairs have been set facing each other. Despite knowing better, I glance over the railing and am instantly sorry when my stomach lurches. "Maybe I should change." I edge back into the safety of the hotel room.

"You look perfect."

Cass is tall, with a lean body clad in all black, leather bracelets lining her wrists and hair that practically glows. If she wasn't a personal assistant, she could be a model, so I'm confident we have very different definitions of *perfect*. I slide onto a chair. "Should I unbraid my hair?"

"Nope. Your dad wants you to be authentic. It's part of the hook."

"The hook?"

"Don't worry about it." Cass sits and turns on the video.

The red light blinks. "So, Danny, tell me about yourself. Start with your full name, what you like to do, friends, et cetera."

"Um. I'm Danger Danielle Warren."

"Danger?"

"My dad's choice."

Cass laughs. "Of course it was."

"I'm, um, sev—sixteen next Friday. I live in Portland, Oregon, with my mom." What do I like to do? My mind goes blank. I'm not going to tell Cass that my favorite sport is bowling because my coordination, while greatly improved, still sucks. As for friends, I thought one best friend was enough, but I might not have her anymore.

"Danny?"

"Um. I don't really play sports. Mostly I read…and I like to make three-dimensional, um, box things." I sink lower in my chair, wishing I could disappear.

Cass puts down the camera. "Danny, it's okay. You're still figuring it out."

But it's not okay. Cougar Warren is my dad. He deserves better. "I'm sorry."

"Don't be. I'm twenty-nine and have no life outside this job. No boyfriend, hobbies, I don't even have my own apartment. When I'm not working, I couch-surf at friends' places."

"And you're okay living like that?"

"Hell yes! I'm putting in my time, showing Cougar I'm dedicated and that I have the skill and drive to someday direct." Cass starts filming again. "Let's just conjure the life you dream of leading. That's the first step to making it happen. Where would you live?"

"LA."

"Why?"

"To be closer to my dad."

"You miss him?"

"He's super busy."

"Are you close to your mom?"

I thought we were, in our way, but she's a liar. "Not really."

"Cougar told me Samantha made it hard for you two to have a relationship."

"I… Yeah." I'm super pissed at Sam but my answer still feels disloyal.

Cass waits a few beats. "Okay. Let's move on. Not sure which way you swing but what about a boyfriend or girl-friend?"

I blush. "Boyfriend. But I've never had one."

"I was a late bloomer, too. Is it fair to say Gus Price would be your type?"

The question makes my insides lurch in a not altogether horrible way. "Well, I guess he's everyone's type?"

Cass laughs. "Pretty much. Last question. What do you hope to get out of this trip to Peru?"

"I want to change who I am," I blurt, "and spend more time with my dad." Cass lowers the camera. Her forehead scrunches, as if she's worried. My insides sink. I should've gone for a joke, like I want to be the next female Indiana Jones.

Cass says, "Danny, hon, you're good the way you are." She hesitates. "You do get that your dad is going to be working, like, nonstop? Most of the crew and the director are already there setting things up, but it's a short trip. Your father won't be free to hang out one-on-one, much."

"I know. Really, I'm just grateful to be here."

"You guys almost done?" Cougar calls. "Because if I tell one more reporter how goddamned excited I am to be working with Gus Price, instead of the other way around, I'm going to throw myself off that balcony."

"Hey, Dad, um, are you sure you want me to actually be in the episode? I mean, I'm cool, really cool, with just helping behind the scenes?"

Cougar roars, "Absolutely not! The world might be most excited about seeing Gus with his shirt off, but I'm more excited about taking a trip with you, buddy, and having you be part of my show. You're my priority."

Cass swings the camera toward Cougar. "Say that last part again."

"I'm more excited about taking this trip with my kid, Danny, than spending time with *Famous Magazine*'s hottest teen of the year."

My dad strides onto the balcony and kneels, hands on my knees. I stare into his face and try to see myself there. Besides a few shared freckles on our noses and the color of my blue eye, we barely look related.

"Cards on the table," Cougar says. "I know you had to fight to come. Your mom hates me."

"She doesn't. She's just…kind of bitter."

Cougar nods. "Our relationship was complicated. Samantha and me, we were just kids when we had you. My dreams included you both, but she had different ideas. I had to respect that. But I sure as hell regret not seeing you more. Commander Sam didn't want me there. In the end, I thought that the fighting would've hurt you more than helped."

He's wrong, but I get it. He didn't have all the facts. I don't tell him what my mom did to him, to us. There'll be time for that later, off camera.

"My biggest regret is that we didn't have the chance to stay close when you were younger. I hope we can change that, now that you're old enough to make your own choices."

"I hope so, too." I feel two things at once—a surge of optimism and a swell of guilt. Like this is the best day ever, but wanting a relationship with my dad is a betrayal of my mom despite the fact that she's the one who betrayed us.

Cougar jumps to his feet. "Now, let's get out of here. I'm starving."

Cass turns off the camera. I'm kind of uncomfortable that she just taped that conversation. If my mom ever hears it her feelings, wherever they're buried, might be hurt. "The pre-interview stuff isn't going to air, right?"

Cass looks at her watch. "Crap. We're late for dinner at Nobu."

"Isn't your job to keep us on track?" Cougar ribs. "Did you call the paparazzi, let them know our schedule?"

Cass nods. "Of course."

I happily scamper off the balcony. "Should I change?" I bought a dress at Goodwill. I'm sure it's not stylish enough for LA, but at least it's black.

"Buddy, this one is just for Cass, my agent, a network guy and me. It'd bore you to death. Loads of planning, logistics, blah, blah, blah, then a heads-up to the paparazzi on our location for a photo op with Carmen Fox."

I can't help asking, "Is she really your girlfriend?"

Cougar laughs. "Our publicists are stoking that fire. Order whatever you want from room service, okay?"

My heart sags. "Um. Sure."

"We'll catch up more on the plane. Promise," my dad says.

I grin. "Sounds really great. Really."

"Good. So chill out for now, enjoy the movie channel and room service. Cass will call when we're back from dinner and we'll meet in the lobby. Right, Cass?" Cougar ruffles her hair. "I can count on you not to mess that up, too?"

She smiles. "I'm on it."

Cougar bounds toward the door, but before he opens it, he looks back and winks. "In a few hours it's off to the airport, kiddo. The beginning of the adventure of a lifetime."

My nerves jangle. *Tomorrow will be the first step to getting back to the Danny before the accident. Someone my dad will be proud to call his daughter.* "I can't wait."

10

We don't sit together on the flight to Peru. My dad and Cass have work to do. I get it. But when Cougar walks by me without glancing back it's a reminder that once we sailed the ocean together but now I'm in a separate boat, desperately attempting to paddle back. *What if I can't get there?* Anxiety tightens my chest. *No. There will be moments to show my dad who I can be.*

It's my first time in business class, and only second time flying, so once the window shade is down, I watch movies to distract myself from thinking about how high we are; that there are only a few inches of plane between me and the clouds; that engines can fail. I skip the late dinner and have a hot-fudge sundae before snuggling beneath a comforter and drifting off to sleep.

We arrive the following morning—a smooth flight without any bumps except for a light one on landing. Still, I feel a surge of confidence that I didn't spend the entire time scared. My dad insists on carrying my backpack while Cass films our walk through the Lima airport past high-end stores like Hugo Boss, BVLGARI and Gucci, then the cramped jeep ride along the airport's mirrored exterior. Our driver turns away from the main airport onto a narrow paved road that cuts through an expanse of yellowish dirt stretching toward distant mountains. Compared to winter in Oregon, this looks and feels like another planet. When we reach a metal hangar set on a small airstrip the driver stops and we get out of the jeep. It's in the low seventies. The wind and harsh sunlight make my right eye tear. I have the urge to put on my glasses. They have lenses that darken in sunlight. But I don't. *Cougar said my eyes are gorgeous.*

The pilot is waiting inside the open hangar. Tan cargo shorts and a white Air Lima Express button-down shirt hang off his bony frame. There are crescents of dirt beneath his fingernails and gray stubble on his chin that matches his white skin's ashen tone. Watery green eyes are red-rimmed. *Is he hung over?* I glance around. The place seems kind of run-down with piles of junk in the corners and cluttered countertops. Instantly my palms are damp.

"Mack," the pilot says, hand outstretched.

"Cougar Warren." My dad pulls the man into a bro hug, then tilts his aviator sunglasses down, peering around. "Where are my camera and sound guys and America's hottest teen actor?"

Mack points us toward the tarmac. "Your people are waiting by the plane. The movie star hasn't arrived yet."

Two guys are stretched out on the pavement beneath a very small plane's wing, their heads resting on duffel bags. One has brown skin with black dreadlocks fanned around his head. He's engrossed in a paperback and looks comfortable in baggy yoga pants and a T-shirt. The other guy is white but very tan, like he spends every day in the sun. A baseball hat covers blond shoulder-length hair and his tank top shows off chiseled biceps. They both look midthirties. I recognize a Dispatch song coming from the small speakers connected to the muscular guy's phone. As for the plane, it's splattered with mud, and the propeller looks like it's drooping.

Cass and my dad walk off to talk, leaving me with the pilot. We wander toward his plane. "Um, how many engines does it have?"

Mack says, "One. But we won't be flying that high so if we crash, the chance of us all dying is slim." He laughs, the sound phlegmy, like he smokes six packs a day.

"Have you… Has it… Have you been flying a long time?"

"This is my first time," Mack says, laughing harder.

"You teasing my kid?" my dad asks.

I jump. He's on my left side—my blind side. He musses my hair like I'm six, not almost seventeen, but I don't mind.

Mack nods at a few clouds building over the mountains. "Rain is coming."

Cougar calls over his shoulder, "Cass, what's Gus's ETA?"

Cass pulls out her phone. "He was on a flight from Manaus, Brazil. It was supposed to be here twenty minutes before ours. I'll call his people."

"You sure about rain?" Cougar asks the pilot.

"It's December in Peru. Rainy season. There're always shit-buckets of water coming down. Forecast is calling for thunderstorms, too. We need to get there and be tied down by 1:00 p.m. to be safe."

"He missed his flight," Cass says. She twists her hair into a knot, fans her neck.

Cougar frowns. "When's he getting in now?"

"Supposedly an hour."

My dad shakes his head, creased lines between his brows.

Cass's smile fades. "Mack, can you work with us on this?"

"It's company policy, not a rule, but regardless I won't go if the weather seriously deteriorates."

Hooray! I let go of the stale air I've been holding in way too long.

"We can make it worth the risk," Cass says. "Double the price?"

Mack tips his head side to side. "If the kid gets here before the weather goes to shit we'll give it a try. But we turn back if I can't avoid the storm cells and you're still on the hook for the flight time."

Cougar fist-bumps Mack. "Deal. Now things are getting interesting!"

I have the urge to run.

"Go meet some of my crew." Cougar pushes me toward the men lounging beneath the plane's wing, calls out, "Guys, this is my kid, Danny."

"Hey, Danny," the blond guy says. He sits up and holds out his hand. "I'm Sean. Man, your eyes are incredible. They'll be supercool in the right light. Mud'll bring them out, too."

Mud?

Cougar calls out, "Sean's the best cameraman in the outdoor film biz. Tie up those laces, buddy, this isn't Rincon."

Sean is wearing worn leather boots with the laces untied. My brand-new hiking boots are a burnt-orange color. My mom brought them home from REI the day before I left. They were marked down 40 percent because they're so ugly. They're tied tight. Double knotted. I make a mental note to loosen the stiff laces when no one is around. "What's Rincon?"

"It's a wave spot in Southern California," Sean says. "In a different life I was a surfer."

"He's sandbagging," the other guy says. "He was one of the top three surfers in the world." He closes the book he's reading, *The Stand*, by Stephen King, and gets to his feet. "There have been movies made about Sean's ability to ride the giants and survive. He has mad balance." He holds out his hand. "I'm Jupiter."

I shake it and say, "Really? Jupiter?" before I can stop myself from being rude. "Sorry."

Jupiter grins. It's the best smile I've ever seen. He grabs a duffel bag and motions for me to sit. "Don't be sorry. Last name is Jones. My mom wanted me to stand out. Guess we have that in common. You gonna live up to *your* name, Danger?"

He knows my real name. "No one calls me that anymore. I'm just Danny. The most dangerous things I do are read and make dioramas." I cringe. Babbling makes me sound like a total loser. Both Sean and Jupiter are probably wondering why Cougar brought me along.

"Well, *Just* Danny, it's nice to meet you," Jupiter says. "All we know about you is that your name is on our schedule."

My stomach tightens. It shouldn't bother me that my dad hasn't talked about me. Still, it's a little like I'm alive but, at the same time, a ghost. "I guess there's not much else to know," I admit. "My life isn't exciting or glamorous. I'm a kid in high school."

"The last time I was in Toronto I saw an exhibit that had some of Louis Daguerre and Charles Marie Bouton's work," Jupiter says.

I can't help grinning. Daguerre and Bouton invented the diorama. "Did you see any boxes that were illuminated on two sides? When it's done right the scenes change."

Jupiter grins. "My little sister gets that same light in her eyes when she talks about a new recipe. Venus is only eleven but she's gonna be a chef—blending different styles, like Mexican Korean or Thai Cajun, is her thing." He laughs. "Sounds weird, but she's rad and so is her food, most of the time. And yeah, the exhibit had a light box of a train traveling through the mountains before and after a crash. Attention to detail, even down to passengers in the train's tiny glass windows, was incredible."

"Tell us about the dioramas you make," Sean says.

His focus makes my skin prickle. "They're nothing special."

Sean shakes his head. "Never say that about anything you love to do."

I glance back to make sure Cougar is out of earshot. "Mostly they're landscapes. Places my dad has filmed episodes, situations he faced. I cut each element out with a scalpel and then paint them or use textured material. Then I place lost objects in the boxes."

Jupiter asks, "Why lost objects?"

My face gets warm. "To give discarded items a purpose, I guess."

Jupiter meets my gaze. "You're a cool girl, *Just* Danny."

Mack wanders over and circles the plane, stained hands running along its side. My mouth is suddenly so dry that when I swallow there's a clicking sound.

Jupiter says, "I've flown in lots of planes that were way more run-down looking than this one. Mack was in the military. He's been flying for forty years and these Caravans are solid machines. You ever fly in one?"

"I'm kind of not a huge fan of flying." I hope he missed the nervous warble in my voice.

"Don't blame you," Jupiter says. "I prefer my feet on the ground, too. But we'll get through this flight together."

My anxiety goes down a notch. "So what do you do for my dad?"

"I'm his sound guy," Jupiter says. "I make roaring waterfalls, tornados, mudslides, flash floods and wild animals sound as dangerous as they are."

Jupiter rubs his right arm in the exact spot where my mom jabbed my vaccinations. Maybe they actually hurt everyone. "Have either of you been in the Amazon before?"

Sean shakes his head. "Like I've told Cougar, too many things there that can kill you."

A chill dances down my spine. "But you ride monster waves."

"I choose the wave. I'm in control."

"So why are you working on this trip?"

"Money. I'm getting married in a few months. My beautiful bride invited three hundred of our closest friends to a destination wedding."

"Why not make it smaller?" I ask.

Sean chuckles. "You're too young to get this, but happy wife, happy life. Plus, I've spent most of my existence pursuing my own dreams. It's time to take someone else's into account."

"And I thought you were just a shallow surf god," Jupiter says. He turns to me. "Sean may be afraid of creepy crawlies, but I've been to Brazil, Colombia, all over South America. Truth is I hated every one of those places. I'm not a fan of heat, humidity or mosquitos. I prefer Cougar's episodes in Alaska, Montana, Iceland—basically, anywhere cold or mountainous. Plus, I'd rather face an angry moose or bear than a coiled snake. Don't know how your dad talked me into going on this shoot." Jupiter shakes his head. "Yeah, I do. He's Cougar Warren."

"Your dad is a force," Sean agrees.

"We haven't gotten to spend a lot of time together. It's not my dad's fault or anything. He's super busy. But I'm hoping to change that from here on, and get to really know him." Jupiter and Sean share a look. I say, "No worries. I know he'll be busy." *There will be moments, I'm sure of it.*

"So, um, if you hate hot and buggy, why are you going to the Amazon?" I ask Jupiter.

"Truth is that, like Sean, if I didn't need the cash, I'd skip this one."

"Are you saving to get married, too?"

"Nah," Jupiter says, watching a plane take flight in the distance. "The money is to help with my sister's private school." He nods his head toward my dad and Cass. "They're right,

the Amazon during rainy season will make for a great episode. But it'll be pretty miserable for you guys."

My fingers and toes tingle. "Why just for us?"

"The crew gets rain gear, mosquito nets, tents, sleeping
bags and blow-up pads. We have a camp stove to make our
delicious meals—you know, the kind in a bag you dump in
boiling water." He makes a face. "We'll have bottled water,
while you guys will be filtering yours in mud holes or boiling
it *if* you manage to start a fire. The crew's experience won't
be luxurious but it'll be bearable. You, Cougar and Gus will
have to make your own shelter, find food and deal with bug
bites. Plus, you guys will be doing all the athletic stuff. Cougar makes it pretty safe, though."

Despite the sunshine, goose bumps break along my arms.
"If it's bad—"

"Cougar loves it that way. The more extreme, the hap-
pier that man is. But I'm sure if you're really miserable he'll
let you tap out."

I shake my head. "No tapping out."

"Like father, like daughter."

I wish.

11

By the time Gus arrives, it's almost noon according to the cheap waterproof watch Samantha bought me. Cougar and Cass have been pacing and constantly checking the matching oversize waterproof watches they both wear. It hasn't started raining yet, but there's a solid layer of slate-gray clouds. The air temperature has dropped low enough that I've tugged on a sweatshirt.

My dad has been swearing a lot, most of it directed at Cass. I haven't seen him angry since I was a little kid. It brings up that awful sense of knowing something is wrong, wondering whose fault it is, but being powerless to change it. I feel bad for Cass, but it's now late morning, and I, for one, am thrilled. We'll definitely have to put off flying until tomorrow. That's a night in a hotel, a bed, shower and fluffy towels. No mosquitos or any of the other horrible things Jupiter mentioned. Plus, it gives me another day with my dad before he starts working.

A jeep speeds down the road and stops where we've all congregated near the plane. Gus Price climbs out, his backpack slung over one shoulder, and closes the distance to the group. "Sorry I'm late. I had a meeting with my director that went long. You know directors," he says with a wry smile. "They like to hear themselves talk."

Cougar chuckles, "Oh, do I ever."

My heart drops a beat, then returns, double time. A lot of people probably think movie stars aren't as good-looking in real life. That it's all about the lights, makeup, angles. Those people are totally wrong as far as Gus Price goes. He's tall, at least six-four, lightly tanned white skin, dark blond hair pulled back into a messy ponytail, a square jaw, broad shoulders. Sunglasses hide eyes I know from the movies are hazel flecked with gold. His black T-shirt has a tiny symbol in the center that probably stands for something too cool for mere mortals to know about. It rests on the frayed waistband of shorts that hang below his hips. He's wearing flip-flops that definitely aren't rain forest approved, but look cool. Trix would lose her mind. *Truth.*

"No big deal," my dad says, giving Gus a hug like he hasn't been pacing and swearing for hours, like everything is super chill.

Gus says, "You must be Danny."

His attention is like getting hit with a spotlight. I haven't quite registered that Gus Price is standing a foot away from me, let alone that he knows my name. Digging for something to say, I find…nothing.

"Don't mind my kid. She's starstruck. Glad you could make it. We're a bit behind schedule, but I worked it out with our pilot."

Cass hits me with a hip bump while still filming. "Say hi."

"Why don't you give the video diary thing a break?" Jupiter suggests. "Conserve your batteries."

"They're long lasting and I have six extras in my case," Cass says.

Terrific. I reach out my hand to shake Gus's but at that exact moment he turns to meet Jupiter and Sean so I'm left with my hand midair. Cass clears her throat. Gus glances over his shoulder, sees me standing there like a big dolt. I blush from the crown of my head to my heels.

Gus says, "The team has told me a lot about you."

Every inch of my skin gets hot and my guess is that I'm red and blotchy, too. Gus waits for me to say something, but my word well is totally dry. There's a tiny scar on his jawline that adds to the overall package. I take a step closer, like Gus is a planet with its own gravitational pull.

Mack barks, "Quit your lollygagging and load up."

Load up? Sean tosses his duffel into the back of the plane. Jupiter follows. Cass is already halfway up the stairs. I'm realizing that when my dad says jump, she asks how high. "Isn't it too late? You wanted to be tied down by one, right?"

The pilot shrugs. "Flight should only take a few hours. I'll spend the night at the airstrip, then head back in the morning."

"Is there a problem?" Cougar asks. His arm is hung over Gus's shoulders like they're old friends.

My hopes are a balloon that's losing air fast. "No problem." I head toward the stairs.

"You're in for a wild ride."

I turn to tell my dad that I'm up for it, but he's looking at Gus, not me.

Gus winks. "GP isn't so precious that he can't get through a little plane flight."

Did he really just talk about himself in the third person? Must be a movie star thing. Rain begins to patter on the tarmac. I want to reiterate what Mack said. *Shit-buckets of rain are coming.* And thunderstorms. I'm not an experienced flyer but torrential rain and lightning in the battered aluminum tube everyone is climbing into does not seem like a good idea. It's a horrendous idea. But if I say something or, worse, refuse to go, then I'll be the one responsible for screwing up the schedule and budget. Worse, my dad will know that I'm still that scaredy-cat kid.

"All good, Danny?" my dad asks.

"Definitely." I run up the stairs like I can't wait to take off. The plane has three rows with two seats on the right side and a single one on the left side. Sean beckons, and I slide into a seat at the back of the plane beside him. Jupiter is directly in front of me. Cass sits across from him videotaping the flight. I don't want a record of me clenching the edge of my seat, eyes screwed shut. Gus scans the plane and his eyes rest for just a second on Sean sitting beside me. Did he actually want to sit next to me? *Not possible.* Gus takes the front row, sitting across from Cougar, both stretching out their legs like this flight is the most relaxing thing they've ever done.

"Buckle up," Mack says as he makes his way to the front

of the plane. "It's going to be a rough flight. People, do not barf in my plane."

That warning is probably for me. Mack is on the radio, then we're taxiing, rolling down the runway at high speed, every bump in the tarmac jarring my spine. We do a U-turn. The engine starts whining. We take off and the plane climbs steeply.

I close my eyes. Beneath the engine noise of the plane, Sean chats with Cass, and Cougar and Gus joke around like they've known each other forever. Don't they all get that we could crash at any moment? The plane drops. My stomach lurches. I breathe in through my nose, then out through my mouth like my mom taught me to do when I had migraines or panic attacks. If I throw up in Mack's plane he'll be pissed, I'll be mortified, and the look in my dad's eyes will confirm my tagline is spot-on. *Defective. Inferior. Embarrassment.*

The next few hours are a series of relatively calm moments punctuated by violent drops and shudders as Mack weaves around the storm cells. At times the noise of rain hitting the plane is deafening. When Cougar points out lightning in the distance, I don't look, eyes clamped shut, hands gripping the armrests, nails digging in so hard that they're probably making holes in the already-ratty upholstery.

Cougar yells back to Cass, "How's my kid doing?"

I open my eyes as Cass peers at me, camera in hand. She's a peculiar shade of green. Sweat beads on her forehead. "She's doing fine." Cass moves up the center aisle to sit beside Cougar, stopping to zip her camera inside a bag and put it in the bin before buckling in. Maybe she's preparing to barf, too.

Every muscle in my body is knotted. I've swallowed vomit

repeatedly. My T-shirt is drenched in sweat. I'm definitely not fine but appreciate Cass covering for me. When the turbulence eases for the moment, I force my fingers to release their death grip on the armrests.

Sean nudges my shoulder. "Looking kinda pale."

"Didn't you hear? I'm fine."

He chuckles. "You surf?"

Seriously? Do I look like I surf? "No."

"Massive wave at Rincon last weekend. Day before, double overhead at Lompoc."

"Terrific."

"Thing about surfing is that when you're paddling for a big wave, everything else disappears. It's you and the monster above you. If you think about anything else, you miss it. If you catch the wave but your mind wanders, you get smashed."

"Are you *ever* scared?"

"Surfing forces me out of my head. Live in the moment or suffer the consequences."

"What about sharks?" The idea of sitting on a surfboard waiting for a wave, legs dangling in the dark blue, seems like a really bad idea. I wonder if there's insurance for that kind of thing. Loss of limbs due to thinking you're higher on the food chain than you actually are.

Sean shrugs. "There's a better chance of me dying in a car accident."

I don't point out that there are way more drivers than surfers. Plus he's in a car more often than the water, so his comparison is faulty.

"Hey, Cougar," Mack calls over his shoulder.

"Yeah?"

"Gotta head back. There are too many damned thunderstorms ahead."

Cougar goes forward between the two pilot seats. "What do you say we give it one more shot?"

"Right from the get-go I had to divert way off my flight plan, but I guess that I could try to fly under the boomers. More turbulence, but it'd keep us outa the storm cells."

More turbulence? I'm definitely going to vomit.

Cougar claps him on the shoulder. "Good man."

"One shot. Fuel is becoming an issue. If I can't find my way through, we head back."

"Deal."

"Tighten your seat belts," Mack orders.

If my seat belt was any tighter, I wouldn't be able to breathe. Glancing to my left, I see that Sean isn't buckled in. "Hey." I nod at his belt.

Sean winks. "Never wear 'em. It's bad form to doubt Lady Luck."

I'm about to tell him about the car accident victims who weren't wearing seat belts that Commander Sam has seen in the ER, people thrown from vehicles, others whose faces went through windshields, but my words are cut off as the plane veers right. The turbulence we experienced before was nothing compared to the brutal drops and violent tremors now rattling the plane. I smell vomit. Probably Cass. Despite how sick I feel, I'm too scared to barf. I'm freezing cold, boiling hot. Cougar whoops. He's enjoying this. Gus holds his arms in the air like he's on a roller coaster. Another thing they have in common besides being great-looking, talented and famous. Thunder explodes and the plane shudders.

"Think of it like a gargantuan wave," Sean shouts over the storm. "Pretend you're riding it, the wave cresting, white water boiling above your head, a massive tube of blue forming. Feel the cold spray biting, curled toes cramping on your board, the wind's fingers snarling your hair."

I do exactly what Sean says. The green-faced puke-monster inside me takes a tiny step back. "Thanks, I—"

There's another vicious drop. I see trees out the window, then we're crashing through the tops of them before lifting again. One wing catches and we start spinning, backpacks, books and computers flying through the air. There's a ripping sound like the world is being torn open. But it's not the world. It's our plane breaking into pieces.

There's open sky...

The front half of the plane spins away...

Someone screams...

12

My world is upside down.

No. I'm upside down, seat belt buckled, feet above my head tangled in a thorny vine that's suffocating a tree's thick limb.

Where's Sean?

Hot raindrops patter down on my face. I look up, a little bit to the left, and then close my eyes, brain scrambling for a different explanation.

My mom orders: *Give your fears a name. It takes away their power. Then tell me what you like and what you want to be.*

I am afraid of heights…

More droplets patter down, dribble into my hair.

I like flannel sheets…

My head is pounding so hard that my skull might explode.

The ground is far, probably twenty feet… My neck will snap if I land on my head… Both ankles will break if I come down on my feet… Maybe only my ribs will splinter if I land on my side, but that could puncture a lung… My vision blurs.

When I grow up I want to be…adventurous. Strong. Athletic. Popular. Brave. A propeller. The solution. Cougar.

I unbuckle my seat belt and drop.

Falling two stories takes enough time for my stomach to leap into my mouth. I twist as I fall so that I hit the rain forest's floor feet first with a bone-jarring thud. Pain radiates through my body as I collapse and roll over sharp sticks and roots until I'm on my back. *I can't breathe.* Rationally, I know that the wind has been knocked out of me. My diaphragm is in spasm, incapable of the simple act of breathing. *Interesting fact: when a cockroach has muscle spasms it sometimes flips onto its back but doesn't have the coordination to right itself, so it dies that way.*

Breathe.

Breathe.

Breathe!

I suck in tendrils of air until I can force down a teaspoonful. Slowly, my diaphragm relaxes. I gulp, feeding my brain and body until my limbs stop tingling.

Commander Sam's no-nonsense voice rockets to the surface, commands: *Assess.*

Wiggling my fingers and toes proves I'm not suffering from a broken back, or at least my spinal cord isn't severed. There was a twinge in my ankle when I landed. Carefully, I roll my foot around. It's not broken, maybe just a slight sprain.

Sitting up, I look around. No plane. No people. *Dad, Cass, Gus, Jupiter—they were in the front part that tore off.* "Sean?" I don't want to look, but I do. Sean hangs facedown over a thick tree bough five feet above the spot where the metal frame of my seat snagged. His torso is partially ripped, purplish intestines dangling. Blood steadily drips from the massive wound. I touch my forehead where beads of Sean's blood have dried. I call, "Sean?" He doesn't answer. *This is happening. I'm alone somewhere in the Amazon. Sean is dead. His body is hanging above me. Lady Luck deserted him.* I should be horrified, screaming, but I'm not. This is real, but it's like my brain has decided it can't be true.

I look up again. Sean's eyes are open but their bright light has drained away. I'm alive and the impartiality of death—that it chose a guy who had everything going for him, not me—is unfathomable. *Sean's fiancée will never marry him.* The finality of that thought, the number of people who will be forever changed—mothers, fathers, aunts, uncles, siblings, friends, unborn children—cuts through the haze. My throat squeezes tight; my hands tremble. With effort, I drag my gaze away.

Trees tower above me, their triangular buttresses, made from partly exposed ground roots, would take ten people with arms outstretched to encircle. Stands of bamboo form impossibly high prison bars difficult to see beyond. Facts from my dad's show flood my brain: bamboo, found everywhere in the Amazon, is a type of hard, hollow grass that can grow as tall as a tree, with polished, jointed stems three feet across.

Focus.

Palms of every height crowd the already-dense vegetation. Everywhere there are flowers—explosions of white, red and yellow, with scribbles of violet, orange and sapphire at their centers. Woody vines hang from limbs, wind around massive trunks, climbing toward the treetops. They create highways of travel for monkeys that chitter overhead. Their sporadic, throaty howls raise the hairs on my arms. The air is crowded with musky scents so rich that they clog my sinuses and drip down my throat like syrup.

It's okay.

A hummingbird hovers over a trumpet-shaped blue flower. Its wings are lavender. A bright yellow bee at least two inches long draws nectar from a bloom more orange than the sun. Its buzz vibrates in my ears. Multicolored parrots wing overhead, then disappear into the foliage. The heavy bass of frogs underscores melodic birds' songs. Each sound pours into my body until I'm overflowing. I spy a motionless, jet-black toad squatting less than six feet to my right. He's the size of a basketball, covered with emerald spots. I slowly back away.

It's…okay.

The canopy is so thick that the light is shadowy, hiding danger in pools of gray. There's deadfall everywhere, and trees that sway hundreds of feet above crackle like they might split and fall at any moment. I've been swallowed by the rain forest. I'm trapped in its swamp-like belly. I hear panting—it's me. My head jerks left and right, like it did in the old days. *Pigeon.* I don't care. I'm desperate to see every threat, figure out how close it is, muscles coiled to run.

It's not okay. I'm not okay.

How will I get out of this place?

What if I can't find my dad?

What if no one else survived?

Am I going to die here?

The air, hot and humid, thick with the stink of rot, makes

me choke. A droning in my ears signals that the mosquitos have found me. The anti-malaria pills my mom prescribed are somewhere in the wreckage of the plane. *I'm going to get malaria… maybe dengue…high fevers…pain…vomiting…death.* Hundreds of mosquitos coat my slick skin, drawn to the heat that goes hand in hand with dread. An impulse to scream and never stop is overwhelming.

My chest tightens. *NO.* I grew out of panic attacks when I was ten. *But this is how they always started.* "Stop it," I hiss. But my skin shrinks like a torture chamber whose walls slowly close in, crushing its occupant. My bones strain under the relentless pressure. *Not now!* My body doesn't listen, beginning to slide down the terrifying slope. The panic attack surges forward, tackles me. My heart struggles under the painful crush of collapsing bones. Sweat soaks through damp clothes. Invisible hands wrap around my neck, tighten. A wave of dizziness hits. My vision narrows until I'm looking through a dark tunnel.

If I pass out something with claws or fangs will find me… hurt me…kill me…

I.

Can't.

Let.

This.

Happen.

Stars rain down like silver confetti.

WWCD?

WWCD?

WWCD?

I push back against the panic attack like it's an invisible adversary. My ribs expand at a snail's pace, giving my heart space to squeeze out a few beats. *WWCD?* Taking deeper breaths, I force my bones to broaden, allow my organs room to function. Next, I focus on reining in the runaway horse that is my pulse. Light-headedness dissipates. The hands around my neck loosen. Gradually, my vision clears.

I'm crouched, arms wrapped around my knees, head buried. It's hard to know how much time has passed. When I was a kid the attacks lasted fifteen minutes at most, but always seemed like an eternity. They left me wrung dry of energy and emotion, with the sense that the next one was right around the corner, that I'd never be free. It's how I feel now—doomed. My mom's strident voice breaks through my dismay: *Concentrate.*

Slowly, the gears in my brain start turning and I uncramp, stand up. If anyone else survived, what's the chance that they'll find me? They could pass ten feet away and I might not see or hear them over the living beat of the rain forest. "Help," I shout, but the word gets stuck in my parched throat. I try again. "Help! Is anyone here? HELP—HELP—HELP!" I'm screaming and the monkeys add their shrieks, the sounds shredding the air. My ears strain for a human voice. No one yells back. "HELP—HELP—HELP!"

I shout until my voice is a hoarse croak. When I finally stop screaming, it takes a while for the monkeys to quiet. The sounds of the Amazon flow around me, cramming every empty space with the noise of leaves rustling, animals shuffling, leaping, running, birds calling and the snap of branches under the feet of predators I don't even want to imagine. If I don't start moving, find help? I'll be alone tonight. *It will be dark*. My only hope is that luck will lead me to other survivors. *I've never been lucky.*

I look up. Sean's feet are bare, tanned from countless days surfing Rincon. "Goodbye," I whisper. I breathe in his essence, then start walking.

13

There's no right direction. My voice is so hoarse from screaming that now my shouts are mere croaks. It's slow going. The forest grows in layers, one upon the next, sometimes so thick that I can't see my hands or feet, a maze with no clues or markers. Thorns tear at my shorts and leave bloody scratches on bare skin. Ants teem over my boots, racing up my legs, bites burning as I frantically brush them off. As I travel, there's this weird sense of being both in my body and outside it, watching the struggle, frustrated at the uncoordinated girl's slow pace.

"WWCD?" *My dad wouldn't give up.*

Sweat from the heat and humidity, the effort required to force my way forward, slicks my body. I'm parched. I've seen my dad find water in tree trunks or vines, but I don't have a machete. When I trip over a root and fall hard on all fours, I stay down, catching my breath. My fingertip touches something soft. It's a worn hiking boot peeking out from beneath a bush—Sean's. The other one is a few feet away. Maybe it's a sign that I'm going in the right direction. Or maybe it's just dumb chance. I tie the laces together and hang the boots around my neck.

My ears strain for the sound of voices. But all I hear is the chattering of monkeys, the incessant whine of insects and countless birdcalls. *Night is coming.* For a girl who hasn't slept without a nightlight since that fateful camping trip in Yosemite, the idea makes me shiver. A scream scrapes together deep in my chest. But just before my mouth opens, a monkey lets out a bloodcurdling screech, probably signaling a predator. I swallow my cries like broken glass and keep walking. *Am I going the wrong way? How much time is left before dark?*

Each time I stop to rest, I count to sixty, then push on despite the ache in my legs. When hanging vines stop me, I gingerly pull them open, afraid of what I can't see on the other side. A thorny bush covered in yellow flowers the shape of upside-down bells blocks my path. The blooms smell like nutmeg and their spikes scrape against tender shins already bleeding from countless scratches.

The curve of a knotted branch stops me. *Shit.* I might recognize it. Have I been walking in circles? Every freaking thing looks the same here. *I'm never going to find anyone!* Huffing fills my ears. It's me. *Think.* If it's the same tree, I veered right last time. I go left, squeezing through a thick stand of bamboo. A massive fallen tree bars my way. I consider going back. *No.*

If I divert then I'll definitely be walking in circles. *But.* The last time I climbed a tree I was seven, unafraid.

Trix whispers, *Danny, it's okay to be you.*

"No, it's not," I mutter. Ochre-colored bark, the texture of a pineapple, tears at the skin inside my thighs as I straddle it, inching my way up until I can find an open spot on the far side to slide off. Even now, only six feet above the forest's floor, vertigo makes me queasy. Something prickly climbs onto my fingers. I blur my eyes. I do not want to see what it is. I just want it to move on, disappear. But instead it slowly picks its way along the back of my hand with multiple legs. *Don't look.* But I do. It's. A. Tarantula. *IT'S A FREAKING TARANTULA!* I'm straddling a tree, my head hanging over a spider whose segmented body, without the brown-and-orange-striped bristle-covered legs, is bigger than my hand.

Burning bile climbs up my throat. *If I vomit it will bite me.* I swallow hard. A bead of sweat drips off my forehead, lands on the spider's body. It skitters an inch left so that only one articulated leg is on my pinkie. I yank my hand away like it's on fire, scramble backward and lose my balance. I land on my side in a thick pile of sour-smelling leaves, then leap to my feet, shake out my sweatshirt, shorts and hair as imagined spiders, stinging insects and scorpions scuttle along my body.

My skin shrinks…pulse doubles…triples…bones splinter… breath strangles…a bird whistles. The song is so harsh that it slices into my freaked-out brain. I hear it again—it's not a bird's call, it's…metallic. Someone is sending a signal for me to follow! *It has to be my dad!*

I'm off, forcing my way through the rain forest, ears straining. Branches lash my skin, leaving angry welts. After leaping over a jagged stump, I bash through brush whose black thorns stab. My heart crashes into my sternum again and again, like a fist pounding on a locked door. The sound of metal under distress gets louder. I duck beneath a tangle of vines…and see my dad.

Cougar kneels beside a mangled metal bin. He finds a seam and pries it open with a machete, reaches inside and pulls out a black case. It's Cass's video camera. My body trembles as I step into a clearing of broken branches, matted brush. "Dad." My voice is a whisper. "Dad," I say again, this time louder. He doesn't turn. "Cougar!" I croak. He whirls, eyes wide. *Run over. Hug me too hard. Never let me go.* But my dad doesn't move. I deflate a little. *Maybe he's in shock.*

Cougar says, "Jesus, Danny, I thought you were gone. Your mom would've killed me!"

I take ten steps forward and then he's gripping my shoulders. His fingers dig in, hurt, but I don't mind. It makes me feel more alive. "I'm not dead."

Cougar's eyes narrow, scanning me head to toe. "Where's the blood coming from?"

"It's not. I'm not. I'm not hurt. Is anyone else? Are they all?"

"Mack, Jupiter, Cass and Gus are alive, just bumped up a bit. But we couldn't find you or Sean."

"I heard you signaling."

"What?"

"The machete on metal."

Cougar nods. "Where's Sean?"

"We were both… We landed in a tree. My seat belt… It saved me. Sean. He was thrown. He's dead."

"Are you sure?"

I meet my dad's intense gaze. "Positive."

A muscle in Cougar's jaw clenches. It reminds me of episode twenty-seven, filmed in Costa Rica. His celebrity guest, a famous pop singer named Mia, was bitten by a poisonous snake. He held her in his arms until she was evacuated. Despite her pain, I remember being jealous of their time together. During the reunion show at the end of season six, we learned that Mia was okay. She said my dad visited her in the hospital every day.

Cougar says, "Sean had a fiancée. They were getting married in May. Dammit." He runs a hand over his face. "He was smart, strong and a gifted athlete. He could've been a big help in this situation, done some of the heavy lifting if things go sideways."

"I'm really sorry." I think I'm apologizing for being the one who survived.

14

I slap at a particularly thirsty mosquito, then another one. Whirling in circles, waving my arms, I try to bat them away.

"Danny," my dad says, "I need you to be a propeller, not an anchor."

My stomach clenches. An anchor is what he accused Samantha of being that night in the woods when they fought. "I won't be an anchor."

"Good."

There's a bruise on his cheekbone, a small rip in the lower left side of his button-down shirt, dirt on olive green hiking shorts. No blood. "Are you okay?"

He nods. "The others are salvaging useful stuff. Food, water, long-sleeved shirts and pants, anything waterproof and first-aid supplies. They're spread in an arc around the main debris. You think you could look around the nose?" He points. "It's about one hundred feet that way."

Alone? Nope. I'm definitely not going anywhere alone. "Sure."

"Good girl." He holds up the machete. "We're damn lucky that Mack had this, a fire-steel, two rain ponchos and some hard-core bug repellent in his flight gear. All my survival stuff went early with the rest of the crew. I'll get to work on a quick shelter, and if there's time tonight, a fire."

"When will the rescue plane get here?"

My dad kicks at a yellow plastic box the size of a bread loaf. "This is the emergency locator transmitter. It tells people where we went down."

"So rescuers are on their way?"

He picks up the box, toggling a black switch. "This thing is dead."

"How can it be dead? Doesn't Mack have to check it every flight?"

Cougar frowns. "Not every flight, but obviously more than he did."

"Meaning?" Gus asks.

I jump, so focused on Cougar that I didn't hear Gus walk up on my blind side, and say, "No one will know where our plane went down." I notice a smudge of dirt on Gus's cheek but his hair, pulled into a ponytail, looks strangely perfect given that he was just in a plane crash.

Gus shakes his head. "No emergency locator? That's not what my team signed up for."

His team?

Cougar nods. "Definitely not, but the reality is that we're on our own. The good news is that I'm here. Also, no one is badly hurt. We can move fast, find our way out of the rain forest before it takes its toll."

No one is badly hurt? What about Sean? I dig my nails into my palm to distract my brain with pain instead of anxiety.

Gus asks Cougar, "Do *you* know where we are?"

"More or less."

I ask, "Do you have a compass?"

"Nope. Interesting fact? Due to magnetic anomalies, a compass differs from true north depending on where you are on the planet." Cougar taps his temple. "I depend on myself to find the way."

Gus looks up at the dense canopy. "Even if there are search planes they won't be able to see us or the plane's wreckage."

Cougar nods. "That's the truth. Plus, Mack was skirting storm cells from the get-go, for hours. Rescuers won't have a clue where to start looking."

Gus says, "The rain forest can't be that big."

"The Amazon basin is 2.7 million square miles, of which 2.1 million square miles are covered by rain forest. It covers nine nations and stretches across 60 percent of Peru," I say. Gus and Cougar stare at me, mouths slightly open, like I'm some kind of alien. "Um. There was time on my flight to LA to do some research."

"You didn't want to watch a movie?" Cougar jokes.

My mouth is too dry to attempt a smile. "Dad, do you think we're still in Peru?"

Cougar's eyes squint for a split second. "Well. There's a chance, given how long we were flying, that Mack might've skirted into Brazil."

"Is that a big problem?" Gus asks.

Cougar shrugs. "It'd make finding us harder, but we're going to rescue ourselves anyway."

Gus asks, "What about locals?"

Cougar crushes a horsefly, leaving a green-yellow-red smear of goo on his arm. "Indigenous people live in the rain forest, but they're only 5 percent of Peru's population, and about the same for Brazil. Regardless, we won't see them unless they want us to."

"How about a fire?" Gus asks. "Signal where we are?"

Cougar points up at leaves hundreds of feet above our heads woven so tightly together that only narrow beams of light find their way through. "That'd have to be some big fire."

"So what are we going to do?" My voice is pinched, way too high.

"Our best bet is to find a waterway before this place eats us alive. We'll travel downhill and look for small channels. The trick is to find the ones that flow into a river that eventually becomes a major waterway," Cougar says like it's obvious. "Then we'll make a raft out of bamboo. Float to safety."

"Safety?" I ask.

"We'll be visible to search planes, ecotourism operations, and there are also random encampments along the banks where biologists study the diversity of this amazing forest." He jerks his head at me, then winks at Gus. "Chip off the old block."

I want to find a place to hide.

"Danny, what's with the hiking boots?"

"Boots?"

Cougar points. I look down at the boots hanging from my neck. *I forgot.* "They're Sean's. I found them while I was looking for you." *Why weren't you out looking for me?* My dad's fore-head creases. *Of course he looked for me.* "I thought his family might want something that was his?" Gus gives me a funny look. It's probably a stupid idea.

Cougar points to Gus's feet. He's wearing one flip-flop. "They're all yours."

Gus pulls on the boots, double knotting the laces. "They fit. I'll try to find some socks in the wreckage. Thanks, Danny. I'll make sure I send Sean's family a thank-you after this."

I don't think a note, even from a movie star, is going to help. Gus reaches for my hand, gives it a squeeze. I can hardly feel the pressure. It's like Gus Price, here, in the Amazon, talking to me, is part of a bizarre dream. *What's next, flying zebras?* I force down the totally inappropriate giggle burbling up my throat.

"Want me to go with you?" Gus asks. "Help you search?"

Cougar shakes his head. "Gus, I need you to help me build a shelter."

"I can do that. If you want?" I've watched my dad's show for years. Haven't missed a single episode. Watched repeats. It was a way to know him. Theoretically, I understand what a clove hitch is, and I've seen him braid palm fronds to make a roof.

"GP and I have it covered."

It's like being picked last for a team in gym class when your best friend is the captain. My body contracts like a snail hiding in its shell and I pretend to watch a bird fly overhead so they can't see my pink cheeks. "Um. Is that bug spray handy?"

Cougar shakes his head. "It needs to last, so we have to save it for dusk and dawn. That's when the mosquitos that carry dengue and malaria are out."

"Sure, of course." I head in the direction my dad pointed, skin crawling with mosquitos. While he can see me, I resist the urge to fight them off.

Cougar calls, "There are a lot of snakes out here. Keep your eyes open. Please don't go too far. It'd be dangerous to search in the dark for you."

It's embarrassing being treated like I have zero common sense. But I get it. My dad remembers who I was. It's up to me to change his perception.

The plane is tipped down, its nose burrowed into the ground. How could anyone survive the impact with only a few bumps? The edges where the front of the plane tore off are jagged, dangling wires, bits of insulation. Sean's mangled body flashes. I push the vision away. There's a half-empty water bottle resting beside bright pink blooms alive with bees. Two full plastic bottles of lemonade peek out from deep inside the flowering bush. *I absolutely cannot do this.* I move slowly. The bees tickle in a not-funny way. Two stings that hurt like hell later, I've got the lemonade plus the water.

I move on. A bag of potato chips and a silver keychain lie side by side. There's a yellow sweatshirt draped on a bush. In its pocket is Jupiter's paperback, *The Stand*. There's also a roll of butterscotch Life Savers. I drop the book, think for a second, then retrieve it. Paper burns. A few feet later, I spy something dull, silver. It's a roll of duct tape. Beside it is an unopened bag of strawberry Twizzlers. I would've rather found my malaria pills. I take a few more steps. Peeking out from beneath a shard of aluminum is a bright red wing. I glance around to make sure no one can see me, then breathe in the dead bird. Stress has buoyed my old habit to the surface, but I need all the help I can get.

Something rustles above. My body flushes with adrenaline, skin prickling with a thousand needles. I move back toward the clearing, the forest's foliage closing around me with each step, like it's eager to absorb what doesn't belong. Dumping my loot in a small pile by the useless beacon, I rest my hands on my knees and focus on breathing as the adrenaline slowly drains.

"You hurt at all?" Gus asks.

Again I didn't hear him, and I jump. *Did he play some kind of ninja in a movie?* "I thought you were helping Cougar build a shelter." My tone sounds a little bit like an accusation. *It's not Gus's fault that my dad picked him.*

"I just wanted to make sure you're okay. It's getting dark. Smells like rain, too."

"No worries. I'm from Oregon." Gus tips his head to one side. He doesn't get the joke. "It rains a lot. There, in the Pacific Northwest. Um. We're in a rain forest?"

"Oh." Gus manages a sympathy laugh. "Got it."

My fingers push glasses up my nose, but of course they're not there. I took them off so that I'd look cool, which is a joke in itself. Now I'm lost in the middle of the rain forest with nothing to protect the only eye I have left. Gus is staring at me. He's probably so used to being around perfect people that I'm like a fascinating lab specimen. There's a piece of blue fabric wrapped around his forearm with blood soaking through it. "What happened?"

"Just a cut. The bruise from my seat belt hurts worse."

He lifts up the bottom of his shirt, revealing a dark purple stain that's at least six inches by three inches. I have a matching one but don't show it to him.

"Secret? I hate flying. Especially on small planes. If I could've driven here, taken a bus, even walked, I would've done it."

"You seemed comfortable."

Gus flashes a million-dollar smile. "I'm an actor. This trip is a job. If I do it well, it'll help my career."

It still feels like I'm only part here, part floating, which is maybe why instead of being overwhelmed that Gus Price is showing me his cut abs and telling me a secret, I'm more focused on the mosquitos bellying up to the blood bar that is my body. With effort, I focus. "Your arm?"

"It's not deep."

"Did you wash it out?"

Gus looks around, laughs. "With what?"

I dig out the half empty bottle of water. It's not totally sanitary since someone drank from it, but it's the only option. "Things in this environment will get infected really fast. That leads to sepsis."

"Sepsis?"

"It's when your immune system overreacts to an infection. You can get a fever that leads to septic shock."

"Is that really bad?"

"Only if organ failure and death bother you." Gus hesitates, maybe waiting for me to say that I'm kidding. But I'm not and a little bit of me relishes that my dad's new best friend is now worried.

Gus says, "Let's wash it out." He sits on the ground and

unknots the cloth around his arm. "How do you know this stuff?"

I kneel next to him. "My mom is a nurse. She talks a lot." I unwind the blood-soaked cloth. The cut is uneven, three inches long and deep enough that I can see a glint of bone. If I had nylon thread for sutures, I could close up the cut, minimal scarring, probably important to a guy whose looks are tied to his job. But that's not an option. There's a lot of dirt in the gash. I prod at the edges while slowly pouring water, doing my best to dislodge the debris. Gus sucks in a breath. "Sorry."

Cougar shouts, "For Christ's sake, Danny, don't waste water!"

My insides lurch like the ground has vanished and I'm in free fall. "I was trying to—"

Cougar dumps the armful of bamboo he's carrying and stalks over. "There's no excuse. Even you should know basic rules for survival," Cougar says.

My tagline roars in my head: *Defective. Inferior. Embarrassment.*

Gus holds up his arm. "My fault, man."

Cougar squats beside us. "Damn," he says, taking in the gash. "Way to be stoic. Looks pretty clean now." He winks at me. "Playing nurse with the hottest teen actor in the world? Best sixteenth birthday present ever, right?"

If you don't count the plane crash, Sean's death, the fact that we're lost in the Amazon and that you don't know I'm turning seventeen.

"You two can get to know each other later, on camera."

Gus and I ask in unison, "On camera?"

Cougar gives Gus's shoulder a squeeze. "We're still going to film this episode as planned. It's an opportunity to make something of this catastrophe, show resiliency and honor Sean. Agreed?"

I'm not sure how filming will honor Sean, but I nod.

"You sure about this, man?" Gus asks.

"Yes. I need you to be a team player."

The muscles in Gus's jaw clench like he's gathering his resources. "GP's always a team player."

"Good. So is Cougar Warren. We'll use Cass's handheld that she was smart enough to bring in a waterproof case. Sound will be shit, but Jupiter can work some magic later. Like it or not, our episode is now about true survival." Cougar nods at Gus's arm. "Wrap that up and we'll finish the shelter."

I mumble, "We should, um, seal it."

My dad knocks his knuckles on my head. "Earth to Danny, do you see a hospital or even a first-aid kit around?"

I pull out the roll of duct tape. "We could use strips of this?"

Cougar throws up his hand. "My kid is brilliant."

I hand him the duct tape, then push the jagged edges of Gus's cut closed while he tears off strips, securing them. It's hard not to smile a tiny bit. Despite everything, I'm being a propeller.

15

The shadowy light in the rain forest fades as dusk approaches. It's not raining yet, but the air smells like ozone. I find Cass beside a thorny shrub. She's digging through a red duffel bag. When she turns, it's hard not to step back. Blood weeps from a gash that runs the length of her forehead. It glues strands of black hair to pale cheeks.

"I need my computer," Cass says.

"O-kay."

Cass shakes her head hard. Red droplets fly sideways. "I have to email Production. Keep them apprised so we remain on schedule."

There's no way she'll get a signal but I get that she's freaked out. Gently, I seat her on the duffel bag. There's a T-shirt on the ground beside her, Dispatch concert dates on the back.

I shake off the dirt, then use it to clean the blood from her eyes. "Cass, did you get knocked out?"

"I don't remember."

Swiping the cotton across the cut, I can see it's not that deep. My mom says head wounds bleed a ton.

Cass starts crying, salt water mingling with blood. "This is my fault—I picked Mack. Cougar is going to fire me."

"He won't. Anyway, Gus was the one who was late."

Cass sniffles, then asks, "Do you think Gus is hot? I thought you might not be open to it. He's *too* good-looking. It makes a difference."

She's lost me. When I look into Cass's eyes, her pupils are dilated from the hit she took. No wonder she's not making sense. I focus on her cut. Hopefully the blood flow is doing an okay job of pushing out the bacteria. I'm not going to make the mistake of wasting water again. Doubling over the T-shirt, I tie it snuggly around her head. Later we can use the duct tape to close the wound.

Cass goes back to her search, discarding useless items over her shoulder. When she tosses a long-sleeved blue sweatshirt, I grab it. She's wearing leggings with a sleeveless top. There's a carpet of insects feeding on her bare skin. "Hey, want to put this on?" I help Cass slide the sweatshirt over bare arms. Curious George stares at me from the back. "If you find any medicine, like malaria pills, that'd be great."

"All our meds are with the team in Iquitos," Cass says.

Great. My backpack is nowhere in sight, probably snagged high in a tree. The bush to my right rustles. Nerves firing, I leap back, but before I can run Jupiter appears.

"Danny! Damn, kid, I was really worried about you."

"I'm okay. But Sean—"

"Yeah." Jupiter kicks at the dirt and blinks. A tear escapes and leaves a shiny track down his cheek. "He's… He was a really good guy." Jupiter clears his throat. "His gal will be devastated."

Again, I feel guilty. My stomach twists into knots.

Jupiter wipes his face, takes a few deep breaths, then gathers his dreads and ties them into a thick ponytail. "I wanted to keep looking for you guys while it was light, but Cougar said our priority had to be staying together, salvaging what we could, building a shelter."

Sticking together, taking care of the essentials, searching in the light make sense. The knots in my belly tighten. *I found them; that's what's important.* "Are you hurt?"

"A bruise from my seat belt, scratches and a sore shoulder. Probably tweaked it trying to get out of the prickly bush I landed in. Who knows what might've been in there with me."

Mack tromps over to us. "How's it going, kid?"

He's dripping with sweat even though the temperature has dropped in the last hour. *How's it going? Seriously? You flew for more money when you should've told Cass and my dad they had to wait until tomorrow. Sean will never get married because you were greedy. On top of that, you forgot to check your safety equipment. Who does that?*

Mack groans, drops to his knees, then collapses onto the ground.

"Cougar!" Jupiter shouts.

The lingering sense that I'm not quite inside my skin vanishes as I kneel beside the pilot. "Where does it hurt?" He grips his chest. When I unbutton his shirt, his entire torso is bruised, the skin dark purple, almost black. I touch his ribs and feel sharp edges.

Samantha once told me about a high school football player who'd been tackled so hard that a rib fractured, lacerating his lung. The kid thought he was having a heart attack—shortness of breath, terrible pressure across his chest. My mom said he would've died if the ER doctor hadn't put in a chest tube to relieve the pressure.

Cougar breaks through the brush, Gus at his heels. He moves me aside, crouches by Mack and asks, "What's going on?"

"Chest feels like a semitruck...is parked on...it."

Cougar scans the pilot's bruised body. "You might've cracked some ribs. I remember breaking three in Utah. Flash flood." He turns to Gus. "Hurt like a motherf-er but I managed to climb my way out of a sheer three-hundred-foot canyon." He pats Mack's arm. "You're gonna be fine, old tiger, just sore as hell."

"I won't...be able to trek...out of here."

"Bullshit. Things will look better in the morning. Promise." He glances over his shoulder at Cass. "Let's make him comfortable for the night. Tomorrow we'll find help."

Cass nods. "Okay. First, though, I'm going to shoot off an email."

I'm starting to wonder how hard Cass hit her head but Mack is in bigger trouble. "Um...it could be a hemothorax?"

"A hemothorax?" Jupiter asks.

"Under each rib is a neurovascular bundle—that's a collection of nerves, arteries and veins," I explain. Everyone is staring like I've grown horns. "Um." I glance at my dad but he looks away. "Sometimes, with rib fractures, the blood vessels can get torn? That causes bleeding into the space between the chest wall and the lungs. It'd explain Mack's chest pain and difficulty breathing." What I don't say is that I'm pretty sure without a tube put in the chest to drain the blood, or emergency surgery, patients with a hemothorax… They die.

Cougar's smile is tight. "Danny, come on, you're not here to play pretend nurse. Gus, help me carry Mack to the shelter. Cass, film us." Cass follows them, computer under one arm, camera recording in the dim light.

Jupiter asks, "You good?"

I stare at the ground wishing I could burrow into a deep hole like a rabbit. "Yeah."

"Danny, he's not… Just don't…" Jupiter trails off. "You think Mack is going to be okay?"

"I don't know." Jupiter hands me a pair of black leggings he found. I peel off my shorts and tug them on. Screw modesty when mosquitos are sucking me dry. It starts to drizzle. By the time we get to the shelter, an angled lean-to tied between two trees with a roof of piled palm leaves and rows of bamboo on the ground to keep us off the dirt, rain is falling in solid sheets. I've never seen anything like it. Cougar has the bottles we found set out to collect water, plus he's made containers from sections of green bamboo. I know from his shows that if we do need to boil water, the bamboo, heated along its thick sides, not the thinner bottom, will work.

"Everyone, make sure you drink," Cougar says. "Mostly in the morning and night. Drinking too much during the day will make your feet and hands swell."

I take several gulps. It tastes like grass. My dad holds a

plastic bottle to Mack's lips, but the pilot can't swallow. When he passes around a neon-red tube of bug repellent, I want to slather it on but dab instead. Even a little bit helps. A lot. We share the bag of potato chips, each getting three chips, a Twizzler, a butterscotch Life Saver and a few swallows of lemonade, plus all the water we can drink.

Cougar says, "I think we can do without a fire tonight." He gives me one rain poncho and Cass the other one. "You two will be colder than us so put them on to keep in the heat. We can share them later if need be."

It's still warm but my clothes are wet and a light wind is sucking the heat from my body. Grateful, I pull on the clear plastic poncho.

Cougar carefully folds the empty chip bag and puts it in his shirt pocket. "Highly flammable. Tomorrow night, once we've collected some tinder, we'll use it to help start a fire."

"Unless we're rescued by then," Cass says with the computer on her lap, tapping at buttons on the keyboard.

Cougar ignores her. "Here's the deal. Chances are we'll find help in a day or two, but if it takes longer we'll be fine. There's plenty of fruit and nuts to eat if you know which plants won't kill you." He winks. "I do. But for now, we conserve our energy and rest. If you get cold in the night, do push-ups or jumping jacks. If something crawls on you, brush it away from the group. If it's a snake, wake me up. I'll take care of it. If you need to take a leak, stay close, watch where you walk. There are long thorns that can pierce your boots, biting ants and bigger threats. Try to get some sleep. Tomorrow will be a long day."

Bigger threats? I slowly lie down, my body stiff, like it's rejecting the entire idea of the rain forest, telegraphing that nothing about this place is appropriate for a one-eyed city girl who thought she could fake it till she made it. A few strands of my hair tug. I try to ignore the feeling. My hair tugs again. *It's nothing.* But nothing has legs and it's picking its way through my hair, trying to burrow toward my scalp, preparing to sting, bite, furrow beneath the skin where it will do something utterly heinous, like lay eggs. My pulse rate shoots to the moon. *Something is in my hair! Something big! Breathe. Do not overreact. DON'T DO IT!* For a few seconds my need to impress Cougar wins out, but then I'm on my knees, tearing at my hair. "Get it out!"

Cougar kneels beside me, bends my head forward, then digs fingers into the place I'm pointing, because I'm too scared to actually touch whatever disgusting thing is trying to make its home on or in my scalp.

He says, "Got it."

I shouldn't look, but I do. In the almost dark, I can still see it's an inch-long bug, its back the shape and color of a turquoise seashell. Bright orange legs and antennae wiggle in the air as my dad inspects the thing, like it's trying to identify him, too.

"Never seen one of these." Cougar grins. "That's one of the most incredible things about the Amazon. Millions of insects and a lot of them don't even have names because they haven't been discovered." He tosses the bug over his shoulder. "You good now, Danny?"

If *good* means embarrassed beyond any chance to save face, then yes, I'm terrific. I pinch my leg hard enough to make a bruise as punishment. *Next time I will not freak out.* "I'm good."

"Okay then, everyone, shut-eye time," Cougar says.

The idea that I can close my eyes; that I'll have the presence of mind to brush whatever spider, scorpion or stinging caterpillar away from the group when I feel it skittering on my skin; the notion that I'm going to get up, walk away from our shelter in the dark should I have to pee when there are things out there capable of swallowing me whole… It's preposterous. Still, I lie down on the bamboo that's covered with palm fronds. We're a wet collection of mismatched clothing, bruises, bloody cuts and probably a dying old pilot. A rivulet of rain leaks through the roof, dripping onto my shoulder. I shift, but another steady drip finds my hip. There's a knot digging into my back. I don't say a word about any of it. No one is comfortable, especially Mack, who moans but has stopped talking.

Cougar asks, "You okay, buddy?"

I'm still his buddy. Tomorrow, I'll do better. "I'm good." I wish my dad were closer instead of between Cass and Jupiter while I'm next to Mack with Gus behind me. I wish we weren't lying on a hard rack of bamboo; that the Amazon wasn't filled with things that petrify me; that there hadn't been a plane crash; that Mack was okay, and Sean was alive; that I was anywhere in the world but here. Cass is tapping on her keyboard. I have to give her credit for hopefulness.

The night is never ending. I do my best not to scratch every bite or slap as insects creep beneath my poncho. The only positive is that the bug repellent has cut down on mosquitos and gnats. I'm not that successful at keeping still, but I'm not alone. Almost everyone, except Mack, is moving around, swatting and flicking off bugs. Only one person is snoring—my dad. We're nothing alike but I'll do my best to keep that a secret.

Gus whispers, "This is miserable."

"Yeah." I'm glad he thinks so, too. Trix wouldn't believe that Gus Price is lying inches from me. But it doesn't really sink in. I'm focused on the soft rustle of wings inside my body. I fold my arms tightly over my chest to keep my inner Pigeon trapped. Gus's breathing settles to a rhythm. He's softly humming in his sleep. The tune is off-key, but I think it's "Redbird," a song from the '70s that my mom used to sing to help me sleep.

Mack shifts, moans. I rest my fingers on his neck. His pulse has gone from hummingbird fast to slow and his breathing is labored. Tears leak from his closed eyes, dribble down his temples. Moving closer, I whisper lines from *The Phantom Tollbooth* in his ear. "'Have you ever heard the wonderful silence just before the dawn? Or the quiet and calm just as a storm ends…or the hush of a country road at night… Each one is different, you know, and all very beautiful if you listen carefully.'" Reaching for the pilot's hand, I hold it tight. I don't want Mack to feel like he's alone.

DAY
ONE

16

Mack is dead.

I didn't sleep the entire night. Part of it was the unrelenting insects and the rest was worry about Mack. When the pilot's breathing began to falter, I couldn't help imagining his organs shutting down, drawing their blinds, locking the door, then turning off the lights for good. Was he married? Did he have kids, a dog or cat, friends? Will anyone miss him? It's partly his fault we're in this situation, but the way he died, in agony, is really sad. I'm still beyond pissed at my mom, but I wish she were here. She might've figured out a way to save Mack's life.

Last night, when I whispered lines from *The Phantom Tollbooth* in Mack's ear, my hope was that he would focus on the story, not his pain. It worked for me after surgery, when I made my mom read that book so many times the pages were worn soft, and then continued to read it on my own once the suffering and nausea went away. When I was eight, I memorized entire passages. I thought that because my dad loved the book, we'd have something new to talk about since I could no longer do the things he loved. But I never had the chance to share my favorite lines with him. Maybe I will now. Maybe getting closer is about creating new memories as well as reclaiming the old Danny.

I withdraw fingers twined through Mack's stiff hand. I've seen death in the ER. When I was ten, doing homework in the waiting room, a guy sitting right next to me had an aortic aneurysm burst, his main artery no longer able to carry oxygen-rich blood from his heart to the rest of his body. He died quickly, quietly. No one even realized it until a nurse came to talk to him. I close Mack's eyes so the others won't be upset by his sightless stare. His skin already feels different, like plastic beneath my fingertips.

Cougar whispers, "I'm sorry I bit your head off last night. I knew Mack was in big trouble, but I didn't want him to worry."

My dad is on his side, head resting on one elbow, watching me. *All I did was scare a dying man.* My chin quivers but I manage to stem the tears before they fall.

"Lesson learned," Cougar says with a sad smile. "Mack went in his sleep. At least it was gentle."

He didn't. He suffered. "I whispered some of our book to him. The part about the wonderful silence before the dawn."

"I'm sure Mack appreciated it."

"It was important to me. That book? It got me through some tough times."

My dad's eyes shine. "I'm really glad."

Cass sits up, one hand pressed against her forehead. "What time is it?"

"Always trying to stay on schedule," Cougar says with a little smile.

Cass looks around. "Shit."

My dad leans in, kisses her on the lips. It's quick, but there's a comfortable intimacy. *Are they a couple?*

"You look like a warrior." Cougar carefully unwraps the T-shirt around Cass's forehead. Her cut has been sealed with dried blood, but where the cotton adhered it tears open and starts leaking again. He rips six inches off the roll of duct tape and gently presses it over the wound. "Good as new."

Cass rests fingers against her temples. "Tell that to the drum beating inside my head."

Gus sits up, looks around. "Not a nightmare." He glances over my shoulder. "How's Mack?"

I say, "He died."

Gus's eyes go saucer wide. "Dead? What? Shit! What? Are you freaked out?"

I shake my head. "When I was a kid, a guy died next to me in the ER. My mom explained what'd happened using diagrams on the whiteboard in the nurses' lounge. It kind of wiped away my fear. The parts and pieces inside a human body make a fragile kind of sense." I sound like a total loser and my shoulders hunch from the urge to slink away.

Gus's ghost-white face says this situation just became very real. "I've never seen a dead body, except in the movies."

It's my turn to ask, "You okay?"

He runs a hand over his face. "I guess. Yeah. I have to be. Sorry, um, if I came off like a dick yesterday. I'm out of my element. I mean, who gets in a plane crash and survives while other people die?" He shakes his head. "And we're actually freaking lost in the Amazon. This is nuts."

For the first time I see Gus as a person and not a movie star. Maybe the plane crash and Sean's and Mack's deaths have evened the playing field. Gus is a survivor now, just like me.

Jupiter sits up, wipes the grit from his eyes. "Thank God it stopped raining." He glances at the pilot. "Damn."

"Yeah. Let's get to work," Cass says, suddenly all business. She hits Record on her camera. "Cougar, we'll film by Mack's head. There's a little more light over there."

Cougar crouches by Mack. "Late yesterday afternoon our small plane crashed in the Peruvian rain forest. Today is *Day One.* Our first full day on this journey of survival. We've already lost our cameraman, Sean, in the initial crash. A few hours ago, we lost our pilot, Mack. Despite Mack's faulty decision to fly during a thunderstorm, we're deeply saddened by both deaths. For Mack, I'm not sure of the cause, but possibly a punctured lung or diaphragmatic hernia. Nothing we could do for either of them in this environment. It's a damn shame." Cougar clenches his jaw muscles. "We spent a sleepless night beneath the shelter Gus Price and I built. I wouldn't wish Gus here, but a strong, positive guy like him is a real help. Dinner was a few potato chips and water. Now we'll pull together what little survival gear we have and head out in search of a tributary of the Amazon, following it to safety. One big worry, it's rainy season. Last night we had a torrential downpour. Too much rain and the rivers will flood, making travel by water impossible. For now, though, we focus on what we can control—avoiding the venomous snakes and spiders that teem in this part of the world. A bite without medical intervention would equal a death sentence. Cut."

Cass lowers the camera. "Change into your lightest clothes," Cougar tells our ragtag group. "It'll be roasting hot in a few hours. Mosquito bites during the day are annoying but it's the dawn and dusk skeeters we worry about, so save the sweatshirts and leggings for nighttime. Wrap them in the ponchos to keep them dry."

Cass peels down to a white men's undershirt with no bra beneath. Her shorts are khaki, just tight enough to show her perfect body. If you discount the duct tape, she looks like she could be in a Victoria's Secret catalog. I peel down to a black T-shirt and shapeless cargo shorts. I do not look like I belong in any type of lingerie campaign.

"Are we going to bury Mack?" Gus asks.

Cougar shakes his head. "No shovel. The rain forest will take care of him."

The idea of the pilot being slowly torn apart by predators, that insects like the botfly will lay eggs beneath his decomposing skin and maggots will feed as he rots, makes me shudder. No one, not even a reckless pilot, deserves that.

"Back to the earth. That's the way I'd want to go," Cougar says. "Actually, I'd want to float out to sea in flame, light up the sky, burn to ash like a Viking warrior."

A black caterpillar marked with yellow stripes inches along my leg. I brush it off, scramble sideways, trip over my own feet, then almost right myself before I hit the ground in a sprawl. Where I touched the caterpillar, my skin is on fire. I'm surprised there aren't blisters.

Cougar pulls me to my feet. "Stings?"

"A little." *A ton!* He gives my fingers a quick kiss. The kind you give a little kid when she scrapes her knee. I'm too old for that, but they instantly feel much better.

Cougar explains, "Some caterpillars repulse predators by vomiting, others attack and bite. Insects have incredible adaptations. Like fake limbs that come off when a predator chomps down, or secreting toxins that make their bodies inedible." He nods at Cass and she turns on the camera.

"There are seven major keys to survival when you're lost in the Amazon. Danny just demonstrated the opposite of the first one. She panicked instead of remaining calm. Freaking out turns off your brain. By overreacting to a little caterpillar, she could've hurt herself, or ended up surprising a true predator, like a viper. Thanks for the illustration, buddy."

I smile but really hope Cougar isn't going to point out my mistakes for future examples.

"Second, make sure you cover as much bare skin as possible at night to protect from bites, scratches, anything that might lead to infection. Third, water is life. Collect what you can. Make sure to boil it when possible. Parasites can cause fatal diseases and there's also a risk of dysentery, cholera and typhoid if the water is contaminated. Fourth, protect your feet. If they get cut, burned or develop nasty, flesh-eating infections, you're hosed. Fifth, always head downhill. Downhill leads to water and rescue. Sixth, build shelters when possible to escape the elements. Seventh, only eat what you recognize."

He smiles. "I recognize most of the fruits, nuts and vegetables in the Amazon. We won't go hungry. Cut. Let's go."

We shoulder our makeshift packs, five individuals dwarfed by the Amazon rain forest. Cougar picks up the machete and Mack's emergency backpack, then gives each of us a Twizzler. I think about making it last for a few hours, but immediately insects attack the sugary candy. Shaking them off, I shove the entire thing in my mouth. Gus does the same thing.

"Single file. Don't lag," Cougar says. "Drink small sips of water so you don't get dehydrated. Gus, you're behind me, then Danny, Cass and Jupiter bring up the rear."

Glancing back, I take one last look at Mack beneath our makeshift shelter. "Sleep with the angels," I murmur. It's what my dad used to say when he tucked me in at night.

Cougar swings the machete in powerful arcs to clear the way. "Assume every step could be a deadly one."

For a second my legs won't move. *What's the alternative?* Taking a deep breath, I somehow follow my dad.

17

After half a day struggling over slick roots, rocks, deadfall, vines and nasty thorn bushes, we stop by a tree that's at least two hundred feet tall, its pale gray trunk as wide around as a redwood tree's. A cramp in my side has taken up permanent residence, its sharp teeth gnawing. Note to self: bowling does not make a person physically fit.

"Kapok," Cougar says, pointing at the massive tree. "The ancient Maya believed it was sacred—that it connected them to the earth, cosmos and underworld—that it was where their gods lived, along with other supernatural creatures."

The kapok reminds me of the Tree of Souls in the movie *Avatar*. Thick boughs reach all the way to the top of the rain forest's canopy, like a giant parasol, with leaves covered in white-and-pink flowers.

Cougar clears his throat, spits. "The indigenous people use kapok to make canoes and coffins. The flowers stink but the bats love them." Cass films as he pulls free a woody vine climbing up the tree's trunk. "These are called lianas." Using the machete, he cuts a three-foot section free, holding up both ends. "Shake it hard to get rid of the insects." Cougar lowers one side. Liquid drips into his mouth. "It's a little bitter, but safe to drink."

My dad hands the liana to me. It's heavy with a rough skin. I drink, try not to grimace at the earthy taste, then give it to Jupiter. "Your turn." He tries a few drops, makes a pucker face. Out here, he's becoming my favorite person beside my dad. Cass passes because she's filming, of course. Gus, on the other hand, drinks until water drips off his chin.

"Let's go," Cougar says.

Shouldering our packs, we follow him. We've been hiking for hours, heading down when possible, but forced to divert, again and again, when the forest closes in on us or the ground turns into a bog. I skirt a muddy spot, but my foot still gets sucked into the muck. "Crap." I struggle to pull it out, but the suction is too strong, and instead, I sink deeper, my other foot now trapped. The funky odor of slimy earth mixed with rot wafts up each time I attempt to break free. I fight the overwhelming urge to thrash. It will just make things worse. I call, "Um? A little help?"

Cougar and Gus turn around. Cougar chuckles. "She's like a rabbit caught in a snare."

My shoulders sag. *Is that really how he sees me?*

"I've got this." Gus jogs back. "Lean toward me."

He wraps his arms around my waist and pulls until my

feet come free of my boots and we're pressed together for a second in a tight hug before he swings me to dry ground. Where Gus's bare skin touched mine, it tingles, like he's made from electricity. Even after a night in the rain forest, he smells good, like clean sweat and soap. I, on the other hand, smell like muck.

"Thanks."

I duck to hide my blush while he digs my boots free. He shakes them off and helps slide my feet back in. Kneeling, Gus ties my laces with a double knot. I'm self-conscious that Cass is filming, that Cougar is witnessing this, that I'm even noticing Gus when a man just died, but I'm also kind of in girl heaven. It's like I forgot that Gus is an incredibly hot guy and that realization is now, literally, in my face.

When we catch up to my dad, he's crouched by a deep puddle, its surface thick with mosquitos. "Drink what's left in your bottles, then fill them up here in case it doesn't rain."

Murky water burbles into Cass's bamboo container. She makes a face. "That can't be clean."

"We'll boil it tonight. Make sure you don't drink it before then." Cass sways sideways. Cougar helps her stand. She brings the container to her mouth, like she's about to drink.

"Hey," Cougar says, stopping her.

My breath catches. "Cass, what's your last name?"

"Akiyama. Why?"

My dad glances at me. "Just curious," I say.

The air is humid and so heavy it's like wearing a water-drenched coat. Even though the sun can't get through the forest's canopy, the heat is stifling. We're all tired, and in addition to my ever-present side cramp, I'm getting a blister on my right heel. Zings of pain intensify, as the skin is rubbed raw by my new hiking boots. There's no way I'm going to ask for a break, though. My dad has been swinging his machete nonstop. If he can keep going, I can, too.

Cass says, "I need to make a phone call."

I'm sure she's joking, but when I glance over my shoulder she's holding a cracked iPhone to her ear. Her level of optimism is getting ridiculous. "You're not going to get a signal."

Cass tries dialing again. "You never know."

For the next few hours I focus on every step and handhold. The air vibrates with the sounds of creatures slithering, hopping and scuttling either just out of sight or in flashes of movement that make me jump. Birds wing overhead, their colors appearing to glow in the murky light. The drone of insects is constant along with sporadic bites, some hot stings, others drawing blood. Every now and then, Gus looks over his shoulder, smiles at me or makes sure to hold a tree branch or vine after he passes so it doesn't snap in my face. He's just being nice. A tiny flame sparks anyway. I know there's nothing about me that would interest a guy like him. "Truth."

"What?" Gus asks.

Crap. "Nothing."

"You said *truth*."

Gus is looking at me like I'm bonkers. "It's what my friend and I say when there's zero BS. When we mean exactly what we said." He's still staring at me. "The rain forest sucks. Truth."

Gus finally nods. "Truth."

Cougar stops and crouches by a dead frog whose underside is bright blue, his slick back neon orange with yellow spots.

I'm surprised that whatever killed the amphibian didn't eat him. "Didn't he taste good?" I ask my dad.

"Good question. This is a poison dart frog. They come in every imaginable color and pattern. The brighter they are, the more toxic. Indigenous people use the frogs' secretions on the tips of arrows and blow darts. Keep your eye out for ones that are a bit smaller, golden-colored. They have enough poison to kill ten grown men. All it takes is prolonged contact wherever you have a cut. My guess is that whatever tried to eat this little guy crawled away and died. Let's move on."

When I pass the frog, I don't breathe him in, because he's poison. Over the next hour, my stomach progresses from little rumbles to full-on growls.

Gus turns and laughs. "I can hear Danny's empty stomach from here. Time to show us your mad skills, Cougar."

"Your wish is my command." Cougar stops below a skinny palm tree. "This is a wasai. You can tell by the thin, smooth trunk." He swings his machete at its base and bark flies. In a few minutes, the palm topples. Birds cry out in protest when it hits the forest's floor. Cougar walks up the trunk. Just below the spot where the palm leaves start, he cuts away pieces of light green wood and hands each of us a chunk. "Heart of palm." He bites into a piece. "Delicious."

It's not delicious, but I'm starving. An ant skitters across the back of my hand. It's over a quarter inch, with a segmented body, legs like a cricket and a curved black beak. I drop the palm and try to shake it off. It bites, drawing a fat dot of blood, sending currents of searing heat through my hand. "Was that a bullet ant?" My voice is way too high.

My dad crouches, pinches the ant's segmented body between two fingers and holds it up. "*Pachycondyla villosa.* Looks like a bullet ant, but with golden hairs on a waspish body. Its bite isn't nearly as painful." He smiles at me. "If it was a bullet ant, it'd literally feel like you were shot. You gonna survive?"

I rest my hand against the trunk of the closest tree, trying to look like the bite isn't still hurting. "Yeah. Of course."

Cougar says, "Danny is teaching us another valuable lesson right now. The way to avoid ants is to keep your eyes open for nests and never lean against a tree trunk."

He chuckles as I whip my hand away. Heat creeps from my chest to my hairline, no doubt making me look like a sweaty tomato. I understand this is a learning moment for everyone, but I've never seen my dad embarrass his star guests. A deep breath and I let it go. *He's just trying to keep us safe.*

"Hey, Gus," Cougar calls, "check this out."

Gus follows my dad as he points out different plants. Cass, trailing like a puppy, films them. When Gus laughs at a shared joke, Cougar slaps him on the back like they're old friends. *Buddies.*

"Earth to Danny." Jupiter nods toward a bush with purple-and-yellow blooms bordered by emerald green leaves.

It takes me a second to see a lizard perched on a flower. He's about ten inches long. His body is made of tiny hexagons that exactly match every shade of the bloom, right down to the whirls of red in its center. His eyes are concentric multi-colored swirls. I don't know if the lizard is poisonous, but he's gorgeous. If I ever get out of here, I'm going to create a large diorama of the Amazon with the lizard front and center. I'll use acrylics to paint his body, so each vibrant color pops. The lizard senses us and moves, the colors of his skin changing as he climbs across leaves and onto the ground, where his body shifts to coffee colors that perfectly blend.

"Chameleon. They change color to hide, escape predators."

"Must be nice." I breathe in the chameleon's essence, even though he's not dead. I need as much help as I can get.

Jupiter wags a dreadlock. "Blending in is overrated. Fly your freak flag high, Danny."

"I don't really have one—a freak flag. The only thing that's interesting about me is my dad."

"Last night you stayed up whispering to Mack so he wouldn't feel so alone. Held his hand. That seems pretty special to me."

I blush. I didn't know anyone could hear me. "It didn't save his life."

"Don't undervalue kindness. It doesn't come naturally to a lot of folks. Mind me asking what you said to Mack?"

"Quotes from *The Phantom Tollbooth*. It's a kids' book my dad sent after my eye surgery."

"'Expectations is the place you must always go to before you get to where you're going.'"

I grin. "You've read it!"

"It was one of my little sister's favorites, too."

Suddenly the monkeys above us go crazy, their screams so sharp my eardrums feel like they're shredding. Clearly, they don't like people cutting down their trees. We tip back our heads, watch them swinging from vine to bough. A brown monkey launches over Gus's head. I ask, "What kind is he?"

Cougar replies, "Howler. Fun fact? They're considered the loudest land animal. You can hear them from three miles away.

We'll probably see capuchins, marmosets, spider, squirrel and, if we're lucky, tamarins. They actually have a mane."

A howler dangles nearby, and then scampers onto a tree branch only a few feet above my head. *Please don't poop on me.* "Do they ever attack people?"

"You sure you're my kid?" Cougar asks.

It's like getting hit exactly where I already have a bad bruise. *What does he see?* Someone who doesn't belong here and could never survive alone. Pinching my leg, I vow to do better.

"Fun fact," Jupiter says. "I don't like monkeys."

Cougar snorts. "You don't like anything in a jungle environment."

"Au contraire. Born and raised in the jungle of Manhattan."

Cougar cracks up. "Let's go, city slicker."

Over the next hour my blister pops. I want to stop, cover the oozing sore with a piece of duct tape. But that'd slow the group, draw attention.

"Hey—hey—hey," Cougar says, staring up at a thick palm tree whose trunk is covered in fat spines. He points at red clusters hanging just below the tree's leaves. "It's a pijuayo palm. See those fruits? They're delicious."

"You're going to cut it down?" I ask.

"Way too much work." Cougar waggles his eyebrows. "Who's up for a climb?"

I look up. The fruits are at least fifteen feet above my head. *This is a chance to prove that I'm no longer terrified of the things that came naturally before the accident.* I say, "Me," over the pounding of my heart.

"I'm taller," Gus says. "I can do it."

"Yeah, but Danny's a great tree climber," Cougar says. "She used to scamper up them in Yosemite. Right, buddy?"

My lips stick to my teeth as I smile. "Let's do it." Cougar makes a sling out of an extra T-shirt and ties the machete around my waist. He squats down so I can climb onto his shoulders.

"You've got this."

My heart drops a beat. "Yes."

Cass films as I take his hands, use a knee, then hip to climb onto his shoulders. I reach for the palm's spines. They're rough, easy to grip if I slide my hands deep. But there are dark pockets between the spines and tree. Bad things hide in the dark.

"Look before you put your hand down each time," my dad says, reading my mind.

I take one foot off his shoulder, find purchase on a spine, then move my other foot onto the tree and start climbing. A few times I misjudge the distance to hand- and footholds, but adjust and get the hang of it. A vibrant blue butterfly flutters by, lights on my right forearm, then floats away. I disturb a spider whose hourglass-shaped back is bisected by a yellow line. It's not as big as a tarantula, but it's still at least two inches across. Sensing me, it springs away, disappearing behind a spine. A shudder runs down my entire body.

Cougar says, "How's it going, Danny?"

"Great." *My heart is hammering against my sternum so hard it might crack. There are venomous spiders, biting insects and deadly snakes. What could possibly go wrong?* I avoid a column of red ants streaming to my left, close the distance to an enormous bunch of fruit. Each individual one is the size of an avocado with skin texture that's a mix between a strawberry and a grenade.

Cougar says, "Daylight's burning, kiddo."

Carefully, I withdraw my right hand, then fumble for the machete. My palm is so sweaty I'm afraid it'll slip away. Holding the handle tightly, I take short whacks at the stem holding the fruit. On my eighth thwack, there's a splitting sound and the fruit drops.

"Great job, buddy. Now climb down."

An ear to ear grin splits my face. *Great job! Buddy!* I look down.

Vertigo is a steamroller that flattens me. My legs begin to shake like sewing machine needles. Sweat drips into my eyes.

"Danny?" Jupiter says. "You good?"

Nope. Not good.

"Come on, Danny," Cougar calls. "Quit the Elvis impersonation. We need to get moving. Set up the next camp and get a fire going."

My hands grip the spines so tightly that my forearm muscles cramp. Pretty soon they'll burn out, like a rock climber's do when he freezes, midclimb, from terror. That means I won't be able to hold on. That means I'll fall.

Jupiter says, "Danny, move your right foot down just a few inches."

Somehow I do it.

"Good, now move your right hand—"

"I can't."

"Sure you can," Jupiter says like he's absolutely positive.

I do it. The climb down, with Jupiter guiding me, seems to take a year. Throughout the ordeal, I know exactly what my dad is recalling: my terror at the entomology exhibit, crashing my bike and giving up, the way I panicked in the ocean and made a scene. *Defective. Inferior. Embarrassment.* When I'm halfway down, hands reach up on both sides, pulling me off the trunk, depositing me on the ground. I'm too ashamed to look up, but I see Jupiter's hiking boots on one side of me, Sean's on the other. *Gus.*

Jupiter gives me a side hug. "Thanks for getting us fruit, D. Way to go."

My dad's boots walk over but I still can't tear my gaze off the dirt.

"Danny, look at me."

I do. Cass stands slightly behind Cougar, the red light on her camera blinking. I want to rip it from her hands. I don't need a record of my cowardice. I'll never forget it, nor will my dad.

Cougar's blue eyes are somber. "In survival situations, it's not brave to offer to do something you're not equipped to handle. It puts you in danger as well as the rest of the group. At home a broken arm or leg is an inconvenience. Out here it can mean life or death. And we'll have to take care of you if you're hurt. That'll slow us down. We can't save ourselves if we're busy saving you."

My body contracts like I'm origami, attempting to transform into something better. I'm certain that I've never been more humiliated than at this moment. A military saying Commander Sam once shared surfaces: *Publicly praise. Privately reprimand.* She was talking about a doctor at the hospital who screamed at a nurse in front of a patient. *Why is my dad being so cruel?*

Jupiter bites into the soft yellow flesh of a piece of fruit from the pile at his feet. "This fruit is amazing."

"Zip it, Jupiter. This is important. She could've fallen. Broken her neck."

Jupiter takes another bite of fruit, the juices dripping off his chin. "I think she gets that."

Cougar glowers at him. "Danielle, see that palm over there?"

Danielle. I nod because I don't trust my voice. He's pointing at a short palm that's lying sideways on the ground. It looks dead.

"Scoop up all the dried fruit at its base and put it in your sack."

Gus asks, "What is it?"

"It *was* an aguaje palm," Cougar says. "The fruit can be eaten after it's soaked in water. But it's even better when it goes rotten."

I'm not sure how that's possible, but I trudge over to the fallen tree and gather as many nasty-smelling pieces of decaying fruit I can find. When I hand my dad back his machete, he meets my eyes. "I won't do it again," I manage.

"Good. I know I'm being tough on you. But I don't know what I'd do if you got really hurt out here." His eyes are netted by worry lines, making him look older, tired. *He was mean because I scared him. He cares.*

Cougar swings the machete to clear our way. "Let's go."

Gus, who has been talking quietly with Cass, comes over and gives me a hug. When I pull away, our eyes meet for a few seconds. It's crazy, but I get the feeling he might actually like me in a *we've been in a plane crash, we're going through traumatic stuff, so for this brief time I'm drawn to you* kind of way.

Cass turns off the camera, stows it in the black case slung over her shoulder and follows Cougar. She calls, "Good job, Danny."

I'm not sure whether she's complimenting me for getting the fruit or for freaking out. The latter makes for better TV. I catch up to her. "Cass, are you and my dad a couple?"

"We dated a lifetime ago."

She's only twenty-nine. Cass seems to be having trouble walking straight. My skin prickles. *I'm not here to play pretend nurse.*

Cougar says over his shoulder, "A few more hours, then we'll set up camp for the night, make a quick shelter, get a fire going and grill some grubs."

Grubs?

18

We set up camp after a full day of hiking with no river in sight. The frustrating thing is we could've been paralleling one but never known because the rain forest is so dense it's impossible to see ten feet in front of you. This spot looks the same as the last one. For all I know, we're just going in circles. I'm not sure if the rest of the group is disappointed, but I was really, really hoping we wouldn't have to spend another night in this place. We've run out of water, except for lianas and the muddy sludge we collected from the puddle that probably has a zillion parasites swimming in it. The mosquitos and biting flies have backed off but my clothes are soggy with sweat and I'm probably starting to grow some kind of tropical fungus.

"We can't assume it will be dry tonight," Cougar says,

cutting down bamboo to make a shelter. "Gus and Danny, collect palm fronds for the roof. Jupiter, get as much dry wood as you can. Cass, you're filming."

Cougar spends the next thirty minutes building the shelter's frame. When Gus and I have a big pile of palm fronds, I carefully braid a leaf, making sure there aren't any holes to let the rain through because the rivulets and drips of water last night were maddening. I've never braided palms before, just watched it on my dad's show, but quickly get the hang of it. Maybe this is my new sport.

"Nice," Gus says. "I stink at this."

He was watching me. I show him how to tighten the weave. He leans forward, his hair brushing my cheek. Our fingers get tangled. We both laugh and my cheeks get warm. It's like I'm just a girl and he's just a guy.

Cougar comes over and crouches beside us. "FYI, weaving the fronds to make a waterproof roof is great if you're setting up camp for days. We're moving on tomorrow. In the future, just collect palms and pile them. Anything else is obviously a waste of time. Got it?"

Obviously. My skin gets hot, tight. *I should've known.* "Got it."

"Good. I'll finish the roof. See that plant?" Cougar points to a low bush with dark almond-shaped leaves. "It's allspice. Pick a handful of leaves. They'll make the suri taste great."

"Suri?" I ask.

"Beetle grubs. They're a great source of energy and fat. We may be out here a few more days, so we all need them. Gus, you can help Danny split the rotten fruits she collected." Cougar hands Gus the machete. "Pull out the suri inside, wrap each in a piece of leaf, then tie it closed with vines. We'll grill them once we have a fire going."

"What if it's too wet for a fire?" Gus asks.

Cougar flashes a cocky smile. "Doubtful. But worst-case scenario, we'll eat them raw."

Raw grubs? "I could maybe collect kindling?"

Cougar shakes his head. "Jupiter will do that while we finish the shelter."

When I dump out the rotten fruit, I try not to think that I've been carrying grubs on my back for hours. The compulsion to unbraid my hair and comb fingers through it in case one of the grubs escaped is an urge I fight. Gus sits down across from me. He raises the machete, bracing the fruit with his left hand.

"Wait!"

"Why?"

"Episode fifty-one?"

Gus raises one eyebrow.

"The rapper, TZ?"

Gus shakes his head.

"He was chopping bamboo in Malaysia and sliced his hand. The cut was super deep. My dad used army ants to close it."

Both of Gus's brows shoot up. "Excuse me?"

I laugh. "They have mandibles—curved jaws. Cougar pressed the ants' heads into the center of TZ's cut, then he broke off the bodies so the ant's jaws pinched together and held."

"That actually worked?"

"Yeah." I don't say that it was totally unsanitary. TZ spent two weeks in the hospital. Intravenous antibiotics, and a gnarly scar because some of the infected tissue had to be excised, clean tissue from his thigh grafted to replace it. The reunion show was filmed in TZ's hospital room. I get the idea from Gus's grimace that maybe if he'd done his research, watched a few episodes, he would've thought twice before agreeing to come to the Amazon.

"You've seen every one of your dad's shows?"

"It was my way of spending time with him." I look away because it sounds so lame.

He touches my arm. "I get it." Gus uses a stick to pin the fruit to the ground before he cuts it open. Inside is an inch-long white segmented worm with a black head. It wriggles in the light, standing on its back end like it's ready to fight. Disgusted, I scramble away.

Gus chuckles. "Get back here!" He holds up the fruit. "Pull out the worm."

"Um. No."

"I cut it open."

"Congratulations."

Gus hesitates, then plucks out the worm, dropping it onto one of the allspice leaves. He shudders, wipes his hand on his shirt. We both crack up. He has a great laugh. His entire body is part of the fun.

"There's no way I'm eating that thing," Gus says.

"You will. I will, too. Neither one of us wants to disappoint Cougar Warren."

Gus looks up from beneath long lashes. "He's kind of hard on you."

I shrug. "When I was a kid, we weren't really in touch. My mom got in the way, kept us apart, but Cougar didn't know she was doing that. He thought that I didn't love him—that I didn't want him around. I need to show him that I do."

"He called you Danielle after the tree thing."

"Danny is short for Danielle. It's my middle name."

"Seems like you don't like it."

I'm surprised he noticed. Kind of flattered, too. "It reminds me of a time, when I was little, that I wasn't the person I wanted to be."

He tucks a loose strand of hair behind my ear and my skin tickles where he touched it. "You were little. It's not your fault."

He's wrong. Gus runs his thumb over the scar on his jaw. "How'd that happen?"

"Skateboarding with my dad."

A zing of jealousy runs through me. Of course Gus does that kind of stuff with his father. I'm sure they're best friends, go on trips together all the time, share secrets, jokes, a lifetime of Christmas mornings and birthday parties. Gus's dad is probably super proud of his son, watches every movie and joins him for award shows.

"Almost dark," Cougar calls. "Speed it up."

We figure out a method with the grubs. Gus cracks the fruit open. I use a stick to flick every grub onto a leaf. Gus folds the packets fast, then I tie them tight with vines. I make the final knot. "All done."

Gus says, "Nice job." He leans over, kisses my forehead.

I automatically lift my chin, like a reflex, and wait for the next kiss. He gazes into my eyes…

"You're a really cool kid."

Cool kid? "Um, thanks?"

He tugs my braid. "Just doing my job. I told Cass we should drop that part but she thinks it still works. Regardless, you're great."

Job? That part? "What do you mean, job?"

Gus's eyes bulge like a cartoon character. He looks like he wants to rewind our conversation, erase it. His smile disintegrates. "I'm exhausted, babbling. Forget it, okay?"

Seconds tick by. Each one is a hammer cracking against my thick skull. "Wait. Are you saying that part of your *job* is to flirt with me?"

Gus, eyes down, wraps a piece of twine around his fingers until it cuts off the circulation. "Danny. Look, it was just meant to be a light thing, fun. Then the plane crash happened. We agreed to keep filming, honor Sean and Mack, document our struggles and survival. Cass said flirting with you was still important for the viewers, a way to lighten this messed-up situation and that telling you the plan would lose the episode's authenticity. I wasn't going to take it anywhere… I mean, you're just a kid."

Fragments of conversations float to the surface like dead fish…

I'm putting in my time, showing Cougar I'm dedicated and that I have the skill and drive to someday direct.

I thought you might not be open to it.

Do you think he's hot?

He's too good-looking.

It's part of the hook.

I'm an actor. This trip is a job. If I do it well, it'll help my career. Truth. Truth. Truth.

My eyes fill. Fun fact? Both my eyes can cry. *I'm here to be the punch line.* That's the hook Cass was talking about back in LA. Shy, uncoordinated, inexperienced, one-eyed freak spends time in the jungle with hunky Gus Price. He flirts. She falls for him. Cue laugh track. My insides convulse, like vomiting will eliminate the poison of Cass and Gus's plan that's currently eating holes through my stomach.

I struggle for control. My brain knows that none of this should matter to me. People are dead. *But it still hurts.* Cass must've planned the whole thing to impress my dad, to show him what a talented director she can be. *And my dad?* Cougar would never have gone along with it if he knew. *I'm his priority.*

Gus mutters, "Danny, I'm really sorry."

"Hey, GP, come help me put the finishing touches on our shelter," Cougar shouts.

Using the heel of my hand, I smash away tears, get up and head into the rain forest.

Jupiter calls out, "Where you going?"

"Bathroom break." I squat behind a tree and cry, my shoulders hunched, silent sobs shaking my body. Through the foliage I see Gus pick up the leaf packets, carry them over to my dad. He glances my way but I duck so he can't see me. I don't need his fake apology. That's probably part of his job, too.

The voices of the kids who teased me form a chorus in my brain: *Pigeon—Pigeon—Pigeon.* I push them away and dry my tears. Nothing has changed. I will make Cougar proud.

19

"You okay?" Jupiter asks.

My eyes are gritty, puffy. "Allergies." I sit down under the shelter and feel Gus's stare but don't give him the satisfaction of looking his way. Girls might throw themselves at him, but I know who he really is—a guy who'd use someone for entertainment.

Cougar works on starting a fire at the edge of our temporary shelter. He's already dug out a shallow hole to keep it from wind that has steadily picked up, and created a roof of palms resting on sturdy branches to protect the flame from possible rain. There's a pile of mostly dry leaves made into a loose nest, and small twigs beside the nest along with larger pieces of wood. In addition, he tears pages from Jupiter's book and crumples them. My dad turns Mack's fire-steel around and cuts tiny slivers off its bulbous handle, then adds them to pieces of the potato chip bag already woven into the nest.

"What's the handle made of?" I ask.

Cougar says, "Mack was a survivalist at heart. He took the end off his fire-steel and replaced it with a natural resin that burns really well. A lot of trees in the Amazon have resin, so if we need more, it's there." He uses his machete on the steel, shooting sparks into the nest. A red-hot flash sends up a single curl of smoke. Picking up the nest, he blows into it slowly, until the embers catch. White smoke begins to billow. Carefully, Cougar puts the now-flaming nest in the center of the hole and begins feeding it with the smallest twigs, leaves and wadded paper. Crackling sounds fill the air. The best part, besides the heat, is that the smoke drives away most of the insects.

Cougar tells Gus, "Next time you can give it a go."

Gus looks over at me. I channel Trix's sharp edges. "I'm sure you'll be great at it. But aren't we planning to carry an ember? That's usually what Cougar does when he moves campsites. It saves time and resources. Have you watched any episodes?" I'm gratified to see splotches of color on the movie star's cheeks.

Cougar leans sideways, plants a kiss on my cheek and says, "My biggest fan." I help him put the leaf packets on a makeshift tray that he fashioned from sticks, and then place our water containers beside them to boil. The scent of allspice, an earthy mix of cinnamon and nutmeg, actually makes my stomach loudly growl.

"I hear you, sister," Jupiter laughs. "I'm hungry enough to eat grubs, too."

"While we wait, dry your sweaty feet and socks by the fire," Cougar says, "and put on some mosquito repellent."

We peel off boots and soggy socks. My heel is bloody but I don't wash it off. Whatever's in the water we collected could turn my popped blister into a bad infection. Instead, I wait until the blood dries, then cover the blister with a piece of duct tape. Jupiter has blisters on both his heels, even though his boots are worn in. I do the same for him.

"You're hired as trip medic," he says.

Gus unwraps the bandage on his arm and starts to pull up an edge of the duct tape used to close his wound.

"Don't. You'll just increase the chance for infection."

"Is it," Gus asks, "infected?"

I glance over. No swelling or angry red lines run up his arm to signal a problem. I'm clearly not a nice person because I'm glad he's worried. "It's fine."

Since I can't look at Gus without crying, I focus on the rust-red ants parading in rows by my feet. They're each transporting torn pieces of leaves. "The leaves are bigger than their own bodies."

Cougar nods. "They're leaf-cutters. They take those pieces to an underground nest where they'll grow a fungus that'll feed the entire colony. See the ones on the edges?"

Gus notes, "They're larger."

"Soldier ants. Their job is to protect the workers. They're aggressive, so steer clear. Got it, Danny?"

I'm right here. How could I miss it? "Got it."

Jupiter nudges one of the smaller ants with the toe of his boot. "Never underestimate the strength of a tiny ant, right, Cougar? They're mighty in their own way."

Cougar flashes a smile. "Enough about ants. Let's eat some grubs."

Everyone gets six grub packets. My dad shows us how to break off the grub's head, then he tosses the crispy body into his mouth and chews it several times before swallowing. "Delicious. Eat up."

Cass films our dinner. Jupiter goes first. "It's actually not bad," he says. "Consistency of tofu, but much, much oilier. Bright side? It tastes like nutmeg."

Gus eats all of his at once. A mouthful of grubs chewed hard, then washed down by the muddy boiled water. I was hoping he'd gag, but no luck.

"Danny, your turn," Cougar says.

I twist off beady black heads and swallow each grub whole while pretending to chew. "Not bad."

Cougar grins. "That's my girl. Impressive, right, Gus?"

"Yeah," Gus says.

I don't look at him. The muddy water is what gets me. I can't stop thinking about parasites; whether the water was boiled for long enough. There have been cases where worms grew in people's bodies for months, then squiggled out of every orifice—mountains of them. I gag but manage to keep everything down as I burp repeatedly, the greasy taste of the grubs I didn't chew coming back to haunt me. Cass is right there, filming.

Jupiter puts a hand over the lens. "Give the kid a break."

Cass says, "I don't tell you how to do your job."

When it's her turn, she eats her grubs like they're popcorn. She has gray semicircles beneath her eyes and skin so pale that the spidery blue veins beneath are visible. "Gotta pee," she says. When she stands, she wobbles, then gets her balance and ducks behind a tree.

"Um, Dad?"

Cougar holds up his hand. "Time for a game. Everyone know two lies and a truth?"

I say, "I thought it was two truths and a lie."

"Not in my version," Cougar explains. "We each tell two lies and one truth. The group has to guess which thing we say is true."

Cass returns and immediately picks up the camera. "Ready."

"I'll go first," Cougar says. "Number one, I've had a candiru swim up my urethra."

"Candiru?" Gus asks.

"It's a parasitic catfish in the Amazon River. They grow to around six inches long, swim into a fish's gills, then, using razor spines on their heads to attach, chew through the host, hit a major artery and drink the host's blood. The smell of human urine appeals to them, so if you pee in the river, they can swim up your penis or lady parts." Cougar grins. "Only way to get them out is surgery."

Jupiter grimaces. "That's disgusting."

"It'll keep you from peeing in the river. Two. I've killed a mountain lion with my bare hands. Three, Carmen Fox and I are expecting twins."

I know the last one isn't true. My dad's not even dating her. "I think it's number two."

"Number one," Jupiter says.

"Cass?"

She asks, "What were they again?"

"I say the truth is number three," Gus says. "Cougar is a legend."

Cougar savors the moment. "Three," he finally shouts. "I'm going to be a dad!"

If my heart were a bird, it was just shot midair. My dad is having twins and he's forgotten he had me first. Plus, now there's even less of an incentive for him to get to know me. Babies are perfect little beings with all their potential in front of them. Not like the almost seventeen-year-old he's understandably written off. "I thought you weren't, that it was just for PR? Um. Cool. Congratulations." I know my smile is too big.

Cougar cracks up. "Kidding! Trying to lighten the mood. Jeez, you look like someone died."

Jupiter's hand inches toward mine until our pinkies touch. "Spill."

"Number two is true," Cougar says, still winding down from his belly laughs. "It was in Colorado. I was trail running above the city of Boulder. Felt the hairs on the back of my neck rise. Turned just in time to see the cat launch." He points to a scar running along his neck. "His canine did that. Didn't want to kill him, but that cat was trying to drag me to his den, feed on me slowly." He shakes his head. "Jesus, shoot me now if I'm having twins, right?"

No one says anything. The silence stretches.

"We're going to get out of here. But you guys need to take a foot off the gas, lighten up. It'll help," Cougar promises. "You're up, Cass."

Cass hands Cougar the camera. She rearranges her long hair, so it flows over one shoulder. "Let's see… One, I buy a lottery ticket every week. Two, I speak five languages. Three…" She stares down at her hands. "I'm in love but the guy doesn't know it."

"Five languages," Cougar says.

She's still in love with him. "Lottery ticket."

Gus guesses, "Languages."

"Love," Jupiter says.

Cass nibbles her lower lip. "Lottery tickets. You're next, Gus."

Gus looks at me like he's asking permission or something. "Go on," I say. "We're on the edge of our seats."

"One, I'm dating Beca Reese. Two, I turned down the lead role in *The Reckoning*. Three, my dad died in a small plane crash."

I don't know how I know, but I do. *It's three.*

Cougar claps his hands. "Beca. Has to be. Lucky bastard."

"*The Reckoning*," Jupiter says. "Sorry, Gus, but I loved that movie without you in it."

"No apologies needed. Jake Hudson did an amazing job."

Cass shrugs, keeps filming. She's probably doing a close-up of Gus's face. Welcome to the club.

"Go ahead," Gus says to me. "Guess."

He's doing this to make me feel sorry for him. Regardless of the answer, he's still an asshole. "Three."

"Winner," Gus says. "Snowstorm in Vermont. I was six." He looks away.

My dad goes to sit by Gus, an arm around his shoulders. "I'm sorry, kid. This was supposed to be a fun game, lighten the mood. Danny? Save us, buddy. You got any funny ones?"

I'm a barrel of laughs. "One, I'm a high-platform diver. Two, I love eyelash vipers. Three, I'll be seventeen on Friday."

My dad laughs. "All lies, but we appreciate the effort." He turns to Gus. "Losing your dad at that age had to be rough. Anytime you need to talk, I'm available day or night. You're a great guy, tough, talented, driven. I always wanted a son like you."

Truth.

DAY
TWO

20

I sleep fitfully, waking again and again in the dark morning hours to insects burrowing beneath my sweatshirt. The worst part is that I have to look at them in the firelight, hairy legs, twitching antennae, stingers and pincers, to make sure they're not deadly before I brush them away. Some sting, some don't. They're all repulsive. When Gus leaps to his feet, shakes out his shirt, shivers in revulsion, I'm glad. He sees me watching in the flickering light, hesitates like he's considering coming over, trying to talk. I turn my back. He can spoon with my dad since he likes him so much.

The rains start like someone flipped a light switch. Rivulets find their way through the piled palm fronds. Each time I shift, another drips on me. It's like water torture. Sometime before dawn, the switch flips again and the rains stop. Without the steady patter of water, I can hear Cass sniffling. She's sitting at the edge of our shelter by the fire, feeding it with branches and pages from Jupiter's book to keep it going. I'm furious at her. Beyond furious. I crawl over. "What's up?"

Cass chews on her lower lip.

"Is it your head?"

She nods, winces. "It's splitting open."

Sometimes a patient will seem fine.

I push away my mom's no-nonsense voice. Maybe it's the cut. But what can I do if it is infected? We don't have any antibiotics.

A patient will appear lucid, but over time have migraines, become confused, lose balance, ask repetitive questions or have seizures.

"How's your vision?" When I had migraines my already-narrow vision would close in. Each time it happened, I was terrified that I'd gone blind and a panic attack would hit hard. My mom would take off work, sit in my bedroom, read case studies aloud because watching TV made it worse but I needed a distraction, one long enough to put me to sleep.

"My vision?" Cass giggles. "Better than yours."

I don't laugh. "Good one."

Gingerly, Cass shakes her head. "You think this is going to change things." She stares into the fire. "Quit trying so hard. The sooner you get it, the sooner I can stop feeling guilty."

"I'm not—"

"There's no room for you. He doesn't even have space for perfect people."

It's like being stabbed, then having the knife twisted.

"Do you want to grab a coffee? Coffee is my umbilical cord."

Despite the fire's heat, goose bumps break along my arms. "Cass, what's your last name?"

Firelight stains the whites of her eyes orange. She frowns. "You asked me that before. I told you."

"I forgot. Can you tell me again?"

Cass crawls back to the shelter, taking my spot between Cougar and Jupiter. I stay by the fire, keep it alive.

If there's bleeding or swelling in the brain it creates so much pressure inside the skull that it damages the brain tissue, sometimes irreparably...

How long does it take until the patient dies?

Minutes to days... But they don't always if a surgeon can put in a shunt to drain the fluid or remove a piece of the patient's skull to give their swollen brain room.

We need to get out of this rain forest, bring Cass to a hospital. I consider waking my dad. *What good would it do?*

I tend the fire until dawn. I could wake someone else to take over, but I can't sleep anyway. "Hey, Danny? Got a minute?" Cass asks after everyone has woken, crept away to do their morning business, eaten a half piece of licorice and started packing to leave camp.

Taking a swallow of water, I don't choke, so that's a win. My dad is showing Gus how to make the bamboo container to carry an ember. "Sure," I say. She looks a little less wrecked. Maybe she just needed sleep. I follow her out of earshot of the rest of our group.

"So. I'm pretty sure last night I said some things that were none of my business?"

Cass hesitates, like she's waiting for confirmation. I don't give it to her.

155

"Anyway, I don't want you to think I'm ungrateful…for your dad's support, or my job."

No apology. She's just covering her ass. "I know what you did," I quietly say, then walk away. Let her worry about what I mean; that I'm going to cry to Cougar; that she might lose her job. The thing with Gus was really cruel. So is what she said about my dad not having room in his life for me. But I won't tell my dad. No one likes a snitch.

Before we leave camp, Cougar hands everyone a twig and tells us to peel the bark off one end with our teeth and then chew that end until it looks like the bottom of a broom.

"Why?" Gus asks.

Cougar says, "I don't know about you, but my teeth are growing fur. These are hibiscus tree twigs—a natural tooth-brush. They even make your breath smell sweet."

The twig actually works well once the end is the right con-sistency. I pocket mine to use again later. We pack up our things and head out single file—Cougar, then Cass followed by Jupiter, me, then Gus in the rear. For the next few hours I focus on not getting stung, bitten, pierced by a thorn or tak-ing any number of opportunities to embarrass myself. The gnats and mosquitos are a constant drone in my ears. There are moments when the sound is so maddening that I want to scream. But I don't. I won't.

When Gus touches my shoulder I jump. As usual he's ap-proached on my left. To stifle a yelp, I bite my lip hard enough to draw blood.

Gus asks, "Danny, can we talk about it?"

I'm a popular girl today. "There's nothing to talk about. I get it."

"I don't think you do."

Jupiter turns around and asks, "Everything okay, Danny?"

"Yeah. Give us a minute?" Jupiter nods, walks ahead. Gus's expression is pure sad dog. It's the look Trix gives guys after she dumps them. My voice is shaky but pitched low so it won't carry. "You were told to flirt with me, get an uncoordinated, homely, one-eyed girl to think you might like her—"

"You're not—"

"Good job, it worked," I interrupt. "Great acting, GP. You should be proud."

Gus shakes his head. "It's not what you think."

Yes, it is. "Would you have kissed me on the lips at the end of the episode to give hope to all the losers out there who will never, ever get attention from someone as good-looking and famous as you?"

"Danny—"

"Stop." I swallow hard, nails digging into my palms to keep from becoming even more pathetic. "Just drop it."

"Can I explain?"

If he tells me I have a great personality my humiliation will be complete. "No."

Gus sighs like I'm the one who did something mortifying to him. "Is there anything I can do?" he asks.

"Yes," I say, unable to stop myself. "Cougar is *my* dad, not yours, so back off. And stop sneaking up on my left. I'm blind in that eye."

Gus flinches. For a second I actually think I've hurt his feelings. Then I remember he's an actor. I catch up with the rest of the group, face burning. For the next few hours I concentrate on the pain in my heel, the bite of mosquitos, gnats burrowing into the wet corners of my eyes and the sweat soaking my clothes.

Half a day into our hike, we see a trickle of brown water running beside a giant kapok tree. The trickle slowly widens. We follow it until it's three feet across, a dark chocolate stream sluggishly moving downhill. Everyone walks more quickly. We're thinking the same thing. This will point to a real river that'll snake through the rain forest, lead away from the relentless bugs, into air conditioning, a bed, decent food.

I'll never have to see Gus Price again.

Cougar says, "Fill your water bottles. We'll boil the water tonight if we need to." He starts whistling. Even Cass smiles. Gus and Jupiter start talking about their favorite college basketball teams.

"Georgetown," Jupiter says.

Gus shakes his head. "So yesterday. Northwestern is *the* team."

"Sad." Jupiter glances over at me. "What about you, Danny?"

I don't watch any sports. "Georgetown."

Jupiter gives me a high five and says, "I knew you were smart."

Cougar points at electric-blue parrots with bright yellow circles around their eyes that swoop overhead, their calls mingling with the constant babble of monkeys. "Macaws."

I watch an iridescent purple-and-gold bird with long tail feathers wing by. "What's that one?"

"Crimson topaz. See that one? Red wings, yellow tail, orange-and-black beak?"

I lean over my dad's arm, looking where he's pointing. "I see it."

"Oropendolas. They make hanging nests for protection from snakes."

A furry brown-and-white creature high up in a leafy tree catches my eye. It has long hair, curved claws, sloping eyes and a goofy smile beneath a button-shaped nose. I point up.

Cougar smiles. "It's a sloth."

I'm transported back to being a little kid. Cougar and I are walking through the woods, hand in hand, as he tells me about the trees, animals and his next adventure. I study the sloth. "Its fur is sort of greenish."

"Algae grow in the cracks of their hair. It's a symbiotic relationship. The algae get a nice place to live, and the sloth is camouflaged from predators."

We could have a symbiotic relationship, my dad and me, if I can figure out what I have that Cougar might need. "What do sloths eat?"

"They're herbivores. The three-toed sloths in the wild are friendly. If I could reach that guy, he'd let me pick him up. But the two-toed sloths are dangerous. They can cut a predator's throat open with the slash of a claw."

I catch Gus looking at me. I'm a two-toed sloth as far as he's concerned. "What?" I ask loud enough that Cougar can hear.

Gus turns away. "Nothing."

Cougar asks, "You two getting along?"

"Sure. GP is supercool." My dad smiles like he's just another father who's happy his daughter is having a good time. I'm sure that he doesn't know what Cass did. This really was supposed to be the best sixteenth birthday present ever, a way for him to reconnect with the kid he believed didn't want anything to do with him.

Cougar swings the machete, cutting away the woody vines blocking our passage. He raises his arm again, then stops. The stream ends in a swamp stretching as far as we can see. It's a flooded lattice of narrow passageways dotted with trees that grow half-submerged, clumps of thick brush, roots twisting out of the water like gnarled fingers and pockets of darkness where the swamp closes in.

All the beautiful birds, monkeys and sloths are forgotten, replaced by the unblinking eyes of a caiman swimming through tall grasses less than twenty yards away. I watch my dad take it in, square his shoulders, then turn with a smile that makes my insides collapse like a sandcastle obliterated by a wave.

21

"The good news," Cougar says, "is that with this much water there's almost definitely a wider stream that leads to a real river."

I strain to see what he's talking about. The soundtrack from *Jaws* fills my head. We have no idea what's hidden in this swamp.

"Can we go around?" Jupiter asks.

Good idea! Otherwise, this feels like the part in a horror movie where the kids run and hide from their attacker in an attic or basement that has no exit.

Cougar scratches the stubble on his chin. "Diverting is an option. But who knows how far this swamp stretches? Could be miles. Everyone can swim, right?"

"We can't go through it," I say. *Shut up.* But that's impossible. Panic is an express train pulling out of the station. Another caiman surfaces, snout first, its armored tail slowly lashing left and right; moss-colored eyes stare at us, unblinking. Its long jaw parts to reveal rows of curved teeth. My breath catches, skin shrinks, ribs compress inward...

Jupiter asks, "Danny, you good?"

Not good. Hands clutch knees. Nails dig into skin. My heartbeat struggles, dizziness creeps forward, sweat runs down my back...

Cougar says, "Look. That's a spectacled caiman. See the bony ridge between its eyes that makes it look like it's wearing glasses?"

I should be wearing my glasses! I have one eye! It's unprotected! In the Amazon! Fingers wrap around my neck, squeeze. I'm about to be the biggest freaking liability my dad has ever seen. I drag down fistfuls of air but they don't reach my lungs.

"I think she's having some kind of anxiety attack," Cass says.

No shit. Her voice sounds like it's coming from far away. I'm sure she's still filming. I struggle not to vomit...pass out... dissolve into hysteria...

"She's fine," Jupiter says. "It's all good, Danny. We're still on dry land. No caimans nearby. Haven't seen a snake in at least fifteen minutes. The rain has stopped. Actually, it's pretty pleasant out considering—high seventies, light breeze and only about ten thousand bugs in the vicinity. Fair to say that I wouldn't want to buy a condo here, but it has its merits. For example..."

Jupiter drones on and on, like we're kicking it at a local coffee shop. Like we're on a vacation. Like everything is cool. I can't hear much of what he's saying, but his tone cuts through the static. My lungs struggle, my heart has compressed to a pebble, beating erratically, but I focus on Jupiter's voice. It's a rope that allows me to pull myself, inch by inch, back to the surface.

When I open my eyes, it's unclear how much time has passed. Hands on my knees, I peer up at Jupiter, panting like I've just run a long-distance race. I'm afraid to meet anyone else's eyes.

Jupiter smiles. "There you are."

Every muscle in my body is overly wound, like those kids' toys that twist rubber bands to propel plastic cars or jumping frogs. Slowly, I uncramp my torso until I'm standing up straight.

Cougar's brow is scrunched, the picture of parental worry. "All good?"

The truth is that my body still teeters on the edge, but there's a note of impatience in my dad's tone that's a warning. I'm dangerously close to being that little kid who made a scene at the beach. "All good," I say.

Cougar looks from person to person. "Here's the deal. Generally, caimans aren't dangerous. They go for small prey—"

"What about black caimans?" I ask, unable to stop myself but trying to sound interested, not terrified. "In an episode you said that they drown animals and children by rolling, then stuffing them under a log until they're waterlogged and easy to eat."

"Thanks for that image," Cass snaps.

Cougar says, "We're in an area where food is plentiful. If

there are black caimans around, they're well-fed and prefer jungle animals to us."

"Prefer? Does that mean they look at a menu that says there's a choice between wild pigs, sloths and Danny, and then choose pigs?" My dad laughs. Score one for me, but I want to go back. I'm not sure exactly where, but not here. Cass is filming this conversation. My weakness again recorded. But we can't even freaking see where this swamp ends. We have no idea how deep it is. The water is dark brown, opaque. There are things beneath the surface that can kill us.

Gus peers into the swamp. "What about snakes?"

I actually forget to hate him for a split second.

"Good question. The great thing about snakes is that we can see them. Plus, it's hard for them to bite you when they're swimming."

Jupiter snorts. "Is that even true?"

"Look, we're doing fine out here," Cougar says. "We could last a long time, safe, relatively well-fed, or someone could get hurt or sick and that'd be a game changer. I'd rather take a calculated risk, get us out of here more quickly. But if you want to go back, try to skirt the swamp, well, this is a group decision."

Cougar wraps an arm around my waist, points to a bird at the edge of the swamp. It has a beak like a pelican's, black head, red ring around its neck and a snow-white body. "Jabiru stork. He's looking for insects and spiders but chances are the caimans are waiting for him to wade in and then he'll be dinner."

My dad is trying to make me feel better. Like I'm not the best food option. Two furry heads poke out of the water near the stork. They have tiny ears, beady eyes and square snouts. They're the size of a Jack Russell terrier and look like monster rats. "They on the menu, too?"

Cougar chuckles. "Who knew you were such a funny kid? They're capybaras, the world's largest rodents. Fantastic swimmers. Today they're the special on the menu for black caimans."

I ask, "Do they bite people?"

"Nope. Scared to death of people, especially little girls." A pack of monkeys chitters nearby. Cougar points up. "Bald uakaris. The smallest monkeys in the rain forest."

I watch the red-faced, brown-furred monkeys swing from liana to liana, then scamper up a tree and out of sight.

"Tell us the real risks," Jupiter says.

Cougar sighs. "Aren't you supposed to be a grown-up?"

"That's exactly what I am. And I want all the facts so I can make a grown-up decision."

"There could be electric eels. They won't bother us if we shuffle our feet, move slowly. If you do get shocked, it's a nasty jolt but usually not much more. Snakes are always a threat. Not the vipers in the water, the tree boas because if they drop, we'll be as much of a surprise for them as they are for us. Good thing, though, is their bite isn't poisonous. If they start to wrap around you, I can get them off."

I ask, "What about anacondas?" Cougar saw one with Malcolm, the EDM DJ, in Brazil. It was almost twenty feet long. *Drop it. I can't.* "You told Malcolm that they can stay underwater for up to ten minutes. That they kill their prey by coiling, squeezing it to death."

"You're like a Wikipedia page for my show," Cougar says

with a forced chuckle. "Anacondas won't be a problem in this swamp because they only hunt at night."

Jupiter says, "It's always dark in here."

"What do you do if one bites you?" Gus asks.

Cougar takes a deep breath. "Believe it or not, the first thing I'd do is bite its tail. They have supersensitive tails. A lot of times, that'll be enough for them to release you. Regardless, fight like hell. No predator wants to struggle for its meal. I'll use the machete to go after its head, and everyone will grab rocks to bludgeon it." He looks from face to face. "Guys, they're on land, too."

Jupiter laughs. "That makes me feel so much better."

Cougar rubs his left shoulder. "On land they move more slowly so they're easy to outrun."

Gus shakes his head. "This is a seriously f'd-up situation."

"Look, there's a lot of things out here that can kill you," Cougar says. "That's just the truth. My job is to get as many of us as possible out of here safely."

Is he insinuating that the remaining survivors might not all make it?

"Anacondas prefer fish, birds and capybaras. There are a lot of those around. They don't want to mess with something as big as us. Also, after a meal they don't eat for weeks, even months at a time."

"So we're hoping that if there's one in this swamp it recently had a huge meal?" Jupiter asks.

Cougar glowers. "You're getting paid to be here."

"I didn't sign up for this catastrophe. I signed up for the normal trip where the crew scouts, sets up each scene, makes sure nothing too nasty is out there."

"I think the best plan is to hunker down, maybe build a

fort, one with no tiny cracks for snakes, spiders or scorpions, and wait for rescue." Everyone looks at me like I've lost it. "What? There have to be search parties scouring the rain forest for us. Cougar and Gus are really famous. People don't just let famous people die."

Cougar holds up his hands. "You're all overreacting. Seriously. Chances are this swamp is only a few feet deep. We'll be back on dry land before you know it, following a river that'll get us out of here. I'll lead. We'll stick together. This is our best option."

"Okay," Cass says.

Of course she agrees. She's a *perfect* person in love with my dad. She puts her camera in its case, slings it over one shoulder. Without looking back at the group she follows Cougar into the swamp.

"I'll stay with Danny," Gus offers, "until you know how deep it is."

So you can look like a hero? "Thanks, but I agree with my dad. We need to get out of this place before someone gets hurt. I can do this."

"I—I wasn't saying you couldn't," Gus stammers. "You take on every challenge, even when you're afraid."

Rolling my eyes at the fake compliment, I step into the swamp and immediately sink to my shins. Every fiber of my being strains to turn back. But if Cougar glances over his shoulder, he'll see me. So instead, mouth as dry as the desert, I put one shaking foot in front of the other, force myself to ignore the danger siren going off in my brain.

I hear splashes as Gus, then Jupiter enter the swamp. *Stop splashing!* We wade through long grasses, around trees with slimy bark, stands of palms and thorny bushes that flower despite the murky light. There are moments when I can't see my dad, when he's hidden around an obstacle or in shadow, and my heart sprints until he's visible again. Every burble beneath the surface makes me flinch, my head whipping left to right, a terrified pigeon desperate to see what's coming for me.

Jupiter asks, "Doing okay, Danny?"

"It's like a hedge maze, except wet." I'm sure my unsteady voice gives me away. Trix and I got lost in a hedge maze during a school visit to the coast. I raised the red flag we were given at the start so an employee could lead us out. Trix went back in with her crush of the moment.

There are half a dozen four- to six-foot caimans in a thick patch of yellow-brown reeds about twenty feet away. As we get closer, their yellow-green eyes follow us. Anxiety prickles along my skin. The water level climbs to my waist, then just below my shoulder blades. It's the temperature of bathwater with a thick carpet of insects buzzing on the surface. The path we've been traveling closes in, thick with brush on one side, thorny bushes on the other. A fallen kapok tree blocks our way. It stretches hundreds of feet in both directions. Neither end is visible in the thick morass of the swamp. Cougar puts a hand on the slimy bark, attempting to climb it. Within seconds he slides right back into the water.

Gus asks, "Do we go around?"

Cougar's jaw clenches, unclenches. "We can, but this seems to be the main channel. I want to stay on it. If we start winding through secondary ones we might end up far from the major river that'll lead us out of here. Hang on." He takes a deep breath, then submerges.

Bubbles rise to the surface. The water ripples, then stills. I hold my breath, count to sixteen before my dad's head pops up.

"Seems like most of the tree is above the waterline," Cougar says. "We go under or we can try to work our way around. Team decision."

The tree is huge. We won't just be ducking under it like it's a telephone pole. We will be *swimming* under it. Swimming. Underwater. In the dark. Holding our breath. Hoping nothing deadly is under there with us. We can't even see the other side. There might be a second tree. *This is a very bad idea.*

"We go?" Cougar asks. No one answers. He takes the waterproof camera bag from Cass and loops it over his shoulder. "Okay. I'll call once I'm out so you know how far it is." He sinks beneath the surface of the swamp.

No one says a word. We wait. We wait. We wait. Ten, fifteen, twenty-one seconds...

"I'm out," Cougar shouts. "Danny first. Take a big breath and go under right where I did. Swim hard to me."

Terror claws my insides like a trapped rat. *If I stay on this side, my dad will know I don't belong with him.* Before I can hyperventilate, I sink under the water.

22

I swim beneath the massive felled tree. Swamp water streams along my body. I'm petrified of contact with anything, everything. I can hear the fast tick-tick of a stopwatch as the air in my lungs starts to evaporate.

Swim hard to me.

I flail forward. Something snags my shirt. Spastically, I reach back, anticipating teeth or an electric jolt. It's a knot of wood. I twist hard and tug free, push forward. I'm thrashing too much. Predators are attracted to vibrations. They can feel panic. Smell it even in water. Episode 173—New Zealand, with Olympic skier JA Barrett. A great white shark circled JA and Cougar's man-made canoe. My lungs ache, oxygen deprivation creating a hungry void.

I'm taking too long.

Something bashes into me. I wait for an anaconda's coils to slither around my body, squeeze the final drops of air from my lungs.

Fight like hell. No predator wants to battle for its prey.

How can I fight a giant snake or a prehistoric alligator? I open my eyes but can't see anything in the muddy water. Still, I want to know what's going to kill me and reach out. It's slimy, solid…a thick branch, way too big to break. I pull my body under it, belly now touching the muck where stingrays and eels burrow. The ache of my lungs has become a scream. I wiggle forward. The branch presses down harder.

Go under right where I did.

I did!

I manage to get free, propel myself forward and up. There's another limb angling down. I shove halfway through the thick branches, but now I'm so tightly wedged that it's impossible to work my way back.

If your mind wanders, you get smashed.

Fireworks burst behind my closed eyes—sparklers of bright reds and blues, all flash, no big boom. The pain in my lungs is now excruciating. The urge to open my mouth, suck in oxygen, even though I know it's water, know I'll drown for sure, is overwhelming.

Don't stay up too late, girls.

Now I'll never know why I was named after a breakfast cereal.

He left, Danielle.

But you can cut open Poppy without a problem?

Pigeon drowning.

Something twists around my wrist. I flail with the last shred of my strength. It yanks me forward so hard my shoulder almost rips from its socket. I'm rocketing through the water, then surface, gasping for air. My dad pulls me toward him. I climb him, desperate to be out of the water.

"Easy," he says, untangling himself. "You're okay."

I splutter, half choking. "How did you know I needed help?"

"Jupiter yelled when you went under. I counted to thirty. Figured that was all the breath you had in you. No Danny, so I went looking."

I hug him hard, overflowing with happiness, gratitude, after my near-death experience. "Thank you for saving me."

Cougar pulls free, grins. "Can you imagine the negative PR if I let my own kid die out here?"

Joy flakes away like old paint. "I wouldn't want to be the reason for bad press."

Cougar kisses my cheek. "Kidding, buddy."

Jupiter pops to the surface, his dreads arcing a spray of water. Gus comes next. The swamp's murky light highlighting the worry etched on his angular face.

"Where's Cass?" Cougar asks.

"She went before me," Gus says.

"Cass," Cougar calls.

She doesn't surface.

Jupiter yells, "Cass!"

Cougar hands Jupiter the camera bag, then pulls the machete from his backpack. "I'm going back."

I want to stop him. We can't risk my dad getting hurt, or worse. But Cass is under the water somewhere, panicking, or worse. Cougar disappears. There are a few ripples, then the water stills. We wait, ears straining. It's warm out but shivers rack my spine.

"Come on," Gus mutters. "Find her."

His ponytail sheds droplets on the water's surface. They sound like the patter of Sean's blood. *Please find her.* My dad emerges, breathless. He drags Cass to the surface. She coughs, chokes and vomits. I don't want to think about how much of the filthy swamp water is now swimming inside her body.

"What happened?" Jupiter asks.

Cass pushes back the hair sticking to her face. "I got lost."

"She was swimming sideways. Underwater." Cougar's face is red, cheeks puffing hard. "Stick together," he barks, then wades on.

"The traffic in LA is a bitch at noon," Cass says, following Cougar.

What? If anyone else registers that Cass is talking nonsense, that she could've easily drowned, they don't say so. *Cass could've drowned!* Sean's eyes, drained of light, flash in my mind, followed by Mack's unseeing ones. Again, the fine line between life and death is a gut punch. *It could've been me. I could've died in the plane crash, gotten badly injured or drowned in this swamp…*

"Danny?" Jupiter asks.

"I'm good." With effort, I follow the others, walking single file through the swamp. When the water reaches my collarbones, I push off the muddy bottom, wishing I were taller, hoping the remaining fruit tied to my back doesn't escape. I don't want to climb any more trees. We pass more caimans swimming lazily off to our right. Their prehistoric pupils track us. If one disappears beneath the surface, I will lose my mind.

Cougar is in front of Cass. I'm behind her. The water is now waist deep. Something wraps around my ankle. I freeze and it slowly releases. Swamp grass. Maybe. I move on. It's about putting one foot in front of the other. To my left a caiman slides by, just its nostrils and bony eyes visible above the water.

Gus splashes forward until he's next to me.

"Danny."

I refuse to look at him.

"Can we talk about it?"

"Just drop it."

Gus wipes the sweat from his forehead, face flushed. "I thought about it all night. If I were you, I'd be pissed, too. I'm sorry. When I agreed to the episode, I had no idea who you were. I'm filming a new movie in Brazil—"

"Seriously?" I hiss. "Like I care?"

"You're right, it doesn't matter. But doing your dad's show wasn't about the stuff with you, it was just a tie-in for some extra publicity."

"I feel so much better."

He sighs. "Flirting with a girl who's younger than me, who they said was sweet, naive… It seemed harmless. I mean, it's not like I was going to have sex with you."

If there is a level of humiliation far beyond mortification, I've reached it. "Unbelievable. Of course not."

"Danny, that's not how I meant it." He shakes his head. "But your theory that this episode is about you being some homely chick who's lucky to have a guy like me pay attention? That wasn't the plan. Seriously, I'm not that big of an asshole and you're not some pathetic loser. We were in a plane crash and you got separated but somehow stayed calm enough, despite Sean's death, to find the group. I'm not sure I could've done that. You tried to help Mack. This situation is messed up but you're doing your best to deal, contributing way more than me."

I snort, try to walk faster but he keeps up. "Don't worry, I won't tell the tabloids what you and Cass did. Your 'good guy' movie star reputation is safe."

Gus pounds at the water. "It's not... I never even wanted to be an actor."

"Wow. I'm so sorry for you. I didn't know someone was forcing you to be famous, star in blockbusters, date beautiful models, get treated like royalty and make tons of money. Boo-hoo."

"So you know everything about me?"

"I know enough. Maybe your dad died when you were a little kid. I doubt even you would make that up. But lots of kids lose their dads." *I lost mine.* "They don't become assholes."

Gus charges ahead. "If you're so smart, use a mirror," he says over his shoulder. "You look like Shailene Woodley. Except with two different colored eyes. They take some getting used to, but they're striking. So quit sandbagging."

I catch up to him, one part furious that he's saying I'm manipulative, another part insulted that's he's calling me a liar, and a tiny piece pleased at the comparison to Shailene, which is a big stretch. "You don't know anything about my life."

"That makes two of us. Just quit pretending you're something you're not for a sympathy vote."

Gus has no idea what he's talking about. "Shut up," I manage. "If I'm going to die in this swamp, I don't want the last thing I hear to be your voice." I wade ahead, knowing that I'm splashing too much, attracting predators.

Jupiter comes closer, asks, "Everything cool?"

"Not really."

"He's right, about Shailene. You do look like her, but your eyes are way cooler. And just so you know, I had no idea about the setup."

I look to see how far ahead my dad and Cass are.

"They didn't hear," Jupiter says. "Situation stinks. I'm sorry. Your dad can be a total ass—"

"He didn't know. It was all Cass."

"Danny, there's nothing that—"

Something splashes hard to our left. My stomach leaps, wedges in my throat. "I didn't see it!"

"It's a turtle. Keep walking, Danny. You're doing great."

He's beyond wrong. Doing great would be sitting at the kitchen table listening to my mom drone on about a case study. Doing great is hanging with Trix and making her laugh, even if I'm the butt of the joke. I just want to go home.

A snake slithers by, its burnt-yellow body making S's in the mud-brown water. When it flicks its tongue at me I freeze. There are triangles above its beady green eyes. Eyelash viper. Its needlelike fangs have enough poison to kill me. I watch it swim away.

Cougar calls back, "How you doing, buddy?"

"She's having a ball," Jupiter says.

I laugh, which is absurd, all things considered. At the same time, I'm not dead yet, so that's something.

"Hey, I have a great idea," Cass says, turning around. "Let's play Marco Polo!"

Jupiter gasps. "Holy hell."

2 3

"What?" Cass asks.

A massive, fist-size leech is attached to Cass's neck, blue pinstripes on a slimy black body bloated with her blood. Revulsion churns my stomach. *If she tears it off there'll be blood in the water. Blood attracts predators.*

Gus yells, "Cougar!"

When Cougar comes back and sees the leech, even he looks disgusted. "Hold still."

Cass's eyes dart to each person's face. "What is it?"

Cougar says, "Just a little leech."

Her mouth peels back, like she's about to scream, but no sound comes out. Cougar uses his palm, tries to roll the thing in circles until it lets go. But it won't. So he grabs one end, rips it off and flings it into the swamp along with a fine spray of blood. He gives Cass a quick hug. "They inject an anticoag-ulant called hirudin so it's going to bleed for a bit. But you're fine." He pulls back, meets her eyes. "Be my propeller?"

Cass wipes her neck, smearing blood onto her chest. She turns, walks on.

That was a leech—a giant leech. There are probably thousands more in here. Right now, under the waterline, they're already attached to my skin, bloated with blood. My blood. I'm horrified but can't make myself reach down, touch my legs. Even if I did find a leech, there'd be another and another...

Be my propeller.

I don't know if I can!

Jupiter asks, "You okay, Danny?"

"Depends on your definition," I reply, my voice shaky. Somehow I take one step, then another. "There's going to be a big river soon. We'll build a raft out of bamboo, like Cougar did in episode seventy-seven with Tawny Raynes."

"I was the sound guy that episode. Tawny was one hot country singer."

"She'd never gone camping and was scared to death of bugs." I avoid a three-inch-long pistachio-green insect with too many legs to count. "By the end of the episode she'd built a tree fort, killed a black widow and eaten a rat."

Jupiter chuckles. "She threw up that rat."

I turn. "They didn't show it."

Jupiter waggles his fingers. "The magic of the editing room. No way her people were going to let the world see the dar-ling of the Grand Ole Opry barf up rodent."

"Did they date, after, I mean?"

"Who knows?" Jupiter says. "I heard rumors, but they

could've been generated by their publicists. In that world it's hard to tell what's real. Sometimes even for them."

Cass slows way down, barely moving through the swamp. Jupiter wraps an arm around her waist and half drags her through patches of long grasses, under lianas and around trees. Lily pads the size of a car tire dot the swamp, vibrant green, sprinkled with delicate purple flowers.

"Does anyone want Thai food?" Cass asks. "I can order. It'll be here in twenty minutes."

Gus murmurs, "What's going on with her?"

I didn't hear his approach, but at least he's on my right side. I snap, "How would I know?"

"It's a concussion, right? But shouldn't she be feeling better by now?"

I quietly say, "If it was just a concussion, yeah. But I think her brain is swelling from the hit she took. There could be bleeding inside her skull. Confusion, loss of balance, migraines, they're all symptoms."

"Can you help her?"

Gus actually thinks I can do something for Cass? "Haven't you been paying attention? I can't climb a tree or walk in a swamp without freaking out."

Gus says, "You did great climbing up."

I actually laugh. "Too bad I had to come down."

"I'm scared, too," he admits, giving a black cricket on steroids with a serrated jaw and red antennae a wide berth. "I'm just better at hiding it."

We watch Jupiter pull Cass over a network of slippery roots. She looks like a rag doll.

Gus asks, "Is there anything we can do?"

I shake my head. "A neurosurgeon would need to place a shunt in her brain to relieve the pressure."

"She's going to die?"

"If the swelling compresses her brain stem, then she might stop breathing. But what do I know? I'm not a nurse."

"Do you want to be one?"

I wave a crimson dragonfly away. "I don't know what I want to be. Understanding all that medical stuff is cool, like following clues, figuring out a mystery. Unlike life, it all makes sense." I pluck a flower from a lily pad and twirl the pink blossom. "What I don't like is feeling pressured by my mom to be like her, not my dad. It's like she's constantly tugging at a rope stretched between us, so I tug back, but I don't even know what I'm fighting for or against anymore."

Gus hisses, "Snake."

A light green snake with a triangular head swims toward us. It's thin and at least two feet long. *Fun fact? Arrow-shaped heads usually mean the snake is poisonous.* Overhead a black-winged hawk swoops through the forest's canopy, hits the water with a thwack, flies up again, grasping the venomous snake in its talons. Life and death happen fast in the Amazon.

"What you said before, about no one forcing me to be an actor?"

I exhale. "It's none of my business."

"After my dad died, a scout saw me in a shopping mall, gave my mom his card, told her I'd be perfect for commercials. I got the first job I auditioned for and kept getting work. It paid really well, so my mom never got a job. I've been acting ever since."

"What you did to me?"

"Sucks. I get it. There's no excuse."

"So why'd you do it? Truth."

Gus meets my gaze. "I'm kind of on autopilot. I take the work my agent tells me will further my career, memorize lines, show up, put the check in our family bank account, then move on to the next job. I'm not saying some of it isn't fun, but I do what's asked and rarely question it. That includes agreeing to flirt with you for the show, even after the crash. It was wrong. I'm sorry, Danny. Truth."

I release the grudge I've been holding tight and it floats away. It's one less thing to carry out here. "Okay. But now that you know, you can't use being on autopilot as an excuse anymore."

Gus crushes a horsefly on his arm, leaving a gooey red-green smear. "Agreed."

He's not off the hook yet. "I know you don't have a father anymore. I'm sorry about that, really. But mine was MIA for a long time. This is my chance to get him back so I need you to stop being the son he always wanted and give Cougar time to see that I'm not so bad."

Gus scoops a handful of water and lets it run down the back of his neck. I try not to notice the way it makes his skin gleam. He says, "I wasn't trying to get between you two. Honest. Your dad, he's this bright light, you know?"

I skirt a neon-yellow water bug with bulging red eyes. "I know. When he shines on you nothing is better."

Gus nods. "Yeah. But I get that Cougar isn't my dad. I'll back off. Promise. Forgive me?"

"Leaning that way. Tell me something embarrassing about you."

"What?"

"Something no one else knows."

Gus's mouth twists sideways, like he's thinking.

"It can't be something lame like the first time screaming girls followed your car or tried to break into your hotel room."

Gus laughs. "I'm not in a boy band. Let me think. Okay. I hear '70s music in my head, usually at pivotal moments. Havana, Jim Taylor, the Hawks, King."

"Seventies?"

"My dad's favorite musical era. He left behind a big collection of vinyl records. I was obsessed with playing them over and over again. Must've driven my mom nuts but she never stopped me."

"What song do you hear right now?"

"King. 'Leave.'"

"Sing a few lines."

Gus shakes his head. "I'm pretty much tone-deaf."

"Even better."

He clears his throat. "'I'm a king without a crown, a man without a home, a pilot flying low, an archer with no bow…'"

It's hard not to smile because his singing is truly horrible. "You *are* tone-deaf. Good. Apology accepted."

Gus lifts the container he's carrying with the ember. Water pours out of the holes poked in the bottom of the bamboo. "Sorry about this, too."

I laugh. "You get a pass for that one."

We move through a section of swamp with a hole in the canopy above. It allows a narrow beam of sunlight to stream in. It makes the water around us appear emerald colored. In the golden light, pink blooms growing along vines wrapped around tree branches come so alive they glow. We stop, tip our faces and soak the magic in. *If we stayed right here, would a search plane see us?* But we can't stay. It's getting late in the day—the crepuscular hours. That's when predators feed. Another fun fact I learned from watching countless *COUGAR* episodes.

The swamp water slowly recedes. It's replaced by deep mud. This isn't good. We're supposed to find a big river, a tributary of the Amazon. None of us comment. We slog through the mud, our legs coated with the rank-smelling stuff, sweat creating gritty brown runnels in the sludge painting our skin. Jupiter stops to peel a leech off his calf. I shudder and scan my skin, beyond relieved to find no leeches. Gus has one on his shin. He grimaces, then rolls it off with his palm, flings it into the bog.

When the ground is firm, the swamp in the distance, Cougar stops us for the night.

Jupiter states the obvious. "There's no river."

Cougar scowls. "Obviously our gamble didn't pay off. We'll find a river tomorrow. Put your layers and bug repellent on. Jupiter and I will build a quick shelter. Gus, scrounge as much dry wood and leaves as you can find. Danny, set out our gear to dry. We'll make a fire, have fruit for dinner and find a river in the morning."

Cass is lying on her back in the dirt, legs coated with dried muck, eyes closed. "What do you want me to do?"

Cougar squats beside her, a hand on her heart. "Rest."

Cass says, "We'll do confessionals tonight." Even injured, her work brain is still churning.

Everybody scatters to respective jobs. I break off some large leaves and cover the ground, then untie each bag and spread out the wet contents. I find a low branch, about six feet long, make sure there're no ants or spiders crawling along it, then use my body weight to break it free. It's perfect for hanging wet socks high above a flame.

"Danny?" Cass says.

"Just a sec."

"No."

I look up. *Shit.* "Don't move."

"I can't… I'm going to…" she hisses.

"Cass. Don't. Freaking. Move." I recognize the snake from watching my dad's show—arrow-shaped head, gray body with a string of black patches in the foreground bordered by gold. Fer-de-lance—an insanely poisonous viper. The snake slithers along Cass's leg, coils by her hip, head up, tongue flicking. *If I yell for my dad, will it bite her?*

Slowly, I back up. This kind of snake can strike a long way.

Cass murmurs, "Don't."

Desperate, I glance over my shoulder, hoping to see my dad, Jupiter or Gus. No one is around.

Cass whispers, "Danny, help me!"

I look at the stick in my hand. *I can't be thinking what I'm thinking.* Tears roll down Cass's cheeks. "Oh, please, please, please, don't move," I whisper.

"I have to."

If the fer-de-lance bites her, she's dead. A little voice in my head says she's probably already dead from her brain injury, says that if I do what I'm doing and screw it up, I'll be toast, too. *I can't help her!* I watch Cass's fingers burrow into the dirt, preparing to push off. The snake is fixated, slightly swaying.

I CANNOT BE THINKING WHAT I'M THINKING.

I lunge forward.

24

I scream.

Cass screams.

The monkeys in the forest canopy add their cries until the air bleeds. The snake thrashes, its tail lashing through the air. I don't know how long the stick will pin its head. If it gets free, it's going to twist around and bite me.

A machete slices through the air. The snake's head is decapitated but its body continues to writhe. I stare at the dead snake, at Cass, rocking, arms wrapped around her knees, at Jupiter's open mouth, Gus's white face. Then I turn away, vomit. There's nothing much in my stomach but bile burns my throat. A hand rests on my back.

Jupiter says, "You're okay."

He's right. I'm okay.

"What the hell were you thinking?" Cougar shouts.

I wait to hear what Cass is going to say but she's silent. When I turn, my dad isn't looking at her. He's staring at me.

"Me? I… It… Cass… She wouldn't… She was going to move!"

"Lay off," Jupiter says.

Cougar glowers at him. "Shut the hell up."

Gus takes a step forward. "Seriously. She saved Cass's life!"

My dad reaches me in two strides. His hands come up fast. *He's going to hit me.* He presses palms against the sides of my head, hard enough to make me wince. "She's the walking dead," he hisses. "You know that as well as I do." When he pulls me into a hug, I can feel the pounding of his heart. "Don't do anything like that again! Do you hear me?"

Behind him Cass scrambles in the dirt for the camera, pulls it from the bag. "Filming," she says, her voice totally calm. It's like she's a robot. Nothing stops her from doing her job.

Cougar returns to the dead snake, its body still wriggling on the ground, and stabs the head with the tip of the machete. Holding it in front of the camera so the snake's gleaming fangs are visible, he says, "A fer-de-lance can still bite, even after it's been decapitated. A typical bite releases 105 milligrams of venom. Fifty is fatal for humans." He flicks the head into the forest, then loops the machete under the still-wriggling snake's body. "We're having fer-de-lance for dinner. Gus, you want to learn how to skin a snake?"

"I'll give Danny the honors."

Once a hasty shelter is built and the fire started with leaves, twigs, Mack's resin and pages from Jupiter's dwindling book, Cass films while Cougar shows me how to cut the fer-de-lance from the anal opening to the neck. It's hard to make myself touch the snake at first, but its skin is dry, not slimy, and I hold it while Cougar cuts away the snake's connective tissue to separate the skin from the muscle so it can be easily peeled away. Once the snake is skinned, I'm more fascinated than repulsed.

"With only one eye, how'd you pin this snake?" Cougar asks. "I mean, the depth perception thing?"

"It took a few years, but my brain adjusts most of the time."

Cougar glowers. "*Most of the time* is an unacceptable risk." He shakes his head like he still can't believe what happened. "You want to take out its guts?"

My dad cuts along the snake's stomach and I remove the tube that holds its innards, careful not to puncture it to avoid getting snake bile on the meat. In an episode with the ballet dancer Julius Khali, he made the mistake of tearing a rattlesnake's gut open. The excretions ruined the meat.

"Good job," Cougar says.

"Thanks. Julius Khali. Nevada."

He gives me a strange look, then nods before looking up at the camera. "Like father, like daughter."

I'm made of helium. I get why my dad was so furious. I risked getting bitten, too. *But what would he have done if he'd been in my position?*

It starts to rain. Everyone washes off the mud caked on our skin, then we huddle beneath our small shelter and wait for the snake to cook. It's hard to believe, but the smell makes me salivate. I get the first piece. People always joke that snake tastes like chicken. It does.

"Time for confessionals," Cass says, her voice slurring a bit. "You're first, Jupiter. What's your biggest fear?"

Jupiter shakes his head. "I'm too tired to play."

Cass snorts. "Baby. You're up, Gus."

Gus licks his fingers. "Before tonight, I'd say eating a snake."

"Bullshit," Cass says. "We're lost in the fucking Amazon. What's your biggest fear? Hit me with it, actor boy."

She sounds drunk. "Dad, I think—"

Cougar holds up one hand. His eyes spark in the firelight. "This is what my show is about, Danny, digging deep, facing your fears, coming out of every situation victorious in body and spirit. Right, Gus?"

Gus hesitates. "I guess... I guess that I'm afraid of not being there for my brothers. My mom, she tries, but she's just not... She can't carry the emotional or financial responsibility of three sons."

Cougar says, "She has *four* sons." He grips Gus's shoulder. "She's damn lucky to have you."

Gus shifts so Cougar's hand falls away. Jupiter takes the camera, turns it on Cass. "Biggest fear?"

Cass pinches her cheeks like she's trying to get some color in them. "Hmm, biggest fear. When I was a kid, it was not getting invited to prom."

Cougar chuckles. "I doubt that ever happened."

"I wasn't exactly popular. My brother took me every year."

"That's embarrassing as hell, but not exactly a fear. C'mon, Cass," he pushes. "Let's show 'em how it's done."

She looks down, plays with the edge of a leaf. "That I'm unlovable." She holds up her left hand. "That no one will ever put a ring on it. That I'll be cursed because of the abortion I had at twenty-three, and never be able to have a baby.

That in the City of Dreams, mine won't come true. I'll end up in a ground-floor apartment with nine cats. I hate cats—"

"Whoa," Cougar says, grabbing her hand, kissing the palm. "You're going off the rails. Come back, babe. You're a beauty. Your personal tagline is: Strong. Smart. Independent."

Cass blinks back tears. "Give me my damn camera," she says to Jupiter. "It's Danny's turn." She looks up from the lens. "Don't you dare say snakes. You're full of shit, acting all shy and scared when you're a one-eyed warrior. So what really scares Danger Danielle Warren?"

A memory rises to the surface. Music pounds so loud the floor vibrates. My cheeks hurt from grinning at Trix as we dance with abandon beneath the flickering of strobe lights. My classmates circle us. We're that good. Then I see they're flapping their arms like wings, pecking their heads side to side, shouting "Pigeon." I run out of the gym, hide in a classroom. If Cougar had seen those kids, watched me run away? My heart wrenches.

"Danny?" Cass prods.

"I don't know."

Cougar says, "Come on, buddy. I'd like to know, what scares my daughter?"

"Disappointing you." *Holy shit.* The truth just slipped out. Now those two words hang in the air. My dad doesn't move. He doesn't say anything.

"You killed a freaking fer-de-lance today, saved Cass's life," Jupiter says. "That's pretty far from disappointing."

"Sure," Cougar says. "Well, technically, I killed it. Not sure what Danny would've done if I hadn't come along. Eventually that viper, mad as hell, would've wriggled free, probably bitten them both. The venom would've stopped their blood from clotting, led to infection, gangrene, amputation at best, an excruciating death at worst."

It's like scoring a goal, then realizing it's against your own team. I stare at the dirt so no one can see the tears pooling and wish that just one freaking time Cougar could give me credit. He reaches for my hand, tugs until I meet his gaze.

"You're learning," he says. "And it's hard not to be proud of a kid whose instinct is to help."

The moment is confusing, like getting kissed on one cheek and slapped on the other. "Um. Thanks."

"Okay, Cougar, bigesh fear?" Cass asks, her slurring worse.

Cougar says, "It's not snakes. Or bears, though that grizzly in Canada definitely got my attention—nine feet tall standing on his back legs. Let me think. Okay. When Danny was eight or so, my biggest fear was that she was going to be a sociopath."

I laugh. "Excuse me?"

"Whenever I visited and Commander Sam allowed me to take you on a tame adventure, I noticed you had a bizarre habit. Each time you found a dead animal, you'd creep up to it, hang your head over the carcass and take a deep breath, holding it until your face turned red. It didn't seem to matter if it was a butterfly, squirrel, bird or even a fish!"

My entire body blazes like I'm being roasted over a fire.

"I thought my kid might start torturing animals," Cougar says, chuckling. "Thankfully, she's terrified of them. Scared of a lot of things—the ocean, harmless bugs, sharks, riding a bike, even the dark. Hell, I've seen her jump at her own shadow. Hard to believe she's my kid sometimes."

Cougar kisses me on the forehead. I can't feel it.

"Danielle, I wouldn't want it any other way," he says. "Your heart is in the right place. That's all that matters."

Danielle.

"You're such a prick," Jupiter says.

Cougar's eyes widen, like he's shocked. "What?"

"You heard me. You'd tear the wings off an angel if it meant you could fly." Jupiter moves away from the fire, lying down with his back to the group.

"Good idea," Cougar says. "We're all tired. Tomorrow will be a better day. Promise, buddy."

I can't peel my eyes off the ground. "I'm going to build up this fire first."

"That's my girl." Cougar lies down beside Cass. "Wake me up if there are any venomous critters to kill."

He's snoring within ten minutes. Cass falls asleep next, then Jupiter. Gus is still awake. He gets up and sits down beside me.

"You all right?"

"Why wouldn't I be?" I push a stray branch into the fire.

"That sociopath thing?"

"He was just kidding around."

"It wasn't funny."

No. It wasn't. "He doesn't understand."

Gus puts a stick on the fire. "Want to explain?"

I hesitate but there's nothing much to lose. I've already been labeled. "When I was a little kid, Cougar told me that everything has a life force, the land, trees, animals."

"My dad said something similar. It was the reason he didn't hunt, rarely ate meat."

I glance sideways. Firelight licks Gus's face. He looks earnest in the orange glow. "After…after I lost my eye, I got this idea that once an animal was dead I could breathe in its essence and maybe, if I did it right, I'd get the eye it wasn't using anymore." I shake my head. "It's so dumb, but I wanted to be whole."

"You are whole."

That's a nice sentiment from a perfect guy. "The *breathing in* thing became a habit, like a tic. I realized I couldn't have my eye back, but maybe, if I breathed in a deer, I could be fast. A cat would make me graceful. A bird might give me the ability to fly. A squirrel would help me climb a tree without a panic attack. Anyway, I grew out of it." I stare into the fire. "At least I thought I did." Gus tips his head, waiting. "Sean. He was a surfer…super coordinated. That's something I could use."

Gus nods. "You weren't lying about turning seventeen?"

"It's not Cougar's fault. My mom made it impossible for him to be around."

"Yeah, but—"

"Don't." *I've heard it all before.*

He puts a few more sticks on the blaze. "Hey, I have a skill that'll surprise you."

"What's that?"

"I know how to braid hair." Gus scoots behind me. "May I?"

I nod. He undoes the elastic holding my hair, combs it through with his fingers, carefully unsnarling the strands. His fingertips massage my scalp, then gently tug. The simple act of kindness brings on tears. He separates my locks, then starts braiding them. When he's done, he wraps his arms around me from behind and I lean back, letting him hold me. Salty rivulets run down my cheeks. I don't bother wiping them away. If Gus notices, he doesn't say anything.

DAY THREE

25

"Are you awake?" Cass whispers. "The fire has gone out." I'm awake, chewing on my twig toothbrush, so I roll over. In the early-morning gloom her face looks haggard. "How are you feeling?"

A tear dribbles across the bridge of her nose. "Worse."

"Your head?"

"That, and everything is fuzzy, like I'm drunk."

My chest squeezes. "You have a concussion."

"I know. It's getting really hard to do my job."

"Don't worry about your job."

"Easy for you to say. If I mess it up, I'll lose everything."

"Does he know you're still in love with him?"

Cass blinks twice. "We both have to think about his image."

"Maybe you should tell him how you really feel."

"How's that going for you?"

"Well, I—" Cass's eyes suddenly roll back until only the whites are visible. Her body stiffens like it's possessed. "Dad!" I slide over and cradle her head in my lap, her body jerking, head thumping against my thighs.

Scrambling to Cass's side, Cougar says, "Get something to put in her mouth so she doesn't swallow her tongue."

"No. She might bite her tongue but she won't swallow it," I say. "Putting something in her mouth could cause asphyxiation if she vomits."

"What's wrong with her?" Jupiter asks, crouching by Cass's feet.

"It's a seizure," I say.

Gus asks, "How do you know?"

"I saw a few when I was a kid hanging in the ER waiting for my mom to finish work."

Gus asks, "Do we hold her down?"

I shake my head. "It should be over soon." The sharp tang of urine fills the air as Cass loses control of her bladder. The spasms slowly ease, then stop. "Cass, can you hear me? Cass?" I rub her sternum like I've seen the doctors do. She doesn't react to the pain.

"What the hell," Jupiter says. "Why'd she have a seizure?"

I ease Cass's head to the ground. "Sometimes they happen after a traumatic brain injury."

"We should've stayed in one place, not pushed her," Jupiter says.

Cougar snaps, "Based on what? A fifteen-year-old kid who's parroting what her mom says? Christ, my ex isn't even a doctor."

Instead of shrinking away, I glare at him for a moment but

bite back the retort that Sam knows more than he does about this and I do, too. *And at least she can keep track of her daughter's birthdays.*

Jupiter throws up his hands. "So what the hell do you suggest we do now?"

Cougar scrubs a hand over his face. "Here are the options. One, we stay where we are, hope that Cass wakes up."

"If we do that, can a rescue team find us?" Gus asks.

"Maybe. But the search area has to be enormous. We're three days into this and haven't even heard a plane. That tells me they're looking in the wrong place. It could be a week before a search team even starts looking in our vicinity."

"Does Cass have that much time?" Gus asks me.

Cougar waves a dismissive hand. "She has no idea. Option two, we leave Cass, mark the trail along the way, find help and bring rescuers back."

"What if we can't find her again?" Jupiter asks Cougar.

Cougar puts a hand on Jupiter's shoulder. "If we stay, she's going to die."

Jupiter steps back. "She won't last a day here alone. There are jaguars, snakes. Hell, even birds will feed on her. And the bugs, they'll eat her alive! Do you even have a freaking heart?"

Cougar kicks a rock, sending it flying into the forest. "It's not about heart. I'm trying to keep us alive."

"By sacrificing Cass?" Jupiter shouts.

"She has a brain injury. Do you see any neurosurgeons around?"

Jupiter shakes his head and says, "That's cold, even for you."

Spots of color explode on Cougar's cheeks. "You think I don't care? I've known Cass for years. She's a damn good assistant and someday she hopes to be a director. She has the intelligence to make that happen. She's sacrificed a lot for this show. We're in talks with several major film studios for a documentary and possibly an action movie. They'll trample each other to sign a deal just to get this footage. It's everything we've worked for. But I've got your life, Gus's and my own daughter's riding on the decisions I make out here. So a little support would be appreciated."

Jupiter shakes his head like he can't believe what he's hearing. We're both probably wondering the same thing. How can Cougar even consider leaving behind a woman he once dated? I ask, "Any other options?"

Cougar glowers. "We set a deadline, a day or two, hope Cass wakes up and is strong enough to continue."

Jupiter says, "We do that."

My dad looks at me. *He wants me to side with him. He expects it.* "We wait," I say. Gus nods.

"Okay then," Cougar says. "I'll go find us some food. Gus, Jupiter, we need firewood."

"What do you want me to do?" I ask.

"Stay with your patient," Cougar snaps.

His words sting but I let them fall away and move closer to Cass, fan her with a leaf to keep away the insects. I think about what Jupiter said about the angel's wings. Cass would've located the angel, torn the wings off, hidden the crime, then filmed Cougar while people cheered his incredible ability to fly. That's how devoted she is to my dad and his show.

There's no room for you. He doesn't even have space in his life for perfect people.

Does that mean Cougar would leave me, too?

I'm not sure.

26

I spend most of the day waiting for Cass to wake while Jupiter and Gus collect armfuls of sticks and add them to the fire that Cougar built despite the rain, a braided palm roof on forked sticks protecting the flame. When the rain goes from a drizzle to a heavy downpour, we all crouch beneath the shelter, cold, disheartened, worried. I've never seen rain come down this hard. It's impossible to see more than a few feet away and the dirt instantly turns to soup, popping as droplets strike like tiny mallets.

Cougar hunts for hours but returns at dusk, soaked through, with only a small black-and-white-striped lizard. He cooks it over the flame, then divides it between us. Two bites of meat aren't nearly enough to quell my hunger. I drink a bottle of water to fill my empty belly. Cass hasn't moved. Jupiter helps me tuck the second poncho around her body. We slide her closer to the fire so she stays warm.

"Confessionals," Cougar says, pulling out Cass's camera.

Jupiter shakes his head. "Not in the mood."

"Come on, what else do you have going on? Think of the kids," Cougar says with a nod at Gus and me. "It'll help pass the time and you can impart some wisdom."

Jupiter grimaces but then nods. Cougar has that effect on people. He's a planet with its own magnetic pull.

"What do you want to know?" Jupiter asks.

Cougar says, "What was the best day of your life?"

"Best day? Lots of 'em." Jupiter weaves his fingers together. "The most recent one was with my mom. She had a double mastectomy. Went through chemo and radiation. Never complained, not even after the surgery or when she was puking her guts out. A month ago, I went with her to a doctor's appointment. We got the news she's cancer-free. Walking out of that building, it was like I was floating a foot off the ground."

"Were you always close?" Gus asks.

"Dad left after I was born. Mom raised me alone. She didn't remarry until I was grown. She was tough as nails, pushed me hard in school, refused to let me be mediocre at anything, insisted on college." He twists a dreadlock between long fingers. "Took me too long to realize her sacrifices, but she waited and I came around. So yeah, we're really close now. Mom and my little sister are probably worried sick."

Cougar turns to Gus. "Best moment? Make sure it's PG. My kid isn't sixteen yet."

Gus looks over, waiting for me to correct Cougar. "Go on," I say. "Best day?"

Gus stares into the fire, his face lit by the dancing flames. "Any night my dad and I took in the stars. He knew every constellation. In the summer, we'd go out to the dock near our house, lie down on the worn wood and he'd tell me stories about Orion, Cassiopeia, the Herdsman and Sagittarius. My favorite was Cygnus, the swan. In mythology he was really the Greek god Zeus. He'd changed himself into a swan to win a beautiful woman's love."

"Sounds like your dad was a cool guy," Jupiter says.

Gus smiles. "Yeah. He was a commercial pilot, but I think he wanted to be an astronaut, see the stars up close."

"Why didn't he go for it?" Cougar asks.

"My guess? He wanted to be a dad more than fly to distant planets."

Cougar nods. "No judgment. It's a tough path—lots of sacrifice. Not everyone is cut out to follow his dreams."

I stare at the dirt. *He doesn't get it.* I blush, but for once it's not for me.

Cougar says, "I thought you were going to say the night you won best actor at the SAG Awards. VeeVee Kellerman was your date, right?"

When I look up, Gus meets my gaze. "Yeah, I guess that was pretty cool."

"Best moment," Cougar asks me.

I hesitate. Not because I don't have one. I do. It's just that I'm not sure how my dad will react.

"Come on, buddy. I really want to know."

I take the leap. "Every day that I'm here. I know that sounds crazy, but it's a chance to get to know you better."

"If a plane crash and getting lost in the rain forest tops your list, your mom needs to up her game," Cougar says.

No one laughs. A trickle of sweat runs down my back. My plan was to have this conversation in private, definitely not on film, but there hasn't been a chance. I'm not sure what's going to happen, when we'll be rescued, if I'll even make it. I need to do this now and hope Cougar will edit it out. No matter what my mom did to me, to us, I don't want to publicly shame her. "You probably think I didn't want you around, or that maybe I blamed you? For what happened?"

"You should've stayed at camp," Cougar says.

I was seven. "I know. And after that, things got really messed up." I swallow, my throat so dry it clicks. "What I'm trying to say is that I *did* want you around. I wrote you letters."

"Never got them," he says, still filming.

This is the moment where everything between us changes forever. "Mom didn't send them." I wait for his reaction.

"What'd they say, the letters?"

"That I missed you, that I wanted you to come back and make me brave again, that I never blamed you for what happened. They were also about the book you sent—*The Phantom Tollbooth.* I thought we could meet in the Lands Beyond. Have adventures, like before—"

Cougar grimaces. "I never realized just how much your mom hated me."

"Um. I don't think Mom meant—"

Cougar snaps, "Don't defend her."

"I'm not! Mom resented you, yes, but she also read me the book you sent every night, for months and months."

"Enough with the book. I never sent a fucking book."

The earth has tilted and I can't find my balance. My mind slows…sticks…repeats. *I never sent a fucking book—I never sent a fucking book—I never sent a fucking book.* "But it was wrapped. There was a card from you. Mom said it was your favorite book as a kid."

"I think we've established that your mother is a liar."

Do you know the definition of a narcissist?

I wait for my dad to say he understands that he didn't just lose those letters; he lost me. I lost him, too. Now we both know. Now we move on, together. But he doesn't say a word. *I never sent a fucking book.* I'm an asteroid hurtling toward earth. Nothing can stop impact.

"After what happened, you moved out."

Cougar snorts. "Samantha made it clear she didn't want me around."

"What about me?" I ask. "After it… After, I was terrified of what was happening to me. By the time my brain had adjusted, I'd changed and you were gone."

"Your mom was better suited to handle things. And we were fighting. That kind of energy wasn't good for you."

I leave my body, float above the fire, watch this conversation between father and daughter from a safe distance. "I thought you stopped visiting because you didn't love me anymore, because I was scared of everything, defective, inferior, an embarrassment. Before, I'd been a tomboy, your buddy."

Cougar lowers the camera. "Danny, things change. Let's leave it at that."

He brushes a red-and-black segmented insect off his leg. It lands on my knee, long antennae twitching. I flinch, then force myself to flick it away. The connection that has been obvious all along happens in a single breath. *You still terrified of bugs?*

That's what my dad asked when he called to invite me on the trip. If my heart is a house, every door slams. The windows shatter. But even though the damage is done, I still need to hear the words. "Did you know?"

"Know what?"

"Cass's plan. To make me the joke of your episode."

"You're upset about that?" Cougar snorts. "Danielle, it wasn't about you being a joke. I'd never let my own kid be a laughingstock. It was meant to be sweet, fun, no harm, no foul. You got the chance to be on my show, spend time with Gus, and we got a little levity and a great hook for the episode. It was win-win."

I recall what Cougar said to Gus, right after the plane crash. People were dead. Others were gravely injured. My dad squeezed Gus's shoulder and said, *We're still going to film this episode as planned.*

Of course Cougar knew. It was his idea. *Truth.*

27

"Get some sleep," Cougar says. "Hopefully Cass will be capable of moving on in the morning."

Even in the orange glow of the fire Cass's skin looks wan, paper dry. Her breathing is shallow like her heart isn't pumping hard enough or her lungs are giving up. I lie down between Jupiter and Gus. The rain continues to incessantly pound the earth. My raw nerves hum.

Too much rain and the rivers will flood, making travel by water impossible.

What does that mean for Cass?

The drone of insects soon mingles with the sounds of sleep. But I can't even close my eyes. My dad's words are a closed fist hitting again and again. But it's not just what he said that's keeping me awake.

If you want to have any type of relationship with me after I turn eighteen, you won't try to stop me.

That was my threat when my mom stood between Cougar and me. I couldn't imagine forgiving her lies. But I've never worried that if I'm less than perfect, my mom will stop loving me. Commander Samantha is a survivor—tough as nails, blunt, caustic at times. But she stayed. Cougar is a different animal.

"Are you up?" Gus whispers.

"I don't want to talk about it." He rolls onto his side, our faces inches apart.

"His loss."

Mine, too.

"You know that movie *American Gigolo*?"

I nod, not trusting my voice.

"I didn't want to do the remake. It was total trash—a way to make money off me being naked. My mom insisted. Told me I was being disloyal if I didn't take the job. It was my biggest payday, raised my rate. She bought a Tesla SUV to drive my brothers around in and a condo on the beach in Mexico."

"Do you hate your mom?"

"Sometimes. Do you hate Cougar?"

I chew on my lower lip, sifting through thoughts. "I don't know. That's the first time I've actually seen who he really is, deep down, you know? To me Cougar was always larger-than-life. But he was willing to embarrass me for great ratings. That's so...small."

My heart droops like a flower without water. I recall the photo I found in the attic of our apartment—the one in the hospital, after I was born. My mom looked like there'd been a huge mistake and she was waiting for someone to correct it. Cougar stared out the window like he wanted to be any-where but there. I say what I've always known, deep down. "Cougar never wanted a child. And if he had to have a kid, he wanted one that was a reflection of him."

"You can't be sure of that."

I meet Gus's gaze. "He named me Danger." A wave of in-adequacy washes over me followed by the realization that I no longer want to be like my dad. It's an enormous loss and my body throbs like a part has been torn away.

"What was it like? After you lost your eye?"

Instantly my mouth goes dry. "It…it wasn't just the pain. Shadows scared me. I thought they hid monsters. Before? Monsters didn't exist. I tripped over curbs, down stairs. For a while, I couldn't figure out exactly where they were. Mir-rors seemed like extensions into other rooms until I bashed into them. I burned my fingers on the stove because the flame was closer than it seemed. Anything athletic was mortifying. Every accident, nightmare, failure led to more fear."

A tear escapes, dribbles down my cheek. "Will I ever be more than I am right now?"

Gus tucks a strand of hair behind my ear. His fingers lin-ger. "You already are."

"What song do you hear?"

"Havana. 'Sanctuary.' 'Find sanctuary in this house,'" he whispers, "'when cold seeps into bone. All doors open to her touch. There is no love when you're alone.'"

Gus leans in, kisses me. No one is recording the moment for millions of viewers. The kiss feels…authentic. He kisses me again and I kiss him back. I'm searching for something to hold on to. I'm not sure what Gus needs but when we fi-nally stop kissing, he holds my hand for the rest of the night.

DAY
FOUR

28

Cass dies late in the morning. She slips away quietly, like even in death she's doing her job—smoothing the way, eliminating problems. The absence of another living person, like a stone thrown in still water, ripples through the group. We sit in a circle around her body, diminished, as the rain, unrelenting through the night, turns to drizzle.

Gus finally asks, "Should we each say something? When my dad died we didn't have a funeral. Friends and family came to a park, stood up and told stories about him."

Jupiter runs a hand across tired eyes. "Yeah. Okay. Thing is, I didn't know her well. But it was clear that Cass loved her job. On set she worked harder, longer and later than the rest of the crew. She drove herself and everyone around her to give more."

"I didn't know her well, either," Gus says, "but she was dedicated to making Cougar's show the best."

What Gus doesn't say is that Cass was willing to trample my feelings to do that. I'm very sorry she suffered and that she's gone, but I can't pretend that I really liked Cass. Mostly, I'm sad for the experiences she'll never get to have—love with someone who loves her back unconditionally, marriage and children if she wanted them, or a kick-ass career directing TV shows and films with tons of awards.

"Cass told me she had no real life outside the show," I say. "She didn't have an apartment in LA. She couch-surfed when she wasn't on location." I swallow the lump in my throat. "She said she was putting in the time so one day she could be a director." I get up, pick a handful of pale pink flowers, crouch by Cass's side and place them on her chest. They smell sweet, like honeysuckle. "You were worthy of someone's love," I say. "Sleep with the angels."

Cougar kisses her forehead, blue eyes gleaming, but tears never fall. Jupiter waits for him to say something, but he doesn't. He just covers Cass's face with a T-shirt. It's not much of a funeral and there will be no burial, but it's what we can do. That a life can end so quickly, that a person can be summed up in so few sentences, makes me want to cry. Instead, I organize my few belongings. The rest of the group follows suit.

"Do you remember me saying that?" Cougar asks as he stows the camera. "When I'd tuck you in at night?"

"Yeah." I'm unable to look at him without wondering if the way my blue eye tracks slightly off bothers him. *Do you hate Cougar?* Maybe. But for the moment, disappointment overwhelms every other emotion. I'm not sure I can forgive who he really is, or his choices.

Cougar rubs his left shoulder. "What's wrong?" I ask.

"Still being nice to your old dad even though Jupiter says I'm a prick? Maybe I did a few things right, huh?" He glances at Gus and Jupiter for support but they're silent. "We leave in five. Daylight is burning."

I walk behind a bush, peel off my sweatshirt and swap leggings for shorts. The blister on my heel looks angry but no red lines travel up my leg. Hopefully we'll get rescued before infection sets in. But I'm not sure of anything anymore.

"Everyone have water?" Cougar asks.

We nod. The heavy rains have washed the sweat and grime from our bodies and filled the containers yet again. At least it's good for something. Cougar begins to clear our path with the machete. I hesitate. Look back. Cass's body is so small and horribly vulnerable under the little shelter.

Conjure the life you dream of leading. That's the first step to making it happen, Cass whispers.

A life where I could've helped you would be a good start, I silently tell her.

Gus asks, "You okay?"

My sigh is ragged. "No. Three people have died for a TV show." Gus's eyes meet mine. Being looked at, really looked at, by a guy who I can't help but like, is new for me. For the first time, I want to be seen by someone even if I'm not perfect. Maybe it's because I might die out here, too.

We follow Cougar through the rain forest, careful of every step, boots slipping on earth made slick by the rain. When we come upon a small stream, my dad goes to fist-bump Gus, but Gus just nods. It should make me feel good. Gus has my back. Instead I feel kind of sorry for my dad. He's paler than yesterday, and he's taking more breaks. The pressure of leading is taking its toll.

Cougar says, "I keep my promises. It won't be long now." Turning to clear the lianas blocking our way, he suddenly stops, machete midswing. There's a giant wasps' nest, at least a foot wide by two feet long, hanging from the limb of a tree inches from his blade. "Back up. Slowly."

Jupiter asks, "Why can't we go around it?"

"That'd take whacking through trees and vines, making vibrations. It'd alert the wasps that there's a threat." When we're a good distance from the nest, Cougar says, "Ask a local guide in the Amazon what he's most afraid of and he'll say those wasps."

Jupiter shakes his head. "There're worse things in here."

"If you piss off a single Amazonian wasp near its nest, it will call out the entire hive for an attack. Thousands will instantly mobilize. They'll swarm your body, stinging again and again. Get enough stings and their toxin will kill you, or you can have a systemic reaction called anaphylaxis. Either way, you can die. Got it?" he asks, looking at each of us.

"Got it," Gus says. "But we need to stay with the stream, right?"

"We'll run parallel to it," Cougar replies.

But, of course, we lose the stream. It's the hottest day yet. Sauna hot despite intermittent rain showers. I'm slick with sweat and twist my hair into a tight bun to get it off my neck.

Cougar stops us by a low shrub with thick branches and

serrated, hairy leaves. Hanging from the branches are what look like yellow peppers.

"*Solanum sessiliflorum*. Cocona fruit. They come in red and orange, too." Cougar holds up the fruit. "Remember the shape."

He splits one open and hands out slices. It looks halfway between an apple and a tomato and tastes sour. We eat a few each, fill our packs and move on.

A few hours later, my dad starts vomiting. The acrid stench threatens to make me barf, too.

"Ate too much cocona," Cougar says.

No one else is sick.

Cougar wipes his mouth. "Let's go."

Jupiter asks, "How about if I lead for a little while?"

I'm surprised when my dad hands him the machete. He waves Gus and me by, then pulls out the camera, holding it at his shoulder to document our progress.

"Your mom ever tell you about our first date?"

A few days ago I would've hung on to my dad's every word. Been grateful. Now? It's like being thirsty but knowing if you drink, the water is probably poisoned. "Rock climbing."

"Yosemite. I was teaching a beginner class, she was my student. It was six guys and Samantha. She'd never climbed before but she was better than all of them from the start. Truth is, she was as good as me two months into our relationship. Watching Sam climb was a thing of beauty. She was graceful, but it was more than that. She was so smart, thought out each move, real economy of motion."

I've never seen my mom rock climb. It was another thing Samantha had to give up.

"I was a summer fling for her. I remember worrying that she was going to move on. She was premed at Berkeley. Never met someone so driven. Commander Sam. Nothing stood in her way. Me? I'd never gone to college. I had no plan besides a beautiful girlfriend, gas in my van and climbing big walls. No way me and your mom were going to last."

"Then she got pregnant," I say without looking back at him.

"Yeah. She was stuck with me. Sam is the reason I even came up with COUGAR. I needed to show her I could be more than a beautiful loser living in his truck."

"She became a nurse to support us."

Cougar says, "Yeah. But as soon as I had some cash reserves, I offered to pay for Sam's medical school. She refused—couldn't get off her high horse, had too much pride."

I didn't know this and let the information settle. It's possible that it was easier for my mom to blame Cougar than to pursue her goals. Maybe she was afraid she didn't have what it took to be a doctor, or her dreams changed. "Mom was young when she lost her parents, only a few years older than I am now. She might've realized nothing in life is guaranteed and wanted to be around for my childhood."

"She was a kid having a kid."

The implication is clear. Samantha didn't want me. Cougar's words are meant to turn me against her. That might've worked a few days ago, but not anymore. "That doesn't mean she didn't grow to love me."

Cougar demands, "If Saint Samantha loved you so much, why didn't she take the child support I offered? Make your life easier?"

I put together what I've already grasped with the new information. "Here's what I know, Dad. Right or wrong, Sam thought you were reckless, and if she said no to the money, she could say no to you wanting to see me. Turns out she didn't need to do that, though, did she? You weren't interested in spending much time with your kid. And you know what? She probably had some pride, too, something you should understand. She needed to prove we were okay without your help. Yeah, sometimes she probably used me to punish you. But she gave up becoming a doctor, and I don't know if you were a convenient excuse or not, but it made her bitter."

"Sam sure didn't make a relationship with you easy."

I whirl and we lock eyes. "Maybe not. But you should've been there anyway."

The memory of my fight with Sam after I discovered the unsent letters floods back...

I was there before, during and after the surgery. I'm the one who got up every night you screamed in your sleep—the parent who held you, read to you, taught you how to adapt to a new normal and get over panic attacks. Cougar didn't deserve those letters!

The last piece of the puzzle slides into place. For a second I consider keeping it to myself. But neither of my parents ever tells the whole truth and I don't want to be like them. "I'm not saying what Sam did was right. But beneath the pride and anger, I think she wanted me to see *her* as the hero. Not the guy scaling waterfalls and climbing mountains, the TV star rubbing shoulders with celebrities, but the woman who stayed behind and did the really hard day-to-day stuff for her daughter."

"And you forgive her for all of that?" Cougar demands.

"I don't know." My eyes burn. Whether or not I forgive my mom, I've never fully appreciated her. "What you said in LA about wanting to get to know me? Was it a lie?"

Cougar says, "I gotta take a leak." He diverts into the brush.

Clearly, this is too much honesty for my dad. *Of course it was a lie.* I walk away.

Before I see it, I hear it: leaves rustling, a branch snapping. My skin instantly tightens. The hairs on my neck rise. A red-and-black-striped snake slithers out from the deadfall. Its body glides under my right foot, raised, midstep. *Coral snake. Deadly.* "Shit."

Gus turns around, gaze moving from my face to the snake. "Danny. Don't move."

Jupiter asks, "Where are you guys?" He tromps back to see. "Holy hell." He raises the machete, hand shaking hard, and slowly advances. A twig breaks beneath his right foot. Grimacing, he keeps coming. The snake, sensing movement, turns to face him.

"Stop," I whisper. "Coral snake."

Through clenched teeth Jupiter says, "I've got this."

He's not quicker than a striking snake. He takes another step. Gus does, too. Cougar rustles along the path behind me. He's whistling. Instantly, I can see how this is going to end. I stomp my foot down on the snake's head. Fangs puncture just above the top of my hiking boot.

I'm dead.

29

Cougar darts forward, plunges his hand into a bush, extracting the snake by its tail. He whips it against a tree, then lunges, pinching the hissing reptile behind its neck. "Machete," he says. Jupiter hands it to him. Cougar lops off the snake's head.

All I can think, sprawled on the dirt, pain shooting up my leg, is that my dad wanted to kill the snake that killed me. It's not the declaration I'd hoped for, but it's something. Gus drags me onto his lap, arms wrapped around my body. It's an ending fit for a movie. I wait for the poison to hit. I hope it's not too horrible a death. Jupiter grips my hand like if he holds it tight enough he can stop the venom from invading my body. My dad crouches in front of me, the still-wriggling snake's body in one fist.

Glaring, Cougar says, "I should let you suffer."

"Stop riding her for one freaking second," Gus shouts.

"She did it on purpose, so you and Jupiter wouldn't get bitten," Cougar says, shaking his head. "Dumbest fucking thing I've ever seen, bar none. But it's not a coral snake. Those have a thin yellow stripe between the red and black. Remember this rhyme: red and yellow, evil fellow, but if red touches black, you're all right, Jack. Got it?"

My dad rolls down my sock, revealing two deep punctures oozing blood and ringed a blue black. Seeing them ratchets up the pain.

"Hurts like a motherf-er, huh?"

"Yes."

"Good." Cougar pulls a T-shirt from his backpack and rips a thick strip of material free. He ties it around the punctures, then uses duct tape to make it snug. "Snakes have an anticoagulant in their saliva so the wound keeps bleeding unless you apply pressure." He clears his throat, spits. "I've seen some stupid shit but congratulations, this takes first prize."

I notice that the stubble on my dad's chin is gray. He looks his age, strangely vulnerable. "You didn't answer the question I asked. Was it a lie, what you said in LA?"

Cougar clears his throat, spits, then says, "Growing up means understanding that you can want something, really want it, but be incapable of getting it."

Is he talking about himself or me? Gus and Jupiter help me stand. The bite is a deep throb. *I'll live.* I grab my dad's arm. "I turn seventeen tomorrow."

Cougar runs a hand over his face. "Cass told me before the trip. Sweet sixteen just played better and you didn't seem to mind." He moves to the front of our group and starts clearing our way.

Gus is glowering at me. "What?"

"Don't ever do something like that again."

"I didn't—"

"Zip it," Jupiter says. "I agree with Gus. Uncool."

My cheeks get hot. "I'm sorry."

Jupiter shakes his head, follows Cougar. "Completely insane," he says over his shoulder. "Like father, like daughter."

Gus asks, "Can you walk?"

Tentatively, I weight my leg. It hurts. "Yeah."

"Good. I'm too pissed off to carry you."

"I was trying to make sure you didn't get bitten, too."

Gus closes the distance. "Who does that?" he demands.

"What do you see?" I ask, standing my ground.

Gus searches my face. "I see Danger Danielle Warren. And I've never met anyone like you."

He leans in, like he's going to kiss me, then spins me toward the trail, gives me a push. I actually smile. Me, the girl who's afraid of her own shadow, was in a plane crash, is now lost in the Amazon rain forest and risked a snakebite to save her friends' lives. My mom would be beyond furious. *Who does that?* I guess that I do.

When we stop to rest it's beside a leafy green tree with yellow fruits that are a bit rounder than lemons.

"Passion fruit," Cougar says, pulling one free. He tosses the camera to Jupiter, who starts filming. "You can only eat them when they're ripe and wrinkled, like this one."

"What if you eat them before they're ripe?" Gus asks.

"They're cyanogenic. That means they produce cyanide

compounds. Basically they'll make you really sick. Understood?"

Cougar waits until we all nod before he splits one open, handing half to me, half to Gus. Inside are seeds that look like they're wrapped in clear goo. I touch my tongue to one. It's sweet. Gus squeezes the fruit and fills his mouth. Juice drips down his chin. I have the urge to lick it off. *Who am I?* I try the fruit a bit at a time. It's delicious. We pick the four remaining ripe ones and Jupiter and Cougar split one of them. My empty stomach cramps, demanding more plus the unripe ones. We're burning way more calories than we're consuming. Hunger is now a constant, pissed-off companion.

Cougar says, "Let's go. I'm ready to get out of this place."

He's moving slowly. *This is taking it out of all of us.* We follow a narrow stream for several hours before it slowly disappears below ground. When I looked at pictures of the Peruvian rain forest, it seemed like there were rivers everywhere. I didn't think about the scale of the forest between them, or how slow it would be to travel on foot.

"We'll make camp early," Cougar says.

We work as a group to make the shelter, Jupiter and Cougar cutting the bamboo and tying a quick frame together with vines while Gus and I pile palm fronds on top of it.

"Not mad anymore?" I ask.

"Still mad. I'll let you know what you can do to help me get over it."

I think about doing more than just kissing Gus and my insides twist.

Cougar asks, "What're you two whispering about?"

"Dinner," Gus says.

"Come skin your nonpoisonous snake," Cougar says, holding it up.

"You want to learn how?" I ask Gus. He nods. This time, I'm not queasy about touching the snake. It's about three feet long but really skinny, not a lot of meat. Still, it's protein. Before I slit the skin I close my eyes, breathe in its abilities. If Gus notices, he doesn't say anything. I show him how to peel the snake, cut open its belly. "Careful," I say as he pulls out the guts.

Gus makes a face. "This is truly disgusting."

The snake's heart rests in my palm. "But also kind of amazing, right? The sac around it is called the pericardium. And I'm pretty sure snakes' hearts can move around their bodies because they don't have a diaphragm." Gus gives me a weird look. "What?"

"Nothing. It's just, you're kind of unbelievable."

The compliment is glitter on my skin. Rain begins to fall. By the time the snake is ready, there's another downpour. We huddle together in the mostly dry shelter and eat our meager dinner.

When we're done, Cougar replaces the camera's battery, pushes Record, then says, "Question of the night."

Jupiter, using a leaf to fan away the gnats, states, "I'm out."

Cougar shakes his head. "You're on the clock."

"Better get double time, then." Jupiter rests his chin on his knees. "Hit me with it."

"Worst moment of your childhood," Cougar says.

"I'd rather tell you my favorite flavor of ice cream," Jupiter jokes. "Mint chocolate chip. Next?"

Cougar says, "You of all people know how this works."

"Fine," Jupiter says. "Probably third grade. I wanted to join the Cub Scouts and the guy in charge said I couldn't without a dad. So I asked my mom to call my dad and that's when she told me that even if she had his number, she wouldn't cause he didn't deserve me."

Cougar didn't deserve those letters.

"Didn't she get that it was about you, not him?" I ask.

Jupiter shrugs. "Moms are human. Turns out he lived two towns over. Had another family. Three boys. My mom told me right before I went to college."

"Were you furious?" Gus asks.

"At first. But I never called him, not even when I got his number. What would I ask? What did those kids have that I didn't?"

Gus says, "That'd be a start."

Jupiter shakes his head. "There's no acceptable answer. Instead, I studied hard. Graduated from film school. Became a kick-ass sound guy." He grins. "Made my mom proud." He reaches for the camera, turns it on Cougar. "Your turn."

"Worst day of my childhood?" Cougar scratches his head.

I notice my dad's hair is thinning. What I know about his childhood is the same bio anyone can look up online. His parents died in a house fire when he was eleven. No close relatives so he grew up in foster care. Had a passion for the outdoors. Read voraciously, mostly true adventure stories. Ran away when he was fourteen and lived off the grid all over the United States. Ended up in Washington State, where he somehow snuck across the Canadian border into British Columbia. In Canada he honed his survival skills, hunting, trapping and fishing. Came back to the US and spent a few years as a climbing guide in Yosemite Valley before creating the concept for his show, growing the brand by filming himself in extreme circumstances beating the odds, defying nature with his personal tagline: Wits. Strength. Ingenuity.

"My parents were heroin addicts," Cougar says.

My insides lurch. *He's a complete stranger.* "What? I never knew that."

Cougar shrugs. "That kind of backstory isn't sexy and definitely doesn't attract fans. Anyway, they weren't the totally gnarly kind of addicts who sell themselves for drugs. They had jobs to pay for their addiction. My dad worked at a gas station in The Dalles, Oregon. My mom was the cashier. One of them fell asleep smoking. I was at the neighbors' trailer playing when our mobile home burned down with them in it." Cougar takes a sip of water. "Worst day of my life. They were shitty parents, but they were mine." He looks at me. "It's something your mom and me had in common."

"She's never said her parents were shitty."

"Maybe not. But there wasn't a lot of affection in her house, either. Regardless, I'm talking about losing your parents young. It's probably what attracted Sam and me to each other. But the absence of something isn't enough to make the glue that'll hold you together."

"Mom is beautiful, smart, capable, driven." *Bitter, angry and vindictive.*

Cougar winks. "We had that in common, too. But she's also an army kid who moved every two years to different military bases and schools. Developing long-term relationships wasn't exactly Commander Sam's forte." Cougar shrugs. "Believe it or not, we both tried. But I wasn't sure who I was yet so the things that initially attracted me to your mom, like her confidence and smarts, ended up repelling me."

It's hard to imagine my dad as insecure. *But.* It explains why he has to put other people down.

"Anyway, after my parents died, I was moved from foster family to foster family. No one wanted to adopt an older kid." His voice catches. "But hey, I survived. What doesn't kill you makes you stronger, right?"

Not always. Cougar's story has the ring of truth, but sharing it, on camera, seems…manipulative. I think back to all the episodes I've watched. There's almost always a moment with each celebrity where my dad taps into their fears or deepest wounds by sharing bits of his own. Now I understand that every moment was calculated.

Cougar takes the camera from Jupiter. "What about you, Gus? Was the worst day of your childhood the day your dad died, too?"

Gus runs his thumb over the scar on his jaw. "Um."

His discomfort makes my skin feel too tight. "You don't have to tell us."

"True," Cougar agrees. "But I'm sure that if Gus's father had been given the gift of more time, he would've told his son that unloading the bad stuff sets you free."

In the flickering light I see the lost kid Gus was when his dad died. He turns his hands over, spreads his fingers, like he's looking at something.

Cougar prods, "Give it a shot. See if I'm right."

Gus sighs. "Okay… I guess… It was… It was a few weeks after my dad died. My mom couldn't function. I mean, not at all. She'd lost her husband and had four boys, ages six, three, and the twins were one, and no idea how she was going to support us." His chin quivers. "I couldn't understand it at first."

"Leave it, kid," Jupiter says. "This is private stuff."

"She was in the bathtub. The water was so red—" Gus's voice snags. "Danny, I lied to you."

Goose bumps break out on my skin. "About what?"

"My scar. My mom? She'd slit her wrists. Her arm was hanging over the edge of the bathtub. I tried to pull her out but I was too small. I slipped on the blood, hit the edge of the tub. Eleven stitches. My mom got seventy-eight and a stay at a psychiatric hospital before she came home, exhausted and tuned out from the meds."

Gus tries to smile, fails miserably. It's tragic. I hug him and whisper, "I wish it was skateboarding with your dad."

"I wish Cass was here," Cougar says. "She would've been all about this moment."

A flint inside me strikes, sparks. "Did you even realize how much she loved you?" I demand. "Like, she'd do freaking anything to be with you?" The monkeys in the forest's canopy ratchet their chatter, as if they're furious at him, too. The rain comes down harder.

My dad holds up one hand. "Easy. I'm just saying this conversation is raw, real, and Cass loved that. It's the stuff that makes people watch my show. They can't be honest in their own lives, but I tear people down to the basics, force them to face their biggest fears so they can get in touch with who they are, at their cores."

Frustration is a fist crammed down my throat. "You're not a psychiatrist!"

"Agreed. But look at you."

"What about me?" I demand, hands balled into fists.

"The kid I recall after the accident was scared of everything. Probably been about the same the past nine years, right?"

Grudgingly, I nod.

"But out here, you've survived a plane crash, been lost but found your way, climbed trees, dealt with lots of shit that bites or stings, waded through a caiman-infested swamp and gone after two snakes in a misguided attempt to save people you barely know."

"You included." My look dares him to correct me.

"Me included."

The spark ignites. Heat floods my veins. "You know what my worst childhood memory is? It's not losing my eye. It's not the migraines that tore my head open or the unending nausea. It's not learning to live in a world without three dimensions, or being called Pigeon by kids because of the way I moved my head. My worst day was waking up from surgery and being told you weren't there. You disappeared after the accident. I knew you were mad—I'd disobeyed and left the tent. But I was sure that you'd show up for my surgery. Mom told me you might have to work, but I didn't believe her because we were buddies. When I woke, you weren't sitting by my hospital bed. The entire day I waited for you to walk through the door so I could tell you that I was sorry for everything. But you never came. You didn't even call. I'd been bad and now I was broken. My little kid brain made the connection. You didn't want me anymore."

Cougar is still filming. It's more important to record this confession than meet his daughter's working eye. *Truth.*

"You want honesty? The thing I've figured out from spending time in the Amazon with you is that you're an insecure guy who can't let anyone shine brighter, and still that foster kid no one wanted. So you spend every second building your brand, getting more fans, trying to be a movie star, making tons of money, but it'll never be enough. It'll never fill that hole inside you. My mom wasn't enough. I wasn't enough. Cass wasn't, either. Nothing ever will be."

Cougar lowers the camera. *Bull's-eye.* We stare at each other, the silence stretching like skin ready to rip.

"How'd you lose your eye?" Gus finally asks.

I can smell the pines, hear the needles crunch beneath bare feet and feel that crisp night's breeze tangle loose hair. "It's anticlimactic," I say. "Definitely not worthy of one of Cougar's death-defying episodes. I was seven. We were on a camping trip. My mom was mad because Cougar spent all day climbing with a friend. She wanted him to spend time with us. Or maybe she just wanted to take something away from him because she was saddled with me." I can see the angry indents between her eyebrows, the compressed white line of her mouth. "When Cougar got back that night, we had dinner in silence but they were both drinking, simmering. My dad told me to stay in the tent and they went into the woods to have it out. I followed them, hid behind a tree. They called each other names, made accusations. Cougar threw his whiskey bottle against the tree. I stepped out at the wrong time and a shard of glass sliced open my left eye."

Jupiter says, "That's messed up."

Cougar is filming again, hiding behind the camera. I stare through the lens. "I was seven, so leaving the tent, even when you told me to stay put? That's what kids do. It wasn't my fault." I take a breath, see the moment like it wasn't me, like I'm a bystander watching a family detonate, each one irreparably damaged by that whiskey bottle. *He didn't know I was there.* I say, "It wasn't your fault, either."

"Your mother blamed me."

"Did you blame yourself?"

"A little."

"But that's not why you left."

Cougar puts the camera down. "No." He swipes at damp eyes. "Danny, it was never personal. As to that foster kid no one wanted, yeah, I'll always fight to be seen as more. Always."

I let his words settle and finally get it. He needed to be Cougar more than he wanted to be a husband or father.

Truth.

DAY
FIVE

30

Two thoughts float through my brain as I wake in the rain forest: I'm seventeen. It was never about me.

I've based my entire life on the idea that my dad ditched because his daughter was bad and defective. That it was my fault my parents' marriage failed and my mom had to give up her dreams. But everything I've come to understand the past few days coalesces. Leaving the tent wasn't my fault. My dad ditched because he needed to be Cougar. He would've done that with or without me around. Everyone, even Sam, had a choice. *So if I've created myself out of those building blocks, and they're lies, who am I now?*

"Happy birthday," Gus says.

I open my eyes. He's holding out a passion fruit.

"Wrapped it myself."

"Song?"

"Marcus Halliwell. 'Chase.'"

"Sing it?"

"No way."

"It's my birthday wish."

Gus leans in, softly sings, "'Sunshine chase the dark away and warm my lonesome heart. Dreams are made from rays of gold. Your touch is just a start.'"

It's horrible, off-key and perfect. He gives me a quick kiss. I'm lost in the Amazon. Three people are dead. I'm dirty, sweaty, hungry, but in this moment? It's the best birthday I've ever had. I'm not sure what that means about me.

"Happy B-day, Danny," Jupiter calls out while simultaneously taking a leak, his back to us.

My dad is watching me. He looks kind of awful. Scruffy, too thin, pale. He pulls a bouquet of yellow and purple flowers from behind his back. "Happy seventeenth."

It's like I'm outside my body, waiting to see what the girl with two different colored eyes is going to do. She takes the flowers but doesn't smile. "Thanks."

"And I'm watching you," Cougar says to Gus. "That's my daughter."

I imagine Cass filming this. Perhaps she did have a director's eye and her footage would've captured profound moments. Maybe, someday, my dad would've seen her as more, given their relationship a chance. I blink back tears. They're for both of us. Cass will never get to live out her dreams and it could've been me sitting in her seat on the plane. I could still die out here. Never have I felt the fragility of my own life so completely. Never have I wanted to live in each moment more. When Cougar isn't looking, I kiss Gus.

The rain starts all at once. It's like the sky is filled with buckets dumping directly on our heads. Our fire is instantly doused. The roof of the quickly built shelter pours water, then caves in. It's hard to see my hand stretched a few feet in front of me.

Jupiter asks, "Are we going to wait it out?"

"It'll be miserable either way," Cougar says. "Just stay close together. It'd be easy to get separated from the group today."

We gather our stuff and follow my dad. The ground slopes slightly downward. No one talks. My feet squish in my boots. The terrain is slick and it's hard to see the dips and roots. Gus trips, falls to his knees, winces. A black thorn sticks out of his shin. I help him up then pull it out, wishing I had something to clean the puncture. As the wind gains force, despite the heat, we're all shivering.

The hours crawl by. We cross a narrow stream but it just ends in a swampy hollow. It's so frustrating. If we could get above the canopy it'd be so easy to find a large river. But we're operating blind and increasingly exhausted. I roll the top of my shorts. They used to fit, but I've lost at least five pounds, and now, waterlogged, they droop from my hips.

"I need a break," Jupiter calls out.

Cougar stops beneath a kapok tree and we huddle in a concave space formed by its roots.

"This blows." Jupiter kicks at a stick. A five-inch-long scorpion scuttles from beneath it, pincers grasping for the enemy.

"Black scorpion," Cougar says, nudging it with the tip of

his boot. The scorpion's tail, segmented with a stinger at the end, strikes his sole several times.

Gus asks, "Are they poisonous?"

"All scorpions have venom. The sting hurts like hell and can cause a bad fever in humans, but the venom is usually only dangerous to their prey. Ever heard the parable about the scorpion and the frog?" Cougar asks.

"Nope," I say at the same time Gus and Jupiter say, "Yes."

Cougar needs an audience of only one. He says, "A frog and a scorpion are at the edge of the river. The scorpion can't swim so he asks the frog for a ride across. The frog says, 'No way, if I let you on my back, you'll sting me.' The scorpion replies, 'Not gonna happen. If I sting you, you'll die and I'll drown.' Makes sense, so the frog agrees. They get halfway across the river, the scorpion stings the frog, and as they're both slipping under the water, the frog asks, 'Why?' The scorpion replies, 'Couldn't help it, it's my nature.'"

I think this is as close to an explanation or apology as I'll ever get from my father. Gus puts an arm around me. The sheer impossibility of that simple act of compassion hits hard. Someone like him doesn't happen to a girl like me. But if everything I thought about myself is a lie?

What Would Danny Do?

I lean into Gus. The scorpion skitters by my boot. It looks like a cross between a miniature lobster and a spider. A week ago I would've run from it.

Cougar tips his head to the side, listening. "Hear that?"

I strain. All I hear is the pounding rain.

"Come on." He leads us back into the storm.

A few minutes later I hear the sound of water throbbing

like a bass guitar. My dad whacks at a mass of hanging vines. In a single breath, we're standing at the edge of a hill that's so steep it's almost vertical. A few hundred feet below us, a river bashes through the rain forest. Water overflows its banks as it rapidly rises from the downpour. Debris is swept into the torrent, trees and rocks torn free from the slope below by the powerful surge of water.

I've never gone rafting. There was a class trip to the lower White Salmon River last year but my mom decided it was too risky. Trix said there wasn't even any white water. Total yawn. What I'm looking at now would not be a bore—it looks like boiling chocolate milk. If one of us fell into that, we'd either drown after getting pinned beneath a tree, or have our heads cracked open by a rock. My faith that we're going to get out of the Amazon flags. We've finally found a big river and it's not navigable.

"We'll have to go downstream," Cougar says, "follow it until the terrain flattens."

I start to ask if we're ever going to get out of this freaking place, but the soaked earth beneath Jupiter's feet disintegrates. Before he can yell he's tumbling down the hillside. As I watch him cartwheel, my throat clamps shut. Part of me wants to race after him, the other part is desperate to back away. Sharp needles of adrenaline jab into my skin as Jupiter tries to grab for rocks or roots. The slope is so steep that few trees have survived and the ground beneath him is slick mud that speeds his plunge toward the river.

"Step back," Cougar warns.

"We have to—" The wet ground shifts. I topple forward, momentarily airborne, then I'm sliding face-first down the hill, stomach flipping, pulse sprinting. I rocket toward the water, hands clutching for purchase but finding none. Debris tears into my skin. I see Jupiter below me. He grasps a scraggly bush, almost stops, but momentum tears him free. A heartbeat later he plunges into the water. His head surfaces once, then he's gone. I hurtle toward a lone tree, terror coiling around my body like a snake.

"Grab it," Gus shouts.

Somehow I hook the rain-slicked trunk with one arm. My right shoulder feels like it might explode but I don't let go as my legs pendulum beneath me.

"Hang on," Gus yells.

His voice is hard to hear above the torrential storm. My breath comes in tatters and my heart is a balloon about to burst. "I can't! I'm going to fall!"

"Cougar is getting a vine. We'll pull you up."

Ribbons of pain unfurl along the arm holding my body's weight. I try to dig my toes into the mud and find a gnarled root for my right foot to balance on. I could slip off any second. I'm pressed against crumbling earth where poisonous things burrow. I tense for a sting or fangs. Something lands above and a little to the left. I cringe then squint in the pounding rain. It's a thick liana. Cautiously, I lift my free arm. The vine is at least a foot above my head.

"Grab it," Cougar roars.

"I can't reach!"

"It's the longest I could find. You'll have to."

He's crazy. The makeshift rope is slick. My hands are shaking, wet. If I let go of the tree, somehow manage to reach it, I'll instantly slide off, fall the rest of the way to the river. My entire body vibrates with dread, skin tightens, ribs protest under pressure as they cave inward…

"Danger!" Gus shouts above the cacophony of rain and river. "You can do this!"

I tentatively lift my left foot, searching for another root. My toe hits something. It's the point of a small rock. This is insane. I can't put all my weight on it while simultaneously pushing off the tree. *I'm not that coordinated!* My right hand is almost numb because the tree is pressed into the crook of my elbow, my own weight cutting off circulation.

I shout, "Will the vine hold?"

"Seriously?" Cougar roars. "Grab it before that tree goes!"

Gus yells, "Use what you breathed in!"

Deer, bird, rabbit, cat, snake, Sean… I launch and push at the same time, feel the rock give way in the moment my hands close on the vine. Before I can slip, I dig the toes of my hiking boots into the sludge. Cougar and Gus pull. It takes every bit of strength to hang on to the vine, push against anything that gives traction. When my feet slip, leaving me dangling in the air, muscles quivering, I summon the sparrow. When my hands start to lose their strength, I'm a cat with sharp claws. A bright yellow gecko scurries across my thigh. I kick into the mud, keep climbing. I'm a red-and-black snake-lizard-rabbit-eagle-Pigeon…

My torso hits the edge of the hill. Cougar and Gus haul me to safety. We crawl along the mud to more solid ground, lie on our backs, chests heaving. The battering rain cleanses bodies painted brown with mud. *Jupiter was terrified.* "Could he still be alive?"

Cougar shakes his head. "He's gone."

There are purple circles beneath my dad's eyes. His hair is plastered to his skull, skin pale beneath a faded tan. *He looks so run-down.* "Jupiter might've been able to grab a branch, pull himself out of the river?"

Cougar says, "The rocks and trees tore Jupiter apart."

I crawl back toward the edge, stop several feet shy and peer down. The rising water attacks massive trees, slender palms and ground cover. Their shallow roots betray them. The river sweeps even the mightiest away, slamming them against boulders where they split from the force and current. My body hurts like it's been repeatedly kicked. *Jupiter.* Tears mingling with the rain, I return to Gus and my dad.

Gus's face is bone white. "Danny, you almost died, too."

"But I didn't."

My dad hugs me really hard. When I hug him back, there's a monumental shift. I'm the one providing comfort. The idea that Cougar might actually love me in his own way is confusing. His love doesn't meet a standard definition. *Does that make it less real?* I break away, not ready to give him any part of me. "Maybe Jupiter—"

Cougar shakes me hard enough to make my head snap. "No arguments. We are going to follow this flooded river. Wherever it gets calm, we'll cut down bamboo, build a raft, float until we find an indigenous settlement or a plane spots us." He stands, one hand pressed to his left side. "Let's get moving."

I reach to help Gus up, but he gives a little shake of his head. Then I see it—bristled legs creeping onto his neck. The spider's gray-black body is covered with tiny white dots, articulated legs at least six inches long, mouth bloodred. It freezes, like it knows we're watching.

"Dad?"

"Dammit! Enough about Jupiter!"

"It's Gus."

Cougar turns, cocks his head to one side. "Wandering spider."

Gus, his body midcrouch, whispers, "Will it wander away?"

"That'd be nice, but probably not. They're hunters, especially toward dusk. Don't move." Cougar draws back his machete, like a bat, and swings. The blade hooks the spider under its belly, flicks it into the air and over the ravine. There's a dribble of red on Gus's neck where the tip of the machete cut him.

Gus asks, "Was it venomous?"

"The most venomous spider in the world." Cougar shoulders his backpack. "Its bite causes loss of muscle control, shortness of breath, violent headaches and death unless you get antivenom fast. Never seen one in the wild before. Cool."

Cool? When I hug Gus, I can feel his body trembling. "You're okay."

"None of this is okay," Gus says. He shakes his head like he's clearing it. "Screw the Amazon. Let's go find Jupiter."

Cougar throws up his hands. "This is not an adventure flick with a happy ending. It's real life. Real survival. I cared about Jupiter, too. Known him longer than both of you. Hell, I know his mother. But we have to move on. We're alive. Jupiter is dead."

Gus squints in the torrential rain. "I am completely fucking aware that this isn't a movie! But you don't know for sure Jupiter is dead." He grabs the machete, slashes at the tangle of vines and brush. "We're going to find him. Then we're going to build a freaking raft and get out of this place because that water below us is a river, not a channel that's going to dry up. It'll lead to air conditioning, a soft bed and food that won't give me the runs. If I never see another spider again—"

"Or a snake, a grub or monster-size leeches," I add, following Gus. I'm not ready to give up on Jupiter, either. We make our way downhill, climbing over trees, around brush, slip in the mud, duck under fallen trunks, soaking wet, half-blinded by sheets of water. I scan the river whenever I have a clear view. *Where are you, Jupiter?*

Cougar follows. "It'll be dark soon," he says. "Danny. Listen to me. We need to stop, make a hasty shelter, eat what's left of our fruit and get through the night."

"No. Jupiter might still be alive, alone in the forest, hurt, struggling. We search until dark. If you don't want to help, then when Gus gets tired, I'll cut trail."

"Holy shit! I see him," Gus shouts.

We peer down a shallow hillside. A tree is wedged across the river, branches stabbing below the surface. Jupiter is wedged between the trunk and a limb, faceup, arms thrashing as he tries to free himself. Dropping to my butt, I slide down the hill...

31

"You can't go in there," Cougar says.

"We have to." I put one foot in the river. The current instantly sweeps it away. Cougar grabs under my arms, drags me back to land. Jupiter sees us. His face contorts as he screams for help.

Gus says, "I'll go." He finds a vine, pulls it to the edge of the river.

Cougar tears the liana out of Gus's hands. "He's a dead man."

Jupiter gasps for air before a wave crashes into him. He struggles to breathe before another hits. "Dad, we have to help him!"

"It's not gonna happen. If we go in, we'll die, too."

"So we just watch him drown?" I demand.

Cougar's eyes narrow to slits. "Grow up, Danny. One death is better than four."

My father comes into complete focus. "So this is the real you? A coward when the camera is off?" He glares but I don't look away.

Handing Gus his backpack, Cougar ties the vine around his waist. Gus and I hold it as he wades into the water, upriver from Jupiter. Two steps and the bottom drops away. He's swimming as hard as he can but still getting dragged toward the fallen tree. He bashes into Jupiter, then somehow manages to haul himself up, wrapping his legs around the trunk. If the river tears the tree free, they're both dead.

My dad leans forward, suspended above Jupiter's face. I can't hear what they're saying over the rain and booming river. Palms, bushes, rocks hurtle past and get pushed under the tree that's trapping Jupiter, then they pop out on the other side. The river makes a right-hand bend, then hairpins back toward the side where Gus and I stand. The larger pieces of flotsam and jetsam are carried toward the shallows at the edge of a bank about fifteen feet below us. A few get snagged in the mud. I count twenty-five seconds before the trapped debris is torn free and the powerful current sweeps it away.

Cougar looks back at us. He points at a massive tree limb rushing toward Jupiter, then at the bend in the river below us. A tremor passes through me. *We were making the same calculation.* Cougar shouts at us. I can't hear but read his lips: *LET GO.*

"Drop the vine," I say.

"But if—"

I tear the liana from Gus's hands. Cougar unties the vine, drops it, then stands on the slick trunk, somehow keeping his balance as it sways beneath him. He raises his arms, then jumps down on the lower limb that pins Jupiter. It cracks. They both immediately get sucked under the trunk.

Gus and I race downstream. We peer into the muddy water, desperate to see my dad's head, Jupiter's body, any sign that they're not pinned beneath the tree. They could be caught in an underwater whirlpool. They might have been knocked unconscious by a boulder. Probability and common sense say they're drowning, dying or dead right now.

A palm pinwheels by, sucked beneath the water, then popping free. It doesn't get carried to where we stand at the bank of the river, instead disappearing, then reemerging on the other side, sixty feet downriver. There's no guarantee my dad and Jupiter will surface near us. My stomach burns like it's filled with acid. There's no guarantee they'll surface at all.

Cougar did it because I called him a coward. If he—

"There!" Gus shouts.

I catch the flash of bodies wrapped around each other. The two men bob up, get pulled under, then surface again. Gus runs into the shallows, fighting to keep his balance, and grabs Cougar's arm as he spins by. I somehow get the other one. Fireworks explode in my lower back as I use every bit of strength to break the current's hold and help Gus haul Cougar and Jupiter, who is wrapped around my dad like a snake, in.

We don't stop pulling until we're on solid ground, then lie on our backs, gasping, choking as the rain continues to batter down. "Too bad you didn't get that on film," Cougar wheezes. "It's the most kick-ass thing I've ever done." He staggers to his feet. "We need to get to higher ground. The river is still rising."

When I sit up, dizziness rocks me. That was a huge expenditure of energy with too few calories. Taking a deep breath,

I stand. Gus struggles to his feet. Jupiter is still on his back. I ask, "You good?" He points to his right leg. There's a glint of jagged bone where his femur snapped and tore through his skin. My heart takes a swan dive. *How is he not screaming in agony?*

Cougar grimaces. "That is a game changer."

Jupiter clenches his eyes shut, pain carving deep grooves in his face. "You're going to…have to…leave me."

Gus says, "No way."

Cougar squeezes Gus's shoulder. "He can't travel with a broken femur. We'll have to bring back help."

My dad's tone tells me that he's already given up on Jupiter. *No.* "Duct tape."

"Danny," Cougar snaps, "duct tape can't solve everything."

Gus digs the tape out of Cougar's backpack. "What else?"

"Bamboo and a liana, for now." I tear strips of tape and keep the gummy side down so it'll stay sticky in the downpour. My dad hesitates, then finds a piece of bamboo. "Put it under his leg." Jupiter moans as Cougar slides it into place. I wrap the tape under Jupiter's thigh and knee, then around the bamboo. "This is just so we can get you away from the river without doing more damage. Then we'll set your leg."

"This is freaking idiotic. Moving him will just make it worse," Cougar says. "And what do you know about setting an open fracture?"

"It could make things worse, but I do know what I'm doing." I grab the vine Gus found and tie it around Jupiter's waist. "Dad, Gus, get him under his armpits.

"Be tough," I tell Jupiter. "This is going to hurt."

3 2

Wrapping the vine around my abraded hands, I pull with everything I've got. Jupiter bites back screams as we drag him up the slippery hill. I try not to think about all the stuff that can go wrong, but worries crowd my mind—unsanitary conditions, a paralyzing nerve injury or a fragment of bone puncturing or severing a major blood vessel, shock and everything I don't know. Oh, and there's one other thing. I've never set a leg before. I've never even watched someone else do it.

My knowledge comes from a case study in one of my mom's journals about a skier who broke his femur in the backcountry. His friends used ski poles to set his leg, then tied him to their skis, slid him down the mountain. The guy ended up dying. My mom said it was because the femur is extremely vascular.

He lost a ton of blood both from the break and then from the jagged bone slashing through muscle when it was set. A blood transfusion would've saved him, but he didn't get one in time.

If Jupiter needs a transfusion…

I push away that fear but new ones flood in. I'm not even sure I remember all the details of that case. *What if I forget the most important parts?* The old Danny flutters to the surface. *Defective. Inferior. Embarrassment. I can't do this. But I'm not that girl anymore. WWDD?* I have a chance, even though it's small, to save a friend. I'm going to try.

We drag Jupiter to the base of a kapok tree. A deep indentation in the buttressed roots shields us from the downpour.

Jupiter's lips tremble. "Am I going…to die?"

I give his shoulder a squeeze. "Here's what I need," I tell my dad and Gus. "Two pieces of bamboo, one the length of Jupiter's body from his armpit to his ankle, the other from his groin to his ankle. Try to cut the end that's going to rest against his groin as smooth as you can."

"Thanks for that," Jupiter groans.

"Hang in there. You'll feel much better once your leg is splinted." That's what the skiers said when they were interviewed following their friend's accident. That they thought he was okay because after they put his leg in traction, the pain went way down. *He still died.* I shake my head, focus. *What am I forgetting?* "Dad, we also need a crosspiece at the bottom of the splint." He's looking at me like I'm a total stranger. "Go!" Gus and Cougar disappear into the rain forest.

I tear open the leg of Jupiter's shorts so the wound is totally exposed—a swampy mess of torn skin, gristle, bone. "Jupiter, this next part is going to hurt like hell. But then you'll feel 'right as rain.'"

His voice is dry, raspy, as he struggles to talk despite the pain. "I didn't…take you for a *Matrix*…fan."

"I'm full of secrets."

Tears leak from his eyes, dribble down his temples. "Yeah, who knew…you're an…EMT?"

"Nothing wrong with being an EMT or a nurse, but I think I'm going to be a doctor, maybe a surgeon." The idea surprises me but there's no time to consider it. I put my rain poncho over Jupiter, hoping to trap some heat because he's starting to shake. We'll need a fire. My dad will have to work some serious magic to get it going.

Gus and Cougar return and kneel by Jupiter. Cougar measures a length of bamboo and Gus holds it while he trims one end square and notches the other. Cougar asks, "What's next?"

I place a splint under Jupiter's armpit, the shorter one between his legs, and tape the crosspiece across the notched ends. "We need to apply traction."

Gus crawls to Jupiter's feet. "Tell me what to do."

"Hang on," Jupiter cries. He sounds terrified.

Fresh wells of blood continue to flow from the wound. *There's too much blood.* "Jupiter," I say, channeling no-nonsense Commander Sam, "Gus is going to straighten your foot, then pull your ankle until the bone that's sticking out of your thigh slides back into place. He's going to hold it like that while I tape the splint."

Jupiter, his teeth now chattering, says, "I don't…think that's…a…good…idea."

"Sure it is," I say. "It's the best idea. One, you can't have a broken bone sticking out of your leg in the middle of nowhere. Two, you won't be in as much pain. Three…" I nod at Gus and he pulls. Jupiter screams. "More," I say, watching the shattered bones slide through the torn skin. "Good, now hold it there." With Cougar's help, I tape the splint, making sure it's tight but not so tight that the circulation is cut off.

"Almost done," I say. But Jupiter's broken leg is a little bit shorter than the other one. One end of the broken bone still pushes against the skin. I ask, "Can you pull harder?" Gus tries but nothing moves. *How do I—*

"Danny," Cougar says, "maybe you should call it good?"

"Shhhh." I search for an answer. "Does anyone have a belt?"

Gus says, "Jupiter does."

Cougar pulls the webbing belt out of Jupiter's shorts and hands it to me. I crawl between Gus's arms, tie a loop around Jupiter's foot and the crosspiece. "Get me a short stick."

Cougar is back in seconds. "This work?"

"We'll see." I put the stick through the loop, then take a breath to steady shaking hands. "Okay, Jupiter, I'm not going to lie. This next part will be awful."

"He passed out a while ago," Gus says.

I twist the stick, drawing Jupiter's foot down the final inch to the crosspiece. When his legs are even, I reach down and push the bulging bone back in line, until the broken ends grate against each other. Cougar tapes Jupiter's boot into place. "Done." I crawl back to Jupiter's head, rest my hand on his clammy cheek. "You okay? Jupiter? Wake up. Please. Jupiter?" I rub his sternum really, really hard.

Jupiter moans. A moment later, he cracks open one eye. "Is it over?"

"Yeah," I say. "Does it hurt as much?"

"'Right as rain,'" Jupiter groans. "Sweet Jesus, that was... freaking torture."

"I'm sorry."

Jupiter rolls his eyes toward Cougar. "Watch out, man, your kid...might get her own...show."

Cougar is filming again. I need to cover the gash in Jupiter's leg. It's still bleeding, but not nearly as much. Using the least dirty T-shirt we have, I make a pressure dressing, duct-taping the folded cotton around Jupiter's wound. "Finished." My gut clenches. I race behind a tree, dry heave because my stomach is empty, rinse out my mouth with rainwater, then return. "Tomorrow we'll work on making him crutches." I refuse to consider that Jupiter may not make tomorrow.

Cougar lowers the camera. He shakes his head like he's just seen a unicorn. "I didn't know you had it in you."

I didn't, either. "Mom left medical journals around the house."

"*You* read them."

A compliment from Cougar still makes me glow a little. "We need shelter, fire. Jupiter is in shock. In a hospital they'd wrap him in heated blankets, have his feet elevated and he'd be given a blood transfusion, IV fluids." I gently prop Jupiter's feet up on Cougar's backpack. "One out of four isn't enough."

"I can do a shelter, but a fire?" Cougar asks.

"You're Cougar Warren," I say. "Make it happen."

"Has anyone noticed that my daughter is getting extremely

bossy?" Cougar asks. "I blame it on the company she's keeping."

I watch Cougar stand, one hand on his side like he has a bad cramp. He heads into the rain forest.

"Kid," Jupiter whispers. "Hate to ask, but I need you…to take a message to my…mom and little sister."

"Shut up," I say.

Gus takes Jupiter's hand. "What do you want us to tell them?"

"That there's no one else I would've wanted for a mom. She made the best cheese soufflé in the world. I did steal a Hershey's bar from Mr. Chevy's store… I'm sorry if I miss her birthday, but I'll light candles wherever I end up. And tell Venus… Tell her that I'm proud of her. She'll…make a kick-ass chef."

"I'll tell them, but I don't think it's going to come to that. Not with Danny around. Can I steal your doctor for a sec?"

Jupiter says, "Sure, kid."

Gus pulls me to my feet, leads me away. We stand beneath the umbrella of a low palm tree as the rain continues to hammer down. There's a smear of mud on one of his cheeks and his hair is plastered to his head. It's like the Amazon has taken off his sheen and there's a more real, way more attractive person beneath the polish.

Gus rests his hands on my shoulders. "I'm beyond proud of you."

"I didn't… We won't know if—"

"For all of it. For forcing Cougar to help Jupiter, dragging him up the hillside, knowing how to splint his leg—"

"You helped."

"Shut up and take the compliments."

We're lost in the rain forest in a torrential downpour. Jupiter might be dying. There's something wrong with my dad. *WWDD?* "Thank you." I go back to Jupiter to make sure he's not bleeding through the makeshift bandage, then tuck the poncho tightly around his body to trap in heat.

Jupiter says, "Gus is a good guy."

I blush. "I think so, too."

"But he's famous. That world? They…have different rules."

From the tightness of Jupiter's features, I can tell he's still in a lot of pain and desperately wish I could take it away. I meet his gaze. "I know."

"Tell Cougar…I want triple hazard pay…for this shit."

"If he doesn't give it to you, I'll tell the media that Gus saved your life while Cougar watched from the shore, crying like a baby."

Jupiter chuckles. "Seems like you've figured out Cougar Warren."

Growing up means understanding that you can want something, really want it, but be incapable of getting it. "Maybe."

"You're a far cry…from the little girl I met…at the airport, *Just* Danny."

"I'm seventeen now."

Jupiter reaches for my hand. The small movement makes him wince. "No matter what happens…you saved me, Danger Danielle Warren. Like I said…when we met, don't undervalue kindness. It doesn't…come…naturally to a lot of folks."

"Rest," I say.

And please don't die.

33

"You try."

Cougar hands me Mack's fire-steel and a nest of leaves, grass and moss he kept dry in a plastic bag. My hands shake as I work for a spark. Nothing happens. I keep trying. Once, twice, ten times. *Nothing.* Tears prick my eyes.

Cougar taunts, "Don't be a wimp."

"Screw you." I shave off resin from the fire-steel's handle, placing bits in the nest along with a page from Jupiter's now very short book. When I finally get a spark, I pick up the nest, blowing gently like I've seen my dad do on countless episodes until white smoke billows. It makes me cough but I keep blowing. When a little flame appears, I place the nest on the ground. Carefully, I put the dry twigs and sticks Cougar dug from the base of thick bushes on the nest. As

I work, my dad shaves the outer layer of wood from bigger branches, their insides dry enough to keep the fire going beneath the shelter we've taped together using the kapok tree and Cass's poncho. The fire grows until it's crackling and gives off enough heat to warm us.

Jupiter's voice is a weak trickle. "Way to go, Danny."

One side of Cougar's mouth crooks up. "If you use up all of Mack's resin, and it doesn't stop raining, we won't be able to make many more fires."

Jupiter is shivering hard. We put him closest to the fire, then boil rainwater so he can drink warm fluids. Slowly his teeth stop chattering. The hot water warms the rest of us, too. Hope floats to the surface. *Jupiter might be okay.* He eats some fruit and leftover grubs. Without the allspice the grubs taste like bile with a greasy finish. Despite hunger pangs, I give Jupiter mine.

The rain stops just like it started—all at once. When the canopy sways, a sliver of the moon is visible. It's like we're trapped in a cocoon and a tiny hole has torn open to reveal the outside world.

"Song?" I ask Gus.

"'Fire.'"

I look over at him. "Nelson Sheer is not from the '70s."

Gus winks. "Sue me." He chants, "'Fire hollow out my soul, polish the sharp edges, build me from the ashes, talk me off the ledges—'"

"'I was dead before you woke,'" I sing. "'Blind but now I see. Shine your light upon me. Make me wild and free…'"

Gus's eyes widen. "You've been making me sing when you have *that* voice?"

Jupiter says, "Sing more…please."

Memories flood back. Before the accident, I sang all the time. To my stuffed animals, with the car radio, in church on the rare occasions my mom took me. After the accident, I stopped. Was it because singing drew attention and I wanted to hide? Or did I just stop believing that I knew how?

"Please," Jupiter repeats.

"'Father, cut the bonds away. Mother, let me roar. Sister, watch me dance in light, say goodbye to dark of night…'" Cougar joins me, effortlessly harmonizing. His voice is rich with a slight rasp. "'Fire hollow out my soul, polish the sharp edges, build me from the ashes, talk me off the ledges. I was dead before you woke, blind but now I see. Shine your light upon me. Make me wild and free…'"

"You have a lovely voice," Cougar says. "You get that from me."

I look over at Jupiter. He's finally asleep. Taking the video camera from my dad's hand, I turn it on him. "Favorite possession?"

Cougar massages his chest. "Don't have one."

Gus presses, "Come on. You must have something."

"Not really. Some fancy interior designer decorated my house with paintings by up-and-coming artists whose names I don't know. I've got a Porsche. Cass picked it out. My clothes all come from sponsors like Armani, Tommy Ford. I don't collect watches or sneakers." He shrugs. "Maybe my knife. I've had it since before you were born."

"What about you?" I ask Gus.

"My dad's flight logbook," Gus says. "I found it a few years after he died. My mom couldn't deal with getting rid of his stuff, so she boxed everything, stuck it in the basement. Clothes, shoes, glasses, you name it. The logbook wasn't from work. He had a Piper Cub he flew for fun. There were little notes beside some trips. One said he'd given me control of the plane, dual controls, of course. I don't remember it but the note said, *Gus flew for the first time. So proud.*"

Gus smiles. He's so much more beautiful than when I met him. He takes the camera from me and asks, "Favorite possession?"

"Well, I don't have a Porsche," I say, chuckling, "but even if I did? It wouldn't be my favorite thing, either. I'm like my dad in that way." Saying we have something in common isn't as bad as I thought. "People, I guess." But my answer doesn't fit quite right. I turn thoughts over like stones. *My mom tried to bend Cougar to her will. It broke them both. She's trying to do the same with me. That's why I reflexively push back. Trix tried to force me into her shoes, and it damaged our friendship, maybe ended it. Cass wanted to make Cougar love her as much as she loved him and he broke her heart.*

Cougar is watching me. Understanding settles on my skin. But instead of weighing me down, it makes me lighter. "The thing is, people can't be possessed." I meet my dad's gaze. "That's what I've been trying to do with you. Make you what I need. But that can never work." *Truth.*

"You're not like me," Cougar says, his voice gruff. "That's a good thing."

Gus smiles—he's kind, gorgeous, mesmerizing. I can't make him mine, either, no matter how much I want what's between us to continue. He's traveling a different path.

"So is there anything?" Gus asks.

Before this trip I would've said *The Phantom Tollbooth*, because it was the most important, thoughtful gift my father ever gave me. It symbolized that he cared. And now? *"The Phantom Tollbooth,"* I say. But the reason has changed. My mom sat by my bedside and read it every night. Despite everything, she told me it was a gift from my dad.

Gus says, "My dad read me that book when I was little. Remember any lines?"

I sift through my favorite quotes. "'What you can do is often simply a matter of what you will do.'"

Cougar grumbles, "Sounds like something I'd say. Guess your mom did okay picking out that gift for me."

That night we sleep around Jupiter, hoping our bodies will help keep him warm. We take turns feeding the fire. When it's mine, I rest two fingers on the inside of Jupiter's wrist, making sure he's still with us.

"Danny," Jupiter whispers.

"Yes," I say, placing my palm on his forehead. It's warm. *Does he have a fever already?*

"You didn't ask me about...my favorite possession."

"What's your favorite possession?"

"The book I brought."

"*The Stand*? Sorry to say it's not much of a book anymore."

"S'okay, I know...most of it by...heart."

"Why do you love it so much?"

Flickers of firelight illuminate the ghost of a smile. "It's about ordinary people working together...to accomplish the extraordinary."

I kiss Jupiter's brow. "Sleep with the angels, my friend. Tomorrow we'll accomplish the extraordinary."

DAY
SIX

34

It's not raining and Jupiter is still alive in the morning, but his skin is hot with fever. Infection has set in. He needs antibiotics. My already-sinking hopes burrow underground as I watch my dad struggle to his feet. There's no denying that something is really, really wrong with him. His face is ashen. His right arm presses against the left side of his stomach. He's shuffling.

I follow Cougar into the forest. "What's wrong with you?"

"Nothing." He glances down. "Hey, hey. Look at that." Crouching, he puts one hand next to a massive paw print in the mud. "Jaguar."

Icy fingers slide down my spine. "Should we... Do we run?"

Cougar shakes his head. "We'll probably never see him.

They move like ghosts. As long as you have fire and travel with another person, you'll be okay."

A shadow passes over me and I shiver. "You mean, *we*."

"What?"

"As long as *we* have fire and travel as a group *we'll* be okay."

Cougar stands and looks away but I catch his wince, reach out and touch his abdomen. He groans.

"Show me."

"Kid, leave it alone."

I summon Commander Samantha's bluntness. "Now."

Cougar lifts up his shirt. There's a massive bruise on his left side between his upper abdomen and lower chest. It's such a dark purple that it's almost black. I close my eyes and picture the body's organs. "Do you remember what hit you?"

"The ground."

He's trying to be funny, but this is no joke. There are so many things it could be. They swirl around my brain—spleen, bowel obstruction, intestinal injury, kidney damage or infection, broken ribs that have punctured an organ. I don't have the knowledge or skills to figure this out. Powerlessness tastes like dirt.

Cougar says, "I can see the wheels turning but don't bother. It's my spleen. A few years ago I was in a car crash and injured it. Felt the same way—pain in my left shoulder and stomach. I spent three days in the hospital. No surgery, just bed rest and monitoring. Superhot nurse, though, so it wasn't a total loss."

"No one told me."

He grins. "The nurse was just a passing fancy."

"I'm not talking about your sex life."

"We kept it out of the papers. Cougar Warren doesn't get hurt, let alone die from something as lame as a bruised spleen."

"What was the pain like compared to now?"

"It's been there since the crash, but today? On a scale of one to ten, it's a thirty-seven."

I push gently on his abdomen. It feels spongy, like it's full of blood. "Your spleen might've ruptured this time." Rescuing Cass, pulling me up the ravine, the Herculean effort to save Jupiter, any one of them could've made him worse. "I shouldn't have—"

"Danny, it's who I am," Cougar says. "And saving people? We have very different reasons, but you do it, too."

Our eyes meet. "A ruptured spleen means you need—"

"Emergency surgery." Cougar chuckles. "You going to show me up, do that, too?"

I manage a little smile. "Not in my wheelhouse." If my dad has ruptured the capsule covering his spleen, blood is pouring into his abdomen. His spleen needs to be sutured or removed to stop the bleeding before he dies. *He could die.*

"Buddy, I'll be fine."

It's impossible to stop my chin from trembling. "You can't... I don't want to... We can't do this without you."

"You know what happens when you take your hand out of a bucket of water?"

I meet his sky blue eyes. "What?"

"It doesn't leave a hole. The water level just goes down a little."

"That doesn't sound like Cougar Warren," I manage to say.

"It's not. It's John Warren." Cougar runs a hand over his face. "Can you make a raft?"

My skin starts to shrink. "I've watched every one of your episodes, most three or four times, but that doesn't mean I actually know how to actually make one."

"Do you or don't you?" Cougar demands.

"I...do."

"You and Gus will leave today. Follow the river. When the water gets calm, build a raft. Either you'll find help or eventually help will find you."

My dad and Jupiter don't have time for *eventually*. A panic attack surges forward. My lungs contract, ribs press agonizingly against organs. *What he's proposing is impossible. Gus and me, alone in the Amazon, is a recipe for disaster. We'll get lost, or worse.* My heart constricts. It hurts to breathe.

"Danny?"

I start to hyperventilate. *I can't... He's going to... This isn't...*

My mom's voice cuts through the static: *What scares you?*

The list has changed. *Failure, pit vipers, Jupiter and Cougar dying, never getting to a place where I can forgive my parents for their weaknesses, not choosing my own path, the absence of knowledge.*

Sam demands: *What do you like?*

Jupiter's kindness, grilled snake, Cougar's strength, my mom's determination, making fire, the sound of frogs at dusk, the taste of Gus's lips.

Samantha presses: *What do you want to be?*

I will be strong, brave, intelligent, driven, kind, the solution.

The weight crushing my chest lifts. My skin stretches and oxygen flows. The spots clouding my vision scatter, then vanish. Cougar is watching me. "I'm okay."

"Then I'll go find something for breakfast."

He walks away, no longer shuffling, putting on a good

show. He has to be in agony. I'm baffled by the mental and physical strength his effort requires. I doubt any surgeon would believe it's possible. But my dad is Cougar Warren. "Try for something more than a tiny lizard," I call after him.

"Bossy," he tosses over his shoulder before disappearing into the forest.

I'm not sure how long I stand alone beside the paw print of a jaguar. But when I'm ready, I square my shoulders and head back to camp. When Cougar returns hours later, he has a headless orange boa constrictor draped around his neck. It's at least five feet long. "Break out the video," he commands.

Gus pulls the camera out of its case, films Cougar holding up his prize. "Pretty amazing," Gus says.

Cougar grins. "I know."

Then he falls to the ground. He's so much smaller than a kapok tree, but the earth shudders anyway.

35

After I tell Gus about Cougar's injury and the new plan, he helps me clean the snake. We're silent as we work, lost in our own worries. While I grill the meat, he goes in search of the fruits my dad taught us were edible. How long, I wonder, has Cougar known we'd be left on our own?

You can only eat them when they're wrinkled.

Remember the shape.

You know what happens when you take your hand out of a bucket of water?

Gus returns with an armful of passion fruits. He pauses, waiting to see if I want to talk, but I don't. He starts collecting kindling. We're not sure how long we'll be gone. Jupiter and Cougar need enough food, water and firewood to survive.

"Don't burn that meat," Cougar calls.

He's lying beside Jupiter, who is recovering from an aborted attempt to stand. Using a crutch, Jupiter could only go about five feet before almost fainting. There's no way he can hike through the rain forest. Neither can my dad. After he passed out, I wasn't even sure he was going to wake up. He did, and tried to get up but couldn't. Witnessing his struggle is like standing at the edge of a pool and watching him drown.

From the corner of my eye I see Cougar try to get to his feet again. He makes it to his knees, sways, then lies back down, glancing around to make sure no one noticed his weakness. I barely know my dad. He's been a fictional character most of my life. What hurts more than the possibility of his death is the missed opportunity to share even a little bit of our lives. Everything Cougar does goes to feed his ego. That's a sad way to live. But I still want to know my father and have the time to forgive him.

Gus drops a pile of wood by the fire, using the machete to take off the wet bark and cut kindling. "More?"

I nod. The rain has stopped, but who knows for how long. My dad doesn't have the strength to collect more wood. Plus, Jupiter is still at risk for shock and now Cougar is, too. My heart thuds faster. My dad was wrong. Without his hand in the bucket, there's a gaping hole. I can't fill it.

I sit down beside Cougar and give him a piece of grilled boa. He takes a bite, makes a show of chewing and then says, "A little overcooked. Next time a minute less over the fire. And it'd taste better if you'd wrapped it in allspice."

"Sure." I tuck most of the remaining pieces of snake in a giant leaf, put it between my dad and Jupiter. Gus brings them boiled water, fruit. We watch them drink, eat, not sure what to say or do next. Cougar tosses me the fire-steel. I drop it.

"Nice catch, Pigeon."

He's never called me that name. But I get that he's pushing me out of the nest. "Did you know that pigeons have the ability to fly up to fifty miles per hour?"

Cougar's eyes glitter. "Oh yeah?"

"Yeah. And they can always find their way home because they have a spatial map in their heads." I wait for him to say something but he doesn't. "Young pigeons wait in the nest for their father to arrive before they take their first flight."

Cougar meets my eyes. "Better late than never."

There's a massive lump wedged in my throat. "Yeah."

Cougar says, "Kids, the plan is to follow the river. When it gets calm enough, cut down bamboo, lash it together with lianas and make a raft."

Gus says, "Got it." He offers Cougar his hand.

My dad tugs Gus down so he's kneeling beside him. "Remember, my kid knows more than you do. *She's* watched all my shows. Listen to her. And don't get her killed." He hands Gus the bottle of bug repellent.

Gus says, "You guys keep it."

Cougar shakes his head. "We already have fire. The smoke will keep away most of the skeeters. You'll need the strong stuff if Danny can't get flame."

It's my turn to say goodbye. But how do I do that? Maybe Gus and I will make it, find help. But maybe we'll get lost, hurt, or die, or return to find Jupiter and my dad dead. There are no guarantees.

Cougar hands a bright yellow T-shirt to Gus. "Before you

take off, tie this around a tree branch that can be seen from the river. That way you'll be able to find us, bring help."

He says the word *help* like it leaves a bad taste in his mouth. Of course it does. He's Cougar Warren. He doesn't get rescued. He's the rescuer. I kneel beside Jupiter and hug him, the heat rising off his skin reminding me there's not much time. "We'll be back soon." When I turn to my dad his eyes are closed. Maybe he doesn't want to say goodbye, either. It takes all my will to stand. I hoist his backpack and walk away.

Cougar calls, "Danger Danielle Warren."

I turn and study the man who was always a giant to me. He struggles to stand, barely five foot ten, his face gaunt, clothes hanging off a body breaking down, no longer bending to his will. I love him more for those weaknesses than I ever did for his strengths. "What?"

Cougar squares his shoulders, blue eyes bright. "Looking forward to telling the world about my death-defying white-water rescue, how I splinted Jupiter's leg and then stayed behind to keep him alive. Deal?"

"Deal."

"That's my buddy."

I wait to cry until Gus and I no longer smell the fire's smoke. He holds me tight but I only give myself a few minutes with my face pressed into the crook of his neck. Gus ties the yellow T-shirt onto a branch hanging over the edge of the steep ravine to our left. I hope we'll be able to see it if… when we return.

Gus says, "They're going to be okay."

We both know that's probably not true.

3 6

I cut trail for hours, hacking down vines, branches and prickly thorns, clearing our way, keeping the roar of the river on my left. I swing the machete long after Gus offers to take a turn, ignore the ache in my arm, step by step forcing a path through the rain forest, using physical exertion to push away thoughts of my dad and Jupiter. This is the only way I can help them now.

By nightfall, slick with sweat, we've kept the river in sight but it's still running too high for us to raft. It hasn't rained all day, so that's something. We slide down a short hill and dunk into a pool of clear water that's overrun the banks, collecting in the deep depression of a rock worn smooth. The sweat and grime of the day wash away.

I lie on my back at the edge of the pool, a flat rock beneath me, and let my hair fan across the water's surface. Gus does the same. The insects aren't as bad down here, only occasionally buzzing in my ears. Along this section of river, the sky is a narrow ink-colored satin ribbon following the water's curves, sprinkled with stars.

"What's that one?" I ask, pointing to a collection of twinkling dots.

"It's the Southern Cross." Gus puts his hand over mine, tracing the kite-shaped pattern. "It's part of a bigger constellation called Centaurus, the ninth-largest constellation in the sky."

"Is there a story about it?"

"A centaur is a mythical creature, half man, half horse. See his front legs?" Gus asks, drawing my index finger to the left. "They're marked by the two brightest stars. See?"

The touch of Gus's hand, his skin skimming mine, makes it hard to focus. "Do you still miss your dad?"

"Yeah," Gus admits. "He didn't just show me the stars, he'd tell me lots of Greek myths, too. I used to like the story about Chiron. He was the son of a Titan named Cronus, who seduced a sea nymph. When Cronus heard his wife coming, about to discover the two of them in bed together, he turned himself into a horse. The sea nymph got pregnant and her son, Chiron, came out half man, half horse." Gus laughs. "I used to imagine that I could've been a superhero if my mom had slept with Superman, Aquaman or, best of all, Spider-Man, instead of my father."

"You were a weird kid," I say.

"I'm still weird. But that's a secret. My team has coached me well. I'm disarming, self-deprecating, cool, always smooth."

He smiles but his eyes remain serious. "I am the perfect picture of a young, talented movie star."

For the first time ever, I realize how much easier it is when no one expects anything special from you. That maybe I've cloaked myself in pigeon feathers to avoid disappointing everyone, including myself.

Gus turns sideways. The light casts his face in silver. We kiss. Moving closer and closer until there's nothing between us but the thin cotton of T-shirts and shorts. Life isn't a promise. Rescue isn't imminent. My father and Jupiter may die. I could be lost in this place forever, abandoned to the elements like Mack and Cass. But Gus's lips on mine are a reminder that I'm still alive, a brief respite from all that's happened.

Gus says, "You're beautiful."

In this moment, as his hands explore my curves...*I am.*

Gus's kisses grow longer, deeper. His hands slide beneath my T-shirt, circle my breasts. He trails kisses down my neck, soft lips tracing the line of my collarbone. My body heats from the inside out. I reach down, fingers in his hair, and draw Gus back, meet his gaze. "You can be anyone you want to be." Gus's face instantly changes. It's like the lights go out. Abruptly, he rolls onto his back, stares at the sky. *What just happened?* "Gus? Did I...? Is something...? What'd I do wrong?"

He won't look at me.

"It's nothing," Gus says and gets up. "I'm just totally exhausted. We should make camp, eat a little and get some sleep. Long day tomorrow."

I pull down my T-shirt, shoulders hunched, and follow him up the slope. In silence, we tie the remaining poncho between two narrow palms in case it rains, make a bed out of bamboo and palm fronds, then eat some of the leftover snake. The meat sticks in my throat. Finally, I say, "You don't get to do this."

Gus drinks some water. "Do what?"

"Shut me out."

"What are you talking about?" Gus asks, his face a placid mask, tone neutral.

"What happened by the river?"

Gus lies down, his back to me. "I told you. I'm just tired."

My throat tightens. "Talk to me. Please."

"Fine," Gus sighs. He sits up. "I don't want to hurt your feelings, but you're not my type. Now will you let it go?"

Defective. Inferior. Embarrassment. NO. "Your type? What's that? Sexy models? Famous actresses? Singers who win Grammy Awards? Or just hot girls who know exactly what to do in bed?"

Gus snaps, "All of the above, plus anyone who gets me in *Famous Magazine*, is a magnet for paparazzi, raises my rate, interests top studios, attracts famous directors and makes me the envy of all the fans who pay to see my movies because they want to be me. Do you finally get it?"

My body is hollow, like every emotion has been carved out leaving a brittle shell.

Guys always tell you who they are up front.

GP isn't so precious that he can't get through a little plane flight.

I'm an actor... I do what's asked.

The suspicion that the Gus I first met, the shallow celebrity, *might be* the real Gus hits. But even as I think it, it doesn't ring true. It makes me even angrier that, for whatever reason, he's resorting to this. "Don't worry. As soon as we get out of the Amazon, you won't have to slum it with me ever again." I lie down, my back to him. I can tell he's just sitting there, staring at me.

"Danny?"

I don't answer.

"Shit. Danny... I didn't mean... It has nothing to do with you. Okay? It's just, what you said? About me being whatever I want to be? I can't do that. And the way you looked at me, like you totally believed I could?" Gus's voice breaks. "You have that luxury. I don't."

"Luxury?" I sit up and face him. "I'm a one-eyed girl nicknamed Pigeon. My father ditched me, then used me as a freaking hook for his show. My mom both loves and resents the hell out of me. The best things I've ever heard anyone say about Danny Warren are that I have a nice smile and an easy-going personality. I'm one step up from their family pet. But I made myself a lot of those things. I let them happen. It was easier to be what people expected, beat them to the punch line. A luxury? To be what I really want to be is a battle I'm just beginning to fight."

Gus shakes his head. "You don't get it. I'm not just responsible for myself. My income pays for my entire family—food, clothing, travel, homes, private schools and my mom's lifestyle."

"I go to public school, live in an apartment, will probably have a ton of debt after college, but one day I'll be a doctor—possibly a one-eyed, kick-ass surgeon. Sounds like you've made enough money to keep your family comfortable. I understand wanting to do that, needing to do it. But the rest is *your* choice. So stop blaming everyone else."

We glare at each other, daring another word, excuse, apology. Neither of us speaks. That night we brush our teeth in silence, then sleep back to back, an impenetrable wall between us.

DAY SEVEN

37

In the morning it still hasn't rained. I collect a nest of grass and twigs and put them in a plastic bag, so tonight, if it gets wet, I can still make a fire. Gus and I eat a piece of fruit, then drink half our remaining water.

A dragonfly alights near my feet, its wings a delicate lattice of indigo and silver. Monkeys babble above. When I look up, I see they have white manes around their faces. *Tamarins.* A red-and-white-spotted caterpillar inches my way. I use a stick to move it along. The thump of bullfrogs has become almost as normal as my heartbeat along with insects' varied drones. A pair of scarlet macaws wing by, their red head feathers made brighter by the green and blue of their wings. Leaf-cutter ants march along a dirt highway carrying their prizes overhead, guarded by soldiers. Everywhere there's life. I'm part of it, existing in this place in a way I never thought possible. Despite last night's fight, Jupiter's and Cougar's terrible injuries, it makes me…proud and strangely grateful.

What do I see? I see a girl who's surviving.

Something is crawling in my hair. I take a long, calming breath. "Spider or scorpion?" I ask, pointing to the spot on my head.

Gus leans over. "Beetle. Do you want me to get it?"

"No." Carefully, I pluck the beetle free. It has orange flecks along its polished brown shell and wriggles between my fingers. I set it down, watch it scuttle away.

Gus asks, "Do you hate me?"

There are dark circles beneath his eyes. He didn't get much sleep. I turn the question over and look for the truth beneath it. I don't hate Cougar for disappointing me, Samantha for allowing old resentments to affect my life, or Trix for wanting me to share her discontent, so why hate a guy with whom I have zero history? *Gus owes me nothing.* "No. I don't hate you." And I don't think he's that totally shallow actor I met the first day, either. That was a knee-jerk reaction to his rejection. He's just the guy he thinks he needs to be.

I work through the snarls in my hair, then braid it tight to avoid trapping more insects. After securing my braid with a vine, I take the machete and start clearing our way. We don't talk at all, the silence filled with the living rain forest, the whoosh of my blade, our labored breathing as we duck, climb and balance inside the tangled Amazon.

"What's your favorite place?" Gus asks when we take a break to drink some water.

I mop the sweat from my face. The humidity is stifling. "I haven't found it. You?"

"It used to be bathrooms."

I actually laugh. "Why?"

"You have a great laugh."

My face gets warm but I know he's just trying to make up for what he said. "Bathrooms?"

"Before I got really famous, but I was getting recognizable? It gave me a break from feeling like people were watching me. That's something you have to get used to."

"I'll take your word on that. Favorite animal?"

"Dog. I got my brothers a vizsla last Christmas. His name is Boone. He loves going mountain biking with them, but inside he's chill. Plus, he's super protective. I'm not home that much so I like knowing Boone is there."

Gus cuts open a passion fruit, hands me half. Slippery seeds slide down my throat. The heat has made me dizzy but the fruit's sugar helps.

Gus asks, "Favorite TV show?"

"Before this luxury vacation? I would've said my dad's show. But that's not the truth. *COUGAR* is fun to watch, but I love shows that document what happens in an emergency room. There's one called *Oakland ER* that has more trauma cases come through their doors than any other ER in the country. Gunshots, knife wounds, RTT with a BBB."

Gus raises one brow. "What's that?"

"Rat-a-tat-tat with a baseball bat."

He chuckles. "So the truth is you like blood and gore. No wonder you could reset Jupiter's leg."

"I don't mind it, but what I really love is watching men

and women in super stressful situations figure out how to diagnose and treat. Also how doctors and nurses have to remember their humanity. *Cases* are *people*. They have wives, husbands, siblings and children. Treat one person, and you affect countless others who love them. It's this amazing, living network, like an electrical grid for a giant city, but human beings are the lights."

Gus stares at me for a long moment, then picks up the machete and begins clearing a path. I follow him through a crosshatch of branches, trying to avoid the ants streaming along the bark. Only one bites me. It's not that bad. Getting bitten by a snake makes everything else pale in comparison. A stick bug is frozen on a low branch. Gus points it out. I wouldn't have noticed. It's slender with a body that's the color of mossy wood, the perfect camouflage. "Cool," I say, no longer jealous of a creature's ability to hide in plain sight.

I ask, "What would you be if you could be anything in the world?"

Gus says, "I used to think an astronaut, but that was my dad's dream."

"You can have the same dream."

Gus whacks at a branch. "Watch it."

A brown snake slithers beneath the brush. Gus leaps onto a fallen trunk, pulls me to safety. I let go as soon as I can. "So?"

"When I was little, there was a farm down the road from our house," he says before ducking under a termite nest hanging off a narrow limb. "I've seen pigs, goats, even horses born. In another life, I'd be a large-animal vet."

"No fans, paparazzi or big payday."

Gus frowns. "You said if I could be anything."

In this moment, I again see the little kid who lost his dad. He stepped into his father's oversize shoes before he had the chance to find his own path. There's a part of me that wants to repeat that Gus can be anything he wants to be. But maybe that's not true. I ask, "Song?"

"'Sailing toward Never.'"

"That's my mom's favorite." I can hear her humming it softly as she does dishes. A surprising ache accompanies the memory. An orange-and-black-striped cricket hops by my foot. He's so small it's a wonder he can survive in the Amazon. He nabs a tiny ant. For this moment he's a predator but at any second he might become prey. I ask, "What if you don't make it home?"

"Life insurance kicks in. My mom and the kids will be fine." Gus chuckles. "Better than fine. And someone will probably make a movie out of this ordeal where I'm the hero that dies in the end saving a gorgeous fellow plane crash survivor in the process."

I joke, "Who'd play me?"

Gus reaches out, brushes a strand of hair off my cheek. "You'd play yourself."

I take the machete and lead on. Fool me once. *Truth.*

"You ever going to totally forgive me?"

"Sure. Sing 'Sailing toward Never.'"

"We've already established I can't sing."

"You start. We can trade off."

Gus groans, "Cougar was right. You have gotten bossy. Okay, fine. 'The wind tells a story the waves underline. The moon lights blue waters. Stars fall from the sky—'"

"'I never did call him and now I know why,'" I sing. "'His

promises burned me, turned to ash in the wind. His love was a boundary, his words poison lies. He promised forever but I'm sailing toward never.'"

I step over the knotted root of a massive tree. The river below is no longer raging. It bends right then abruptly widens until it's at least three hundred feet across. It's not white water. It's not a channel that will dwindle into nothing. It's a tributary of the Amazon we can navigate. A cobalt blue butterfly the size of my hand floats along currents of hot air. Maybe it's a sign. The chrysalis has broken open. Hope that Jupiter and my dad will both live surges through me.

"Come on," I say. "We have a lot to get done before you can return to your world and I can get back to mine."

38

It's late in the day by the time we've cut enough bamboo and vines to make a raft. We make camp above the river, just in case there's another rainstorm and the water level rises, and build a quick shelter using the poncho and remaining duct tape. When we finish, we haul the bamboo we've cut down to the river.

"Ideas?" Gus asks, hands on his knees, breathing hard.

I catch my breath, too, and wait until the spots dancing across my vision clear. "Episode sixty-seven. Lie down."

Gus smirks. "Excuse me?"

I ignore the implication. "We need to make the raft long enough that if we're on it for days, we can lie down. When the bluegrass singer Abby Tucker joined Cougar in the Everglades, it took them two days to navigate out of the swampland.

They took turns sleeping. Luckily Cougar slept with one eye open, because Abby almost slipped off the raft into crocodile-infested waters."

Gus looks at me like I'm a freak. "Just do it." He stretches out on the dirt. I put a piece of bamboo beside him, whacking a notch with the machete, satisfied to see him flinch. I cut through the bamboo, a one-eyed girl teaching a movie star how to make a raft that's going to float us out of the rain forest. "After you cut all the big ones this length, we'll place the crosspieces. Make sure you save the narrower bamboo for that. Got it?" He nods. I give Gus the machete. "I'll start a fire. When you're done, we can lash the raft together." Over my shoulder I add, "We're out of duct tape, so don't cut yourself."

Gus calls, "I'm flipping you the bird."

I don't look back. "I figured." With dry tinder it doesn't take me long to start the fire, breathing into the nest of grasses until there's a strong flame, then setting the ball of fire in the hole I've dug out and adding wood. I watch the fire burn for a few minutes, slowly feeding it until it gathers together, gets hot. Gus doesn't look up from his work as I fill our bamboo containers, then carry them back to the fire to boil.

"What's next?" Gus shouts an hour later.

I walk down to the river, hand him a water bottle and try not to notice how the sweat on his upper body glistens. *Does this guy ever look like crap?* Gus downs half his water in one swallow. He's gathered his hair into a bun to get it off his neck. The shorts he wears, ripped and stained with mud, hang lower on his hips. He's lost weight, too. But instead of making him gaunt, it just accentuates his muscles. *Stop staring.* "It doesn't matter," I mutter. *Truth.*

"What?"

To hide my red face, I turn away, place the skinny pieces of bamboo perpendicular to the larger ones, evenly spaced. "Now we lash them together. Do you know how to make a clove hitch?" Gus shakes his head. I don't tell him that I don't, either. In almost every episode of Cougar's show, knots come into play. I've seen Cougar make square knots, clove hitches, end loops, stoppers and slides thousands of times. *How hard can it be?*

The clove hitch takes me several tries, but I pretend it's the vine's fault, not mine. If Gus notices, he doesn't say it. "Ready?" Gus nods. "Okay, put the length of a vine by the bamboo, cross one end under and around, like a figure eight, then tuck the short end under the diagonal," I say, demonstrating. "Now you try."

Gus messes it up not once, not twice, but five times. Finally, I put my hands over his and guide them through the knot, ignoring the heat radiating from his skin, the not-unpleasant tang of his sweat and the loose strands of hair that brush my cheek. Once we make the hitch, I undo it. "Again," I say, rocking back on my heels.

"Who made you queen?" Gus asks. On his second try he makes a decent clove hitch.

"Okay, now after you do a hitch holding the two pieces of bamboo together, add a few frapping turns—"

"Frapping?"

"Tightening, like this." I demonstrate. "And then finish with a square knot." I work through making a square knot, show Gus. He gets it the first time. "We have to do that at each spot the bamboo crosses. Got it?"

"Aye, aye, Commander Danny."

The name makes one side of my mouth crook up. We mostly work in silence. When we finish with our knots, we have a roughly eight-by-six-foot raft that I wish my dad could see. He'd tell me all the things that were wrong with it, explain how he'd do it much better, but there'd be a tiny place, deep inside his leathered heart, where he was proud. Tomorrow we'll take this raft down the river, paddling with the extra bamboo, until we find help for my dad and Jupiter. *Please let us find help.*

The mosquitos, always swarming at dawn and dusk, give up their full frontal assault for the night. The river is so wide here that a large expanse of sky is visible. The stars, with no ambient light, are brilliant. Kneeling at the edge of the river, I splash water on my face and neck, washing the day's stickiness away. Gus kneels a few feet away, splashing water on his chest, dipping his head, then shaking off like a dog. I spy a caiman's eyes in the river, watching. *We're not for dinner*, I silently tell the prehistoric creature. It slides beneath the surface like it understood me.

Together, Gus and I pull the raft away from the water's edge, then head back to our fire for what I hope is our last night in the wild. After finishing the snake Cougar caught, we wash it down with water that now tastes sweet to me. We dab on insect repellant, then chew on our hibiscus twigs.

Gus leans back on his elbows, the twig resting on his lower lip. The flickering fire makes the flecks in his eyes glint like fool's gold. He asks, "Truth or dare?"

My stomach flips. "Pardon?"

He points his toothbrush at me. "You heard me. What else is there to do tonight? Truth or dare?"

He's trying to embarrass me. "Truth."

"What's the biggest lie you've ever told?"

I sift through the ones I can remember, find the most innocuous. "When I was ten, I cheated on a math test so I could get an A. When the teacher caught me, I said I hadn't looked at someone else's paper."

Gus makes a cheesy, surprised face. "Wow! You're a total rebel. Did you lie about stealing a pack of gum, too?"

"Sorry I don't live up to your high lying standards."

Gus shrugs. "If you're not going to really play, we can forget it."

The way he says it, like I'm incapable of being honest, or too afraid, pisses me off. "Fine. Here's my most horrible lie. There was a girl in fourth grade named Sarah. She rarely showered or changed her clothes. Turned out her mom was an alcoholic. When we were freshmen, her mother drove drunk and killed a college student. But no one knew about Sarah's mom back in elementary school. A group of kids made a chart showing the days Sarah showered and how many times she wore the same stinky clothes in a row." My face gets warm. "Back then? I was getting teased enough that I didn't want to go to school. Anyway. Every kid in my grade was called into the principal's office when a teacher discovered the chart, asked if they made it or knew who did. I lied, said I didn't know."

"But?"

"I didn't make the chart, but it was my idea. I wanted to turn the spotlight on someone else."

"Pretty rotten. But you were just a kid."

It's hard to look at Gus but I do. "It was cruel. If I ever get out of here, I'll apologize to her. Your turn."

"Truth."

"Same question."

"There are so many. Every time I had to promote a movie I hated, or talk about a costar who was a pain in the ass and rude to the crew, or—"

"Totally lame. Tell me a lie that really matters."

The muscles in Gus's jaw clench and unclench.

"Quit posing and say it."

"Fine. I didn't miss my plane because of a meeting with a director. A few buddies came to Brazil with me. We partied all night. I was hung over, slept in. That means everything that happened, the plane crash, Mack, Cass, Jupiter, your dad? It's on me."

My jaw drops and the planet stops spinning. Despite the heat, goose bumps break out on my skin. Any words I might've uttered dry like dust and blow away. It's a huge lie. Monumental. *If… If… If…* Gus is watching me, waiting for a meltdown. But instead I turn away from emotion and analyze what he's said like it's a case study.

There are countless factors that produce any result. Life isn't a controlled experiment in a laboratory. Long before Gus, there was Samantha, Cougar and our messed-up family dynamic. There was Cass and Cougar's unbalanced relationship. Jupiter's and Sean's work schedules. A production crew already in Peru, with a director who made myriad decisions about the proposed episode that impacted all of us. There was Mack, the experiences that shaped him and made him willing to take risks another pilot would've avoided. It's ridiculous to think that Gus is responsible for every dynamic and decision made over decades or in the past months, weeks or hours. And he's certainly not in control of nature. Gus is a small dot on an enormous timeline that started long before he became involved with my dad's show, long before our plane ever crashed.

Gus blinks and tears roll down his cheeks, drip off his chin. "Say it."

"You have as big an ego as my dad."

Gus's eyes widen. "What?"

"*Cass* pushed Mack to fly late in the day, despite the weather. *Mack* agreed. When he wanted to turn back, *Cougar* prodded him to fly under the clouds. Maybe we wouldn't have crashed if you'd been on time, but the storm was brewing before you got to the plane. No guarantee we wouldn't have been caught in it earlier, maybe more of us killed. And that's just taking into account what happened on the day of the crash, not the countless decisions before you or I ever got on a flight to Peru. Don't get me wrong. It'd feel good to blame you, especially when you're acting like such a self-important ass. Actually, it'd feel stupendous, but you're just one small, and not very important, piece of this giant cluster fuck."

Gus wipes his face with shaky fingers. "Thanks—"

"Don't. I'm just being honest."

Gus clears his throat. "Truth or dare."

"Truth."

"Have you ever been in love?"

"No. Truth or dare?"

"Truth."

"Have you?"

"I thought so, but she traded me in for the lead singer of a band. Not even a great band. Truth or dare?"

"Truth."

"How many people have you slept with?"

I consider lying. Trix has slept with seven guys and given me the details, so I could probably pull it off. The purple chameleon Jupiter pointed out flashes through my mind. *Fly your freak flag.* "None." Gus's eyes get big, like he can't believe he's sitting across from an actual living, breathing virgin. "You?"

"I don't know."

"Guess."

"Fifteen, maybe?"

It's my turn to be shocked. "I'm done playing."

"One more."

"Fine. Truth or dare?"

"Dare."

What can I possibly dare Gus Price to do that he hasn't done a million times already?

Gus says, "If you can't come up with one, you lose your turn."

"Fine. I lose my turn."

"Truth or dare?"

"Dare." This time Gus is the one who's speechless. "If you can't—"

"I dare you to go skinny-dipping."

I shake my head. "It's the crepuscular hour."

"The what?"

"You really haven't watched a single one of Cougar's episodes, have you?"

He shakes his head, half smiles.

"It's when predators feed."

Gus licks his lower lip. "Okay, Miss Wikipedia. I dare you to kiss me."

WWDD? I stand up, quickly peel off my clothes, slip on my hiking boots because I'm not a total idiot and run down the hill to the river. Halfway to the water, it starts to rain, hard, like someone turned on the faucet, full force.

"What the hell," Gus yells after me.

But I don't look back. I'm flying. My feet slip as the rain makes the ground slick. Twice I almost fall but manage to regain balance. When I get to the edge of the water, I kick off my boots and wade in, shuffling my feet in the desperate hope that whatever is hidden beneath the mud won't sting, bite or constrict. The surface of the water pops as the rain comes down harder. I can see glowing yellow-green caiman eyes in the distance, as the creatures weigh in their walnut-size reptilian minds whether I'm worth the effort.

Taking a breath, I dunk under the water. The current weaves around my body. After so much time in the Amazon, it's the silence that has the most impact. Despite everything, it's beautiful, peaceful.

Hands reach beneath my arms and drag me out of the river, swing my body through the air in an arc, water spraying. I'm standing, totally naked, in the pouring rain, in front of Gus. He's drenched, cheeks ruddy, eyes scanning, like he's looking for blood, a wound.

"What the hell were you thinking?" Gus shouts.

"You dared me."

"I didn't mean it! I was trying to shock you, get a smile, a laugh, find a path to forgiveness, maybe steal a kiss—"

"Yeah, right." I turn to find my boots, which are already full of water. "I'm slow to catch on, but not a total dolt."

Gus grabs my arm, pulls me back. "Danny, you're not my type because you're better than my type. You're mind-blowing! You're fierce and fragile and perfect. Truth."

The rain slows to a drizzle, then fades away. Gus is out of breath, chest rising and falling fast. He hasn't let go of my arm. We're standing inches apart, the air between us electric. Everything he just said, everything that's happened, what I've done in the rain forest, comes together. "Let go," I say. Gus's eyes momentarily close, like those two words were bullets. I study his smooth brow, golden hair, full lips and imperfect, perfect scar. The rain has washed away the Amazon's grime and his skin shines. He is beautiful, talented, lonely, sometimes unsure and insecure, other times wise, and always compassionate. He's watching me but I no longer wonder what he sees. What matters is what I see in myself.

I recall the promise made at a trendy LA hotel before this trip began: *I will get to know my father on this trip and become the person I was meant to be.* I now know John "Cougar" Warren. But there was never going to be a way for me to be totally fearless again. Life is made of deep wounds, different kinds of love, invisible scars, disappointment, surprises and hope. I'm the product of losing an eye; an intelligent, resentful, but loving mother; a selfish, charismatic, sometimes caring father; a friend who both elevates and demoralizes; people I couldn't save; others I try my best to help; plus all the dreams and desires inside me.

No longer do I want to be who I was before the accident. That girl was seven years old and lived in the past. I'm seventeen and live in the present. Gus said Cougar is a bright light, and that's true. I thought I wanted to live in his glow. But you can't hitch a ride on someone else's star. Cass tried that with my dad and it left her miserable. I tried, too, and all it did was make me feel flawed. You have to be your own star. If I survive, the world is filled with possibilities. There's no limit to how bright I'll shine.

A quote from *The Phantom Tollbooth* surfaces: "You can swim all day in the Sea of Knowledge and not get wet." I set down my fears and responsibilities. They will still be there tomorrow morning, when I will do everything I can to save Jupiter and Cougar.

"Danny?"

I say, "I'm not perfect. But I'm kind, smart, determined, loyal, brave when I need to be, sometimes striking, and I have a really pretty singing voice. You have to know that I know that now."

Gus's expression is solemn. "I do."

"Then kiss me." And he does, our mouths tasting, testing, asking, then taking. My hands run down his back, skimming over each defined muscle. A mosquito buzzes past my ear. I wave it away. Gus slaps at a biting fly. We kiss again. He takes my hand, leads me to the raft and we lie down. My pulse takes off like a runner at the start of a race. "Just so you know? I have no idea if I'm about to make a total fool of myself. I'm afraid of what I don't know, but more scared to miss this moment." *WWDD?* I kiss Gus again.

He traces the line of my jaw with light fingers. "Just so you know? I'm afraid I'll disappoint you. But I can't let you go."

He runs his lips along a bruise inside my forearm, sending ribbons of heat into my body. A tickle interrupts the sensation. "Ah, Gus?"

He looks up. "Yeah?"

"Something is crawling across my back."

Gus peers over my shoulder. "Beetle. A red one." He flicks it away, then rolls sideways, winces.

"You okay?"

"Yeah, one of the clive hitches tried to burrow into my kidney."

I laugh. "Clove."

We kiss again, our limbs twining together. I forget about the mosquitos, beetles and the hard bamboo beneath us as Gus's lips travel across every cut, bruise and abrasion, tickling away the pain. He leaves a trail of kisses to my nipples, tracing, teasing. His tongue outlines the semicircle bruise my seat belt left behind, and my insides knot. I pull him back toward me and we kiss again, like we're sharing a secret no one else will ever know.

"I'm breathing you in," Gus whispers in my ear.

He weaves his fingers through my hair, his face above mine, eyes searching. I ask, "What do you want to know?"

"Why did you choose to have two different colored eyes?"

"I wanted to be more like Cougar. Now I understand that the decision made me more *me*."

Gus wraps me in a hug, holds tight, his eyelashes brushing against my cheek. He says, "I don't ever want to hurt you."

I understand what Gus means. But this isn't about taking anything. This is about living, right now. "Tonight we both get to be the people we want to be," I say. "No promises. No future. No sins or need for forgiveness. Just this." I kiss him. "Who do you want to be, Gus Price?"

"The guy you love," he says, voice catching. "Who do you want to be?"

"The girl you love."

And we are those things and more somewhere in the Amazon, beneath a canopy of twinkling stars.

"Will you be sorry in the morning?" Gus asks when our heartbeats have finally slowed.

His arms hold me close, fingers trailing along bare skin. "For loving a guy who loved me?" I shake my head. We tumble into sleep, wake before dawn and love each other again.

DAY
EIGHT

39

I slide onto the raft, a bamboo pole in hand while Gus pushes it off the bank. The moment of truth—it holds together, floats well. Gus hops on and we glide with the current. For the first time in a week I feel the steady heat of sun on my skin. Head tipped back like a flower, I take a few seconds to drink it in, then join Gus, paddling hard.

Gus and I haven't talked much this morning. I'm not embarrassed—everything we did together was everything I wanted to do and we didn't risk pregnancy. I've seen what an unwanted baby does to the parents *and* their child. A little smile plays across my lips. Last night was magic. Nothing can ever take that away, but at first light the weight of Jupiter's and Cougar's lives settled back onto our shoulders. We need to find help for them soon.

Gus points to a flash of pink in the water. "Look!"

I count five dolphins. They weave around our raft like they're playing with us. I trail fingers along the water and the palest of the dolphins comes close, touches my palm with her nose. "Pink dolphins are actually a species of toothed whales," I say. I'd planned to impress my dad with that fact. Gus leans over my shoulder, kisses my neck, a remnant of who we were last night.

The dolphins stay with us for almost an hour, putting on a show of spins and leaps as we relentlessly push through the river. Sweat stings my eyes, but I don't stop to wipe it away. Time is running through Jupiter's and Cougar's hourglasses. As I paddle, I constantly scan the shores for any sign of the small indigenous population that lives in the rain forest, but either they don't want to be seen, or they're not near us.

Traveling in the river on a raft is entirely different than wading through the swamp. When a grass-green snake slithers by I don't cringe. I count the orange lines across its back. We see capybaras and they look like guinea pigs with tiny ears, not big rats. Caimans dot the edge of the river. "Look," I say, pointing to a black one that has to be twenty feet long. At one point I see a fin that doesn't have the gentle curve of a dolphin. "Shark."

"It's fresh water," Gus says, using his paddle to steer us clear anyway.

"There are bull sharks in the river."

"Please tell me that you're kidding."

"Nope. They can swim in fresh water, too."

Gus asks, "How does that work?"

"They have special kidneys that can adapt." I don't say that they're considered some of the most dangerous sharks in the world because they frequently attack humans.

When the shark is hopefully an hour behind us, we take a paddling break, drink some water and dip our heads in the river to cool off. My skin is getting red so I pull on a sweatshirt even though I'm sweltering. Gus leaves his off and stays bare-chested, his hair pulled into a ponytail, still looking near perfect despite a week in the rain forest.

We paddle on, early morning turning to midday, arms aching, neither of us willing to take more than a few minutes' rest. A hawk wings overhead, its auburn body tipped with black wings. It dives toward the water and skims the surface, then soars up, a massive blue-green fish wriggling in its talons. On the far shore are white birds with blue beaks. Coral-colored birds with bright yellow breasts peck by their feet. We push on, ignoring the blisters on our hands and the throbbing in our backs.

"What song do you hear?" I ask.

"'The Chance.'"

"I don't know it."

He says, "'Grab the chance of tomorrow. Choose the road you don't know. Take a leap once you've fallen. Blood will still flow. Hold her too tight, like she might fade away, love like she's gold and there's no way to pay. Pray when you die it wasn't a lie 'cause the flame is snuffed out in the blink of an eye...'"

I close my eyes and let his voice lap against me like the small waves hitting our raft.

And then I hear it, lower than the chatter of monkeys,

deeper than the bass of bullfrogs, sharper than the snap of a thousand crickets.

It's a motor.

Neither Gus nor I wave. Not at first. We watch the canoe round a bend in the river. After the plane crash, Sean's, Mack's and Cass's deaths, Jupiter's leg, and Cougar's grave injury, this moment is still a shock. But in a way, it's not. The real world was always out there waiting for us to find it.

"Jupiter and your dad have a chance now," Gus says.

My tears fall. But there's an emotion waiting beyond relief. Surprise. This rescue doesn't elicit the sense that *I've* been saved. Maybe it's because I no longer feel lost.

Gus's arms tighten around me, like he's trying to keep *us* for a moment more. He breathes three words into my ear. I say them back, then wave at the canoe with one hand, the fingers of my other still woven with his. Two men and a woman come into focus as the canoe nears. When they reach us, I let go of Gus's hand.

40

The man driving the large motorized canoe, dressed in a T-shirt, shorts and hiking boots, his brown skin deeply tanned, is a Peruvian guide named Carlos. He immediately gives us a thermos of water, then offers us sandwiches. I drink but decline the food. In this moment, my hunger has faded away. Names are shared. The two passengers, wearing worn khakis, long-sleeved shirts and sun hats to protect age-spotted white skin, are French botanists on a three-week trip to study native plants. Anthony has serious dark eyes behind round, gold-wire glasses. Paulette has a sweet smile. The red scarf wound around her neck gives her a strangely stylish look in this environment. We quickly learn that they've heard about our crash. Given Cougar and Gus's celebrity, it's all over the news. We're still in Peru, not Brazil, but Carlos tells us that the search is going on much farther south, along what would've been our route if Mack hadn't diverted.

"How many survivors?" Anthony asks.

Gus says, "Four. Our cameraman, Sean, died on impact. The pilot, Mack, and Cass, Cougar's personal assistant, soon after."

"Of course Cougar Warren is still alive," Paulette says in heavily accented English.

Deal. "Yes," I say. "He stayed behind to help one of his crew who was badly injured."

We explain that there's a bright yellow T-shirt hanging from a tree near our camp as a marker and that we've been roughly following the river. Carlos uses his satellite phone to call for help. I don't understand Spanish, but after he hangs up, he explains, "Your families will be alerted that you're safe. A team in Iquitos is being pulled together and a helicopter with medics will be sent out as quickly as possible. In the meantime, I can take you back to our base camp. From there, rescue workers will transport you to safety."

"We need to get back to my dad and Jupiter," I say. "Please."

"How long have you been traveling since you left them?" Carlos asks.

"We bushwacked for about twelve hours. It was slow going. As soon as the river calmed we made a raft." I turn to Gus. "How long have we been on the water?"

"Four or five hours," he says.

Carlos looks at the botanists. "By motor-canoe it might take half a day if the river stays relatively calm. If it doesn't, we'll need to bushwhack our way in. You two okay with that?" Anthony and Paulette nod their agreement.

It's hard to grasp. All the effort we put into fighting our

way through the Amazon, the time it took to build a raft and paddle, collapse into a compact, direct, motorized trip back up the river. *But still, Jupiter and Cougar may be dead when we arrive.*

Conversation fades after a few more minutes. The drone of the motor, the sound of waves slapping against the fiberglass canoe, is a welcome respite to answering their questions. Without the rain, the river has receded from the banks and is no longer tearing trees and boulders free. While it's still moving quickly in places, the motorized canoe manages to push through the current and we need to portage around obstacles only a few times. Now and then I glance at Gus. What will happen to the guy who loves constellations, sings '70s music off-key, laughs like his entire body is in on the joke? Will he ever become the person he wants to be, not just the guy he thinks he needs to be for everyone else?

It's early evening when we finally spy the yellow T-shirt. While the botanists and their guide pull the canoe onshore and call the authorities with our exact location, Gus and I run up the hillside. I smell the fire's smoke. It's a good sign. Someone has been keeping it alive. When we hit a tangle of vines and thorns, Gus swings the machete, clears our path. We reach the edge of our campsite. Jupiter is feeding the small fire from the pile of kindling we left behind. He looks up, eyes burning bright with fever. Cougar is asleep beside him. My dad's face is covered with the Curious George sweatshirt Cass once wore. His arms are flung wide, like he's embracing the rain forest's canopy.

I look at Jupiter. He's crying now, big, shaking sobs. "Danny—"

"Shhh." I kneel beside my father. With shaking fingers I feel for the pulse in his wrist. The utter stillness, the total absence of life, is a silent earthquake. *If we'd just traveled faster, paddled through the night, found help sooner, pushed harder.* "When?"

Jupiter says, "A few hours after you left."

For the past nine years all I've wanted is a relationship with my dad, to prove to him that I'm worth loving. *I am, and he's gone.* My dad was wrong about a lot of things, especially that his absence wouldn't be felt. I will never stop feeling it. An empty space where my larger-than-life father once lived.

My dad's hand is clenched into a fist. I gently pull the fingers open, wanting to hold his hand one last time, be his seven-year-old buddy even though I finally understand there was never any chance of going back. At first the splash of bright gold makes no sense. But then I see what remains of a webbed foot squeezed between my dad's second and third fingers. Poison dart frog. Beneath it is torn flesh, to allow the frog's toxins to enter his bloodstream quickly. *Cougar Warren doesn't get hurt, let alone die from something as lame as a bruised spleen...*

"Danny," Jupiter says, holding out a scrap of paper torn from his book. "He wanted me to give you this."

The damp page trembles in my hand as I read the sentence my dad wrote in charcoal: **BE YOUR TRUE NORTH**.

Cougar whispers in my ear like he's still alive, like he's right beside me: *A compass differs from true north depending on where you are on the planet. I depend on myself to find the way.*

"I do, too," I say softly, then give the scrap of paper to Gus, watch him read.

Gus says, "I haven't found mine, yet."

"You will."

"Truth?"

Overhead, I hear the drone of a helicopter. I ignore it and kiss Gus to seal the promise, salt water on our lips. "Truth."

41

We carry a barely conscious Jupiter to the water's edge. The helicopter, hovering above, drops a basket by cable. Gus helps Carlos pull it sideways and I kiss Jupiter's hot cheek before we lift him into the basket and he's swept through the air, disappearing into the belly of the helicopter. He'll be flown to a hospital in Iquitos, maybe in time to save his life. I wipe away tears. Kindness is underrated, and Jupiter Jones overflows with it.

Gus and I ask Anthony, Paulette and Carlos for their help getting Cougar to the edge of the river. His body is heavy, like he decided to weigh more in death to remind us that Wits. Strength. Ingenuity…wasn't just a tagline. They were a responsibility that only the strongest could shoulder.

Carlos says, "I'm so sorry for your loss. We'll stay with you until the helicopter returns at first light tomorrow to transport you, Gus and your father's body to safety."

I meet his gentle eyes. "Thank you, for everything. But we're fine now. Really. I'm sure Anthony and Paulette want to continue their journey, and I'd like some time alone to say goodbye to my father."

Carlos's brow wrinkles but he nods. "Is there anything else you need?"

"Yes. Can you spare some food, water and gasoline?"

Gus and I stand side by side as the group pushes off from shore and motors down the river. When they're gone, we cut down bamboo and make a quick raft, lashing the pieces together with vines. Neither of us talks. We're both trying to sift through the wreckage and use what we find to start building our own constellations.

Night falls and moonlight illuminates Cougar's body as we shift it onto the raft and tie lianas around his chest, waist and legs to keep him in place. I try not to feel the sharp jut of his hip bones, notice the narrowness of his rib cage, the gray stubble on his chin, choosing to see my dad like he always saw himself—unbeatable, a force of nature. Gus takes all of Cass's tapes and smashes them with a rock. I wedge them under Cougar's body. What happened between all of us, and the secrets we shared, will stay in the Amazon.

"You'll tell everyone about the dart frog? That Cougar died from its poison?"

Gus says, "Yes."

Gathering a handful of wild orchids, I rest them on my dad's chest, then take hold of his hands one last time. "People are flawed," I say. "You were no exception. But in your own way, you tried." I smile through my tears, kiss my dad's cheek, then breathe in his essence. "I forgive you, Dad." Tearing the final pages from Jupiter's book, I crumple and slide them into Cougar's pockets, the folds of his shirt, beneath shoelaces and under movie star sunglasses so that his eyes can light up like fireworks. We pack branches around his body, sprinkle his clothes, the tapes and kindling with the gasoline Carlos left us. I use Mack's flint-steel to spark the last shred of paper by my dad's feet. A flame catches.

"Will he burn?" Gus asks.

"I don't know. But we'll say my dad ignited the sky like a Viking hero." I untie the raft and push it into the current. "Sleep with the angels," I say, watching John "Cougar" Warren burn bright.

The Pigeon inside me stirs. I open my arms wide, tip my head to the velvet sky and set her free.

EPILOGUE

I called Samantha during my transport to the hospital where Jupiter was being treated. She was at the airport with Jupiter's mom, about to get on a plane to Peru. I asked her not to come. It was an awkward conversation since we were barely talking when I left for LA. The last thing I wanted to do was hurt her feelings, but I needed to finish my journey without any help or distractions. I also wanted some time to absorb all that had happened. Sam agreed to give me that space. I slept in Jupiter's hospital room and when his mom arrived, she was kind, super tough, and together we were Jupiter's advocates.

For a few days it looked like infection might kill Jupiter, but massive infusions of IV antibiotics, a great surgeon and luck saved both his leg and his life. He will walk with a limp, but the doctors told me he would've certainly died if Cougar hadn't reduced his fracture, treated him for shock and if Gus and I hadn't gotten help so quickly. In his press conference about Jupiter's injuries, the chief of surgery called Cougar a "wild cowboy hero." He would've liked that.

Gus's team whisked him out of Peru once he'd given his statement about the crash to the authorities. One minute he was at the hospital, then he was gone. We didn't get the chance to say goodbye and I haven't heard from him since. My heart aches, but I figure that a heart that doesn't hurt has never loved or been loved.

I do know that Gus hasn't spoken to the press. Nor have Jupiter or I. The media is ravenous for the inside story, even sneaking into the hospital and later my hotel in Lima. On my flight home, this time in coach, the guy seated beside me was from *Star Variety Magazine*. A really nice flight attendant moved me to business class so that I could have privacy and get some sleep. I'm really tired, like everything that happened has caught up and filled my bones with cement.

My mom is waiting, along with a dozen reporters holding cameras and microphones, as I walk through Portland International Airport's arrivals gate. Commander Sam and I stare at each other while flashes go off around us. We're only a foot apart but miles stretch between us. Then she pulls me in, hugs me tight, for longer than I expect.

"Having you didn't ruin my life," Sam says, her breath warm in my ear. "You gave me a life. I'm sorry I never told you that."

My throat constricts. "I heard your voice in the Amazon. Sometimes it was annoying, but other times it gave me strength."

She lets me go but doesn't step back. "You look thin."

"I'm not a huge fan of grubs."

My mom actually laughs. She's not wearing her hospital scrubs; instead she's in a long sweater, black leggings and boots, like she dressed up to see me. From the sharp jut of her shoulder blades when we hug, she's thinner, too. A red scarf accentuates the paleness of her cheeks. There are dark smudges marring the skin beneath her gray eyes. For the first time I notice they're a shade lighter than mine. "I missed you, Mom."

She blinks away the shine in her eyes. "I missed you, too."

There's so much to talk about, things I want to know, stories to share, boundaries to set, truths to tell, but that will come in time. For now it's enough that I'm closer to understanding. My mom is a woman who made tough choices, sometimes failed, always tried, never left. Just like Cougar couldn't get beyond being that insecure foster kid, my mom may never let go of her anger or resentments. Regardless, I forgive her. Letting go and redefining who you are isn't just a choice. It's a battle. Not everyone sets her pigeon free.

"Danny, tell us about the crash," a reporter says.

Another journalist pipes in, "Are there any photos?"

"Are there?" Trix asks. "I'd love to see pictures of you kicking the rain forest's ass."

My stomach drops. I didn't see Trix hanging behind the reporters. Her hair is blond today, close to her natural shade. There's a new piercing in her lip but she's wearing a baggy sweater, loose jeans and sneakers. *What do I see?* A best friend abandoned at birth, working out how to fill that void and find her place.

Trix says, "I asked your mom if I could tag along."

THE SPEED OF FALLING OBJECTS

"Hey." I wave her over, turn my back to the reporters and lean in so they can't hear. "I said some things that were unkind."

She exhales hard, like she's been holding her breath for weeks. "You get that from me. I said some stuff, too. Maybe I didn't want to be alone."

This is Trix's version of an apology. "You're not."

She nibbles the hoop in her lip. "Really?"

"Truth."

Turning back to the reporters, I tell them the story that Gus and I decided on before we left the Amazon. "This will be my only statement. Our small plane went down in the Peruvian rain forest during a storm. There were seven people on board. Sean, the show's cameraman, and Mack, our pilot, both died in the first twenty-four hours from impact injuries. Cass, Cougar Warren's assistant, died a few days later from a traumatic brain injury. The authorities had difficulty finding us because our pilot diverted well off course to avoid storm cells and the plane's emergency locator wasn't working. So we set out to find a river to carry us to safety." I take a deep breath. "I'll take questions now. This is all a bit overwhelming, so please ask one at a time."

"Danny, I'm Scott Horsley from NPR. I'm sorry for your loss."

I hear Cougar's voice singing harmony with mine. *You have a lovely voice. You get that from me.* Grief and gratitude mingle. When a tear escapes, I don't wipe it away. "Thank you."

"Where are Sean, Mack, Cass and Cougar now? Did you bury them?"

The perfumed scent of flowers weaves around me. "It

wasn't possible. The Peruvian authorities are working to recover their bodies." *They won't find Cougar's.* At some point I'll share that my dad blazed like the brightest star. For now, that memory is mine. I point to the next reporter.

"How'd the rest of you survive?"

Cameras whir and click but I don't rush. It's important to fulfill my promise, get this right. "We wouldn't have without my dad. He found food, taught us how to make fire and build shelters to avoid hypothermia. He protected us from deadly snakes, spiders and caimans, and led us to the river that ultimately saved us. Who's next?"

"*Celebrity Magazine.* Good to have you home safe, Danny. Sounds like your dad was a superhero."

There's a hard lump in my throat. "No. He was human. Next?"

"Were you terrified?"

"Yes. But wits, strength and ingenuity weren't just Cougar's motto. They were the code he lived by. He showed us how to dig deep and stand on our own. He truly was—" my voice cracks "—he was *Cougar.* He died the night before our rescue from the toxins of a poison dart frog. My dad… He'll be missed more than he realized. Next, please?"

"Are there any videos from your ordeal?"

"No."

"Chris Richards, the *Oregon Times.* What's your plan for the future?"

I take a deep breath. "Both my parents have made a difference in people's lives. I'd like to do that, too. My plan is to go to college, premed."

The reporters follow us all the way to the parking garage.

The Christmas decorations and blinking holiday lights we pass on our way make my reentry feel all the more surreal, like maybe the Amazon was the real world. Once the three of us are in the car, the journalists race to theirs and trail us out of the Portland airport. They'll probably camp out in front of our apartment for a few days before they give up.

"Medical school?" my mom asks as she pulls onto the highway.

"She's really good at the science stuff," Trix says from the back seat.

"I am. And yes, med school."

One side of Commander Sam's mouth crooks up. She hands me a small FedEx package. "This arrived for you yesterday."

Her eyes flick from the road to watch me open it. Inside is a new iPhone. No card. She's not the sentimental type. I turn it on. It's already fully charged. "Thanks, Mom."

"It's not from me."

The phone lights up. The ringtone is the '70s song "Chase." Butterflies take flight. "Hello?"

"Hey."

In an instant I'm transported to the Amazon. The exotic perfumes, thrum of wildlife, roar of the river flood my senses. I can see the gold flecks in Gus's hazel eyes and feel the weight of his hands as they run along my body. A million thoughts join the butterflies, but what I say is, "How'd you know when to call?"

Gus laughs. "Always pragmatic. I have people. And if you didn't answer, I would've kept calling until you did."

"Are you okay?"

"Better now that I hear your voice. You?" Gus asks.

"Same." The line is silent except for the sound of his breathing. "Gus?"

"Truth or dare?"

A spark ignites. "What if I don't want to play?"

Gus says, "I'll go first. Truth."

WWDD? "Do you miss me?"

"Yes. Your turn."

I smile. "Dare."

★ ★ ★ ★ ★

ACKNOWLEDGMENTS

The Speed of Falling Objects was a team effort and I'm incredibly grateful for the support, guidance, input and intellect of a wealth of people.

First, always, is Henry, my partner in all things, best friend, husband and dream come true. Thank you for believing in me, reading my very rough first draft, telling the truth even when it's hard, supporting my passions and always knowing when I need a long bike ride or kitesurfing session to put things into perspective. Kindness is underrated and you're overflowing with it.

Thank you to Natashya Wilson, editorial director at Inkyard Press, champion of authors, determined, talented, insightful editor who (I think) harbors the same secret dream I have of being a pop star. You have made *The Speed of Falling Objects* a stronger novel with every idea and editorial suggestion while always giving me the space to find my way. I truly appreciate and love working together.

Thanks to the whole Inkyard Press team! Line editor Libby Sternberg. Art director Gigi Lau. Publicity director Shara Alexander; publicity manager Laura Gianino; library marketing manager Linette Kim; and Natashya's wonderful assistants, Gabrielle Vicedomini and Connolly Bottum. Copyediting, proofreading and production team: Tracy Wilson-Burns, Ingrid Dolan, Tamara Shifman, Kristin Errico, Allison Draper, Nicole Rokicki and Peter Cronsberry. The marketing team: Bess Braswell, Brittany Mitchell and Olivia Gissing. The sales team: Jennifer Sheridan and Jessie Elliott, Andrea Pappenheimer, Kerry Moynagh, Kathy Faber, Jennifer Wygand, Heather Doss, Heather Foy, Marianna Ricciuto and the digital commerce team, and everyone else at Inkyard, Harlequin and HarperCollins who committed their time and energy to make *The Speed of Falling Objects* the best book possible and to put it in the hands of readers. Big thanks as well to Megan Beatie, book publicist extraordinaire!

Stephanie Kip Rostan of Levine Greenberg Rostan, every writer needs a terrific literary agent in her corner and I'm beyond lucky to have you! Thank you for your insight, wit and smarts. You made my dream of becoming an author possible and I'm so happy we're on this adventure together.

Thanks also to LGR's agent Sarah Bedingfield, for your support and input; foreign rights director Beth Fisher; business manager Melissa Rowland and contract attorney Kristen Wolf.

I'm so fortunate to have a group of friends and family who are willing to listen to my book ideas, share their own stories, read early drafts, give honest opinions and invite us to delicious dinners as my own cooking sometimes falls by the wayside. Apologies if I'm forgotten anyone! Big thanks to Carol Holdsworth, Judy Frey, Michelle Goguen, Karen Ford, Dr. Erin Burnham, Dr. Stephen Parker, Colleen Jones, Sue Bishop, Jane and Art Richardson, Trent Burgess, Daryl Young and Doug Turich. Thanks also to Shannen Fogarty (Boone's other mother) for your kindness and support. And a big hug to Jackie Skakel and Elda Orr, who are always game for chats and dog walks, rain, mud or snow, and put up with our mostly good but sometimes naughty vizsla, Boone.

AUTHOR NOTE

The Speed of Falling Objects is the story of a young woman who faces hard truths about her past and her parents' flaws, and flourishes despite the deeply ingrained belief that she's defective, inferior and an embarrassment.

Many of us, especially as teens, face a moment like Danny does, when we see our parents for who they truly are for the first time and must decide whether to pardon them for not being the superhero we imagined. It's only by developing the ability to empathize and forgive that we're granted the freedom to become our own person without carrying the baggage of anger, regret and guilt. Maybe Danny's journey will help readers find their way through that difficult transition. She'd like that, as she truly does overflow with kindness.

I think most people, at some point in life, have an internal voice like Danny's, though the negative messages vary in type and decibel level. Maybe you don't think you're pretty, smart or talented enough. Maybe you don't believe you're physically or emotionally capable, lovable or deserving. That voice can, at times, be overwhelming. It casts a long shadow, not just for those brilliant, tender, terrifying and thrilling teen years but also, if not addressed, for an entire life. Truth.

Perhaps Danny will inspire readers to think about their inner voice and question whether or not it's actually true, or based on misperceptions and faulty memories. Even if what that voice says is valid, remember that you get to choose how you live your life, regardless. Ask yourself: WWYouDo? Then make the conscious choice to pursue each goal despite insecurities and fears. You will never regret the things you try to accomplish, only the missed opportunities.

At the end of each novel, I have a wish for my readers. For *The Speed of Falling Objects*, my wish is this: open your arms and set the pigeon inside free, no matter how daunting the process, so that you can shine brighter than you ever dreamed possible.

RESOURCES

I have never had to survive in the Amazon rain forest. I'm terrified of spiders, snakes are a close second and I've been known to melt down under a horsefly attack. In my defense, there were a ton of horseflies that day and we were on mountain bikes so there was no quick escape. The worst part was that they were so slow that when I smacked them, *after* those buggers drew blood, I was left with giant globs of green-yellow goo on my skin. All this is to say that everything you read in *The Speed of Falling Objects* comes from research I did on my computer in a safe, clean and air-conditioned writing room…though at one point I did have a spider dangle over my desk that sent me running.

I've done my best to be accurate about the rain forest, its myriad challenges, threats and beauty. Please do forgive any mistakes and remember that this novel, while set in the Amazon, is about a young woman's journey to quell her internal narrative and find her true self. I took a few liberties when necessary, as *The Speed of Falling Objects* is not meant as a manual for hard-core survivalists!

Research for this novel was both incredibly fun and fascinating. At the start, I could barely look at photographs of all the creepy crawlies. Today I can identify venomous spiders at first glance, describe the sensation of a bullet ant or scorpion bite, tell you which kind of snakes can end your life or make it *miserable*, and, if you're lucky enough to survive, exactly how to gut a snake so the meat won't be ruined. Learning about the birds, caimans, sloths and capybaras (rodents of unusual size) made the Amazon come even more alive and gave me so many opportunities to challenge Danny. Best of all were the caterpillars, scorpions and poison dart frogs, which look like the creations of a mad scientist. Their brilliant colors, intricate markings and venom are part of the perfect puzzle that is survival in an environment teeming with threats.

In the safety of my writing room, I learned how to build shelters from videos made by folks willing to live in the rain forest, weave palm fronds and huddle beneath them despite really desperate conditions. Those videos also taught me how best to start a fire in soggy weather, the way to transport coals, how useful lianas are to tie together shelters, rafts or for a quick drink of water, and reinforced my decision that firsthand research was best left to the professionals.

The World Wildlife Foundation was a great resource for the vegetation and plant systems of the Amazon along with the ParksWatch park profile of Alto Purus Reserved Zone.

Peru Travel's *Handbook for Survival in the Rain Forest* provided details for various insect bites and stings and the best way to find and purify water. Additional guides educated on how to identify trees that are actually food, the fruits to eat and the ones to avoid at all costs. Various reptile sites, articles about the most dangerous animals in the Amazon, as well as firsthand explorer stories supplied even more details.

I also consulted with emergency room physicians and nurse practitioners to make sure that the plane crash injuries made sense, the best ways to treat them, the types that might be sustainable for a time, like a head injury or a partially ruptured spleen, typical symptoms and where there might be an opportunity for Danny to showcase her medical abilities. Those same medical professionals also stopped me from going overboard, like when I wanted to stuff Jupiter's open leg wound with maggots. In my defense, I read that maggots (fly larvae) are used in some hospitals to clean out necrotic (dead) tissue. They do work, but, among other issues, there wasn't enough time in the story to get the job done.

Also invaluable were the pilots who helped me figure out the type of plane, Mack's decision-making process, possible reasons for the accident and how, exactly, Mack's bird would go down. Those pilots included my husband, Henry, and our friend Russ.

Finally, I want to give credit to the television show that provided great visuals for some of the challenges and discomforts of untamed environments. While I steered clear of the individual survivalist shows, as I was afraid they'd influence the creation of Cougar's unique personality, I was fascinated with *Naked and Afraid*. That's the reality show where two "normal" people, one guy and one gal, agree to go into the most demanding environments—deserts, islands, jungles, forests, mountains—NAKED. They don't know each other, generally come from radically different backgrounds and are given only one tool each to aid in survival—commonly a big knife and a fire starter.

The challenge is to last twenty-one days in dangerous conditions. There are poisonous snakes, venomous spiders, flash floods, crocodiles, tigers, leopards, electric eels and even sharks that threaten their lives. On top of that, these naked and many times terrified people suffer food poisoning, hypothermia, dehydration, life-threatening infections and bites from every kind of insect...in unimaginable places.

Why do they do it? The challenge. If they don't tap out before twenty-one days, they can say that they faced their biggest fears, struggled with intense hunger, discomfort or horrible pain. Their takeaway: they are far stronger and more capable than they ever imagined.

While the individuals participating in the show face real hardships, there is always a medical team on hand to transport those who are in dire condition to a hospital. How absolutely terrifying it would be to find yourself alone, with no backup, where a single error in judgment, a fall, a cut, a bite or a bone break could easily result in death. That sense of imagined dread helped inform me that a place like the Amazon was the perfect location to test Danny with very real consequences, and to allow her unique abilities to surface.

My hope is that my research has resulted in an exciting and fulfilling novel about an insecure girl, whose experiences and internal narrative supported her perception that she was defective, as she transformed into a young woman who faced tough truths, found her voice and claimed her power.

Finally, if anyone is inspired to spend time in the Amazon rain forest after reading this novel, please do send me a postcard detailing your adventure!